Praise for ,

"*Slumberland* is laugh-out-loud funny . . . and its wit and satire can be burning, regardless of where they are pointed: blackness or whiteness . . . It is rife with sex (particularly interracial sex as weapon, as guilt and celebration, but never as love), music (it is, in fact, a love poem to music as identity, as savior, as self, as the perfect language) and religion, whatever mask it wears." —Chris Abani, *Los Angeles Times*

"With its dictionary delight mixed with cheerfully raunchy, tossed-off outrageousness, *Slumberland* is like a trip-hop *Myra Breckinridge*. (If Myra were plying her libidinous philosophy in contemporary America, it's easy to imagine her, like Sowell, dreaming of a 'ménage a noir.') What Gore Vidal did for sex and gender constructs, though, Beatty does for race and prominent black Americans, with sacred cow–tipping on nearly every page." —Kevin Allman, *The Washington Post*

"One of the hip hop generation's most lyrical writers spins a tale that traces an introspective DJ from his Los Angeles home to Berlin in search of a sublime sax player he hopes will bless his latest sonic sculpture." —*Vibe*

"A charming barrage of linguistic playfulness that is some of [Beatty's] best work to date." —Saul Austerlitz, *The Boston Globe*

"The final message, romantic but deeply felt, is crystal clear—music might not pave the way for reunification, but in many ways it's the best possible option." —*Chicago Sun-Times*

"With laugh-out-loud parodies of everything from the SAT's cultural bias to neo-Nazi musical tastes, *Slumberland* shows that Beatty can still crank out the acerbic riffs . . . As inimitable as ever. Beatty's outrageous novel aims to provoke, and it succeeds." —*Time Out New York*

"Whether he's warning against the 'cutie-pie cabal' of *The All-New Mickey Mouse Club*; spinning a track for a philosopher skinhead; hypothesizing about Harriet Tubman or Nabokov or Big Daddy Kane; rhapsodizing about every sound he's ever heard (he has a 'phonographic memory'); or brilliantly spinning an analogy between East Germans after reunification and African-Americans during Reconstruction, DJ Darky brings the full funk . . . Marvelous."

—*Kirkus Reviews* (starred review)

"The narrative touches on oppression and the inexplicable, transcendent power of music, both of which translate to the American race struggle. Beatty's rolling Faulknerian prose has been praised for its 'dazzling linguistic flights' (*Salon*), and this newest novel is no different; the dense imagery and sound create a synesthesia carnival."

—Stephen Morrow, *Library Journal*

"With its acerbic running commentary on race, sex and Cold War culture, the latest from Beatty . . . contains flashes of absurdist brilliance in the tradition of William Burroughs and Ishmael Reed."

—*Publishers Weekly*

"Furiously written . . . Another bravura performance from the searingly talented Paul Beatty. A no-holds-barred comedic romp that crushes through the Fulda Gap of Black/White, East/West relationships like an M1 tank."

—Junot Díaz

PAUL BEATTY

SLUMBERLAND

Paul Beatty is the author of four novels—*The Sellout, Slumberland, Tuff,* and *The White Boy Shuffle*—and two books of poetry: *Big Bank Take Little Bank* and *Joker, Joker, Deuce.* He is the editor of *Hokum: An Anthology of African-American Humor.* In 2016, he became the first American to win the Booker Prize. He lives in New York City.

ALSO BY PAUL BEATTY

FICTION

The Sellout
Tuff
The White Boy Shuffle

NONFICTION

Hokum: An Anthology of African-American Humor (editor)

POETRY

Joker, Joker, Deuce
Big Bank Take Little Bank

SLUMBERLAND

SLUMBERLAND

a novel

PAUL BEATTY

PICADOR

NEW YORK

Picador
120 Broadway, New York 10271

Published by arrangement with Bloomsbury USA,
an imprint of Bloomsbury Publishing Plc.
Printed in the United States of America
Originally published in 2008 by Bloomsbury
First Picador paperback edition, 2021

2004 BONDE assembly instructions used with permission of Inter IKEA Systems B.V.

Cal Worthington radio jingle used with permission of Cal Worthington.

"Tom Sawyer," words by Pye Dubois and Neil Peart, music by Geddy Lee and
Alex Lifeson, copyright 1981 Core Music Publishing. All rights reserved.
Used by permission of Alfred Publishing Co., Inc.

The Library of Congress has cataloged the Bloomsbury hardcover edition as follows:
Beatty, Paul.
    Slumberland : a novel / Paul Beatty.—1st U.S. ed.
    p. cm.
    ISBN-13: 978-1-59691-240-3 (hardcover)
    ISBN-10: 1-59691-240-5 (hardcover)
    1. African American men—Fiction. 2. Musicians—Fiction. 3. African
Americans—Germany—Fiction. 4. Berlin (Germany)—History—1945–1990—
Fiction. I. Title.
    PS3552.E19S57 2008
    813'.54— dc22
                                                              2007045049

Picador Paperback ISBN: 978-1-250-78941-9

1 3 5 7 9 10 8 6 4 2

For Yvonne W. Beatty, my mother

PART 1

THE BEARD SCRATCHERS

CHAPTER 1

YOU WOULD THINK they'd be used to me by now. I mean, don't they know that after fourteen hundred years the charade of blackness is over? That we blacks, the once eternally hip, the people who were as right now as Greenwich Mean Time, are, as of today, as yesterday as stone tools, the velocipede, and the paper straw all rolled into one? The Negro is now officially human. Everyone, even the British, says so. It doesn't matter whether anyone truly believes it; we are as mediocre and mundane as the rest of the species. The restless souls of our dead are now free to be who they really are underneath that modern primitive patina. Josephine Baker can take the bone out of her nose, her knock-kneed skeleton back to its original allotment of 206. The lovelorn ghost of Langston Hughes can set down his Montblanc fountain pen (a gift) and open his mouth wide. Not to recite his rhyming populist verse, but to lick and suck some Harlem rapscallion's prodigious member and practice what is, after all, the real oral tradition. The revolutionaries among us can lay down the guns. The war is over. It doesn't matter who won, take your roscoe, the Saturday night special, the nine, the guns you once waved fuck-a-white-man drunkenly in front of the kids, take those guns and encase them in glass so that they lie passively on the red felt next to the blunderbuss and Portuguese arquebus and Minuteman musket. The battle cry of even the bravest among us is no longer "I'll see you in hell!" but "I'll see you in court." So if you're still upset with history, get a lawyer on the phone and try to collect workmen's comp for slavery. Blackness is passé and I for one couldn't be happier, because now I'm free to go to the tanning salon if I want to, and I want to.

I hand the receptionist the coupon. On the front is a glossy aerial photo of a Caribbean coastline. She flips it over and her eyes drop suspiciously from my face to the back of the card, which reads, ELECTRIC BEACH TANNING SALON. BUY 10 LIGHT BATHS, GET 1 FREE. Underneath the promotion, in two rows of five, are ten pfennig-sized circles; and rubber-stamped in each circle is a blazing red-ink sun wearing a toothy smile and sunglasses. Today is the glorious day I redeem my free suntan. But somehow this woman, who has personally stamped at least seven of the ten smiling suns, is reluctant to assign me a tanning room. Usually she stamps my card and under her breath whispers, *Malibu, Waikiki,* or *Ibiza,* and I go about my business.

A look of bemused familiarity creeps across her face. A look that says, *Maybe I've seen you somewhere before. Didn't you rape me last Tuesday? Aren't you my son's tap dance teacher?*

"Acapulco."

Finally. She pencils my name into the appointment book. I point to the sunscreen in the display case behind her.

"Coppertone," I say.

A tube of Tropical Blend skims over the countertop like a miniature torpedo. The sun protection factor is two. Not strong enough. If the receptionist's white vanilla frosting lip gloss has an SPF of three, my natural complexion is at least a six. I return fire and send the lotion back. "Zu schwach. Ich brauche etwas Stärkeres," I say, asking for something stronger.

Maybe mammals should be classified by their sun protection factors. Married SPF3 female, 35, seeks nonsmoking, spontaneous SPF4 or lighter for discreet affair. SPF7 Rhino Faces Extinction. I'm the Head SPF50 in Charge. *It was the SPF2ness of the whale that above all things appalled me. But how can I hope to explain myself here; and yet, in some dim, random way, explain myself I must, else all these chapters might be for naught.*

The windowless Acapulco room has the macabre feel of a Tijuana cancer clinic. Like the liquor stores, ball courts, and storefront churches back in the old country, Berlin tanning salons are ubiquitous sanctuaries. Places of last resort for the terminally ill, the terminally poor and sinful, the terminally pale. Places where you go when the doctors tell you there's nothing more they can do. When the world tells you you're not doing enough.

A ceiling fan churns efficiently through the musty air. On one dingy aquamarine wall hang two framed, official-looking pieces of parchment, one an inspection certificate from the Berlin Department of Health and Safety, and the other, written in ornate script, a degree from the College of Eternal Harvest in something called Solarology. In the middle of the room sits the tanning bed, a glass-and-chrome-plated panacea from heaven or, more accurately, Taiwan. I undress and lotion up, leaving the door open just a crack.

After years of tanning, my skin has lost much of its elasticity. If I pinch myself on the forearm, the little flesh mound stays there for a few seconds before slowly falling back into place. My complexion has darkened somewhat; it's still a nice, nonthreatening sitcom Negro brown, but now there's a pomegranate-purple undertone that in certain light gives me a more villainous sheen. Half of my information on what's new in African-American pop culture comes from Berliners stopping me on the street and saying, *Du siehst aus wie . . .* , and then I go home and look up Urkel, Homey the Clown, and Dave Chappelle on the Internet. Lately the resemblances have been to the more sinister, swarthy characters from B-movie adaptations of Elmore Leonard's pulp fiction.

I rent these movies—*Jackie Brown*, *Out of Sight*, *Get Shorty*—and watch them while running back and forth from the TV screen to the bathroom mirror. I think I look nothing like these men, these bad, one-note character actors whose only charisma seems to be the bass in their voices and the inflection in the way they say *motherfucker*. Sam Jackson, Don Cheadle, the chubby asshole from *Be Cool*, they're always smart and dark, but never smart enough to outwit the white guy or dark enough to commit any really heinous crimes.

I often think it would've been easier to have grown up in my father's generation. When he came up, there were only four niggers he could look like: Jackie Robinson, Bill "Bojangles" Robinson, Louis Armstrong, and Uncle Ben, the thick-lipped man in the chef's hat on the box of instant rice. Today every black male looks like someone. Some athlete, singer, or celluloid simpleton. In Daddy's day, if you described a black man to somebody who didn't know him, you'd say he looks like the type of nigger who'd kick your natural ass; now you say he looks like Magic Johnson or Chris Rock, the type of nigger who'd kiss your natural ass.

Most liniments are cool and soothing, but this isn't the case with sunblock. The stuff smells like brine and has the consistency of rancid butter. My dingy skin seems to repel it. No matter how hard I rub, I can't get the cream to disappear, much less moisturize. The greasy swirls just sit there on my skin like unbuffed car wax. I silence the ceiling fan with a firm pull of the cord. If the fan has slowed down or sped up, I can't tell. One more yank. Same difference. Clumsily, I climb onto the tanning bed and raise my hand until the fan's blades skip across my fingers and gradually come to a stop. There's an oily, linty residue on my hand, which I wipe off on the wall.

I put on the goggles. The tanning bed is cold but soon warms up. Like a childhood fever, tanning heats you from the inside out. My ash-white bones become calcium coals, briquettes of the soul. Soon I'm back in my bottom bunk, the ultraviolet radiation substituting for my overprotective mother piling blanket after quilt after blanket on her baby boy. The warmth from the lamps becomes indistinguishable from that of my mother's dry, calloused hands. My own skin seems to vitrify, and while I have any range of motion in my arms I slip a CD into the built-in stereo and press play.

Music. My music. Not mine in the sense that backseat lovers have songs or fifties rock 'n' roll belongs to the devil, but mine in the sense that I own the music. I wrote it. I own the publishing. All rights are reserved. The song is titled "Southbound Traffic Jam." It opens with a rumbling melody, ten lanes of bumper-to-bumper morning rush-hour traffic over a sampled Kokomo Arnold guitar solo. In the background, two exits away and tailgating the guitar riff, is the intermezzo, a Peterbilt eighteen-wheeler that merges into the tune with grinding gears and a double blast of its air horn. After sixteen bars of bottleneck guitar and bottlenecked cars (no one ever gets the joke), a Japanese sedan suddenly slams its brakes. The wheels lock. The skid is ominously long and even. I can't count the number of times I've heard this track, and yet that high-pitched screech still makes me brace for impact. Steel myself for the sound of sheet metal folding in stereo. A windshield explodes and ten thousand cubes of safety glass fall to the fast-lane pavement with the digitally crisp tinkle of a Brazilian percussion instrument. Sun Ra's saturnine falsetto bespeaks the urgency.

So rise lightly from the earth.
And try your wings. Try them now.
While the darkness is invisible.

The guitar comes up, the traffic chugs on. Kokomo hums and moans. The knees of the receptionist pop. She's at the door, peeking through the crack. Staring at the bulge in my Speedo, listening to my music, and wondering why. How does it come to this? You'd think I'd be used to it by now—this lack of sunshine. But winter in Berlin isn't so much a season as it is an epoch. Eight months of solid prison-blanket-gray skies that, combined with the smoky nightlife and the brogan solemnity of the Berlin footfall, give the city a black-and-white matinee intrigue. If it weren't so cold I'd think I was doing a cameo in an old Hollywood melodrama. To shake the leaden September-to-April monochrome I find myself colorizing things. Ingrid Bergman's eyes, the Polish prostitute's language, the pastry sprinkles on the *Schoko-Taler* in the *Bäckerei* window, the patches of sky on a partly cloudy to mostly cloudy afternoon are all a false-memory shade of blue. A blue that doesn't exist in nature, but resides only in my mind and the twang of Kokomo's guitar.

On days when the skies are clear and that stark blue I'd long forgotten, I sprint out of the apartment and into the blinding afternoon looking for affection and serotonins. For an instant I forget where I am, then I notice the narrow wheelbases on the cars parked along the street with showroom precision. At the intersection of Schlüterstrasse and Mommenstrasse, dogs, dog owners, and unescorted schoolchildren, all equally well behaved, patiently wait for the walk signal. I look down at my funny-looking shoes and I remember where I am. *Berlin, yup, Berlin.*

The quirky functionality of the German shoe, like that of Volkswagens and Bauhaus, grows on you. If one is a creationist, the Adam and Eve of German cobblery are the bowling and nursing shoe, respectively. Shoe Darwinists such as myself believe the lungfish of the species is the three-hundred-year-old Birkenstock.

I own a highly evolved pair of Birkenstocks, all-season Hush Puppy–hiking boot hybrids that adapt to the ever-changing environment like suede chameleons. It is in these sturdy marvels of natural selection that I traipse around the city frantically searching for the sun in the same panic-stricken manner in which I look for my keys. The deductive clichés run through my head: *When did you last see the sun? Are you sure you had it when you left the house?* I work my way backward from the shadows of the Cinzano umbrellas that front the outdoor cafés and head for the Ku'damm shopping district. The crushed quartz in the sidewalk sparkles. Tourists wave from the tops of the double-decker buses. The sun is indeed "out," but I can never find it in the sky.

None of the Germanic tribes had a sun god. Pagan as philosophy professors, the Visigoths, the Franks, and the Vandals knew better than to believe in something they couldn't see. Ra, Helios, Huitzilopochtli—my name for the sun is Charlie. I weave in and out of pedestrians imagining that two thousand years ago some Hun idler shod not in Birkenstocks but straw sandals trod the same path looking for solar spoor in these now-concrete wilds. But I catch only glimpses of the yellow deity, the corona shimmering through the leaves of the tree blossoms in Tiergarten Park, the herbalescent shampoo sheen in a tall blonde's hippie-straight locks, maybe a reflection in a skyscraper's glacial façade. My sightings are never more than partial eclipses; castle parapet or church steeple, something is always in the way.

Knowing the Egyptians haven't done anything of note in three thousand years, the Berlin civil engineers must have taken a cue from the ancient ones. Giza's men of science built Cheops's pyramids to align with the celestial pole, and so too did Berlin's urban planners, establishing a zoning code that seemingly stipulates every structure, be it building, billboard, street lamp, or bird's nest, be erected to such a height or in such manner as to prevent any person of normal stature standing at any point within the city limits from having a clear and unobstructed view of the sun.

I always conveniently abandon the search at Winterfeldtplatz, the bells of Saint Matthias ringing in the dusk and signaling an end to the hunt. The sky darkens. The acrid smell of charred pita bread and shawarma lingers in the air. An old man rides a creaky two-speed. A woman curses her uncooperative daughter. The lights inside the Slumberland bar flicker on. In all the time I've lived here I've seen one sunset. And if it hadn't been for the reunification of Germany it wouldn't be that many.

The buzzer goes off but before I start to climb out the receptionist resets the tanning-bed timer for fifteen more minutes, restarts my song, and beckons me to lie back down. Retaking her seat, she listens to the music, one corner of her mouth raised in a deeply impressed smile. Suddenly that corner lowers into a pensive frown. Her fingers stop dancing. Her feet stop tapping. She wants to know why. Why I tan. Why I came to Germany. I tell her it will take more than fifteen minutes to answer that question. It will take the two of us having one of those good horizontal relationships, the kind that the day-to-day verticality of dating, jogging, and window-shopping eventually destroys after two years. By the time I got to the point where I mailed her postcards with accidental haikus scribbled hastily on their backs . . .

In bed we cool. Kiss.
Soon as my feet hit the floor—
The shit go haywire.

. . . her question would remain unanswered, then I'll call her whining, "I sent you a postcard, please don't read it." She'd want to break up with me, but wouldn't go through with it because she still hadn't found out why.

She shifts her plump behind in the chair. The chair squeaks. My sphincter tightens. Other than that I don't move. To move would mess up the comfort level, and I haven't been this comfortable in years.

On our way out of the Electric Beach my freshly irradiated face quickly loses its battle against the brick-cold night. Always a clean city, on winter nights Berlin is especially antiseptic. Often, I swear, there's a hint of ammonia in the air. This is not the hermetic sterility of a private Swiss hospital but the damp Mop & Glo slickness of a late-night supermarket aisle that leaves me wondering what historical spills have just been tidied up.

The ubiquitous commemorative plaques, placed with the utmost care as to be somehow noticeable yet unobtrusive, call out these disasters like weary graveyard shift cashiers. *We have a holocaust in aisle two. Broken shop glass in aisle five. Milli Vanilli in frozen foods.* These metallic Post-it notes aren't religious quotes and self-help affirmations like those pasted onto bathroom mirrors and refrigerator doors, but they are reminders to never forget, moral demarcations welded onto pillars, embedded into sidewalks, etched into granite walls, and hopefully burnished onto our minds. WAY BACK WHEN, AND PROBABLY TOMORROW, IN THE EXACT PLACE WHERE YOU NOW STAND, SOMETHING HAPPENED. WHATEVER HAPPENED, AT LEAST ONE PERSON GAVE A FUCK, AND AT LEAST ONE PERSON DIDN'T. WHICH ONE WOULD YOU HAVE BEEN? WHICH ONE WILL YOU BE?

At the Nollendorfplatz U-bahn station we catch ourselves staring blankly at a marble plaque memorializing the homosexual victims of National Socialism. People whom the inscription described as having their bodies beaten to death (*totgeschlagen*) and their stories silenced to death (*totgeschwiegen*).

"What did you do last night?"

It's an odd question. One that is usually only asked by a best friend after a drag on a borrowed cigarette or the pulling of a strange hair from a familiar shoulder. I'm thankful for it, though. She doesn't want to dwell in the not-so-distant past, and neither do I. "Nothing. What about you?"

"Nothing."

"What about the day before yesterday?" she asks, pulling in close enough to squeeze the air from my down jacket.

"The day before yesterday?" I say, reaching behind my back and breaking her grip. "I was really busy the day before yesterday."

She's hurt that I refuse to share, but the day before yesterday is too personal. The day before yesterday was the most important day of my life.

On the elevated tracks above us her train brakes to a halt. She's trying to hold my gaze; however, my attention is focused on a place I can't see but know is there. A place two blocks and a left turn behind her—the Slumberland bar. My patronizing good-bye kiss on the forehead is quickly countered with a kiss of her own. A lingering smack on the lips that gives me a glimpse into what could be our future, a long stretch of day after tomorrows that would be soft, impulsive, slightly salty, and an inch and a half taller than me. *Bing-bong.* The two-note electronic chime sounds, the pneumatic doors hiss to a close, and in a sense we've both missed our trains.

Not getting the anticipated response from me, the receptionist quickly folds her arms in disgust, her hands tucked tightly into her armpits. I want to ask her to do it again. Not kiss me, but fold her arms. The sandpapery sound of the linen sleeves of her lab coat rubbing together makes the tip of my penis itch. It's time to say good-bye. I reach out to lift the name tag poorly fastened to the receptionist's lapel. It reads, *Empfangsdame,* German for receptionist.

I begin to backpedal, expecting her figure to recede into the night. It doesn't. Her lab coat is too bright. She stands there like a stubborn ghost of my satyric past, present and future refusing to disappear.

It's a slow Monday night; the Slumberland is gloomy and quiet. Only the jukebox's flickering lights and a Nigerian trying to impress a blonde with his Zippo lighter tricks punctuate the musty stillness. I order a wheat beer, then insert some money into the jukebox. I punch in 4701, "In a Sentimental Mood." Duke Ellington's languorous legato soft-shoes into the bar and, as advertised, puts me in a sentimental mood about the day before yesterday.

Most languages have a word for the day before yesterday. *Anteayer* in Spanish. *Vorgestern* in German. There is no word for it in English. It's a language that tries to keep the past simple and perfect, free of the subjunctive blurring of memory and mood. I take out a pen, tapping the end impatiently on a bar napkin as I try to think of a English word for "the day before yesterday."

I consider myself to be a political-linguistic refugee, come to Germany seeking asylum in a country where I don't have to hear people say "nonplussed" when they mean "nonchalant" or have to listen to a military spokesperson euphemistically refer to a helicopter's crashing into a mountainside as a "hard landing," and I can't begin to explain how liberating it is to live in a place where I can go through an autumn of Sundays without once having to hear someone say, "The only thing the prevent defense does is prevent you from winning." Listening to America these days is like listening to the fallen King Lear using his royal gibberish to turn field mice and shadows into real enemies. America is always composing empty phrases like "keeping it real," "intelligent design," "hip-hop generation," and "first responders" as a way to disguise the emptiness and the mundanity.

Ironically, though the sound of American rhetoric is one of the reasons I left, it's the last remaining tie I have to the country of my birth. The only person back home I correspond with is Cutter Pinchbeck III, senior editor for the *Kensington-Merriwether Dictionary of Standard American English*. Our relationship is contentious, and like some exiled word revolutionary I try to improve the linguistic repression from afar. To date I've submitted four words for inclusion in the next edition: *etymolophile*, *Corfunian*, *hiphopera*, and *phonographic memory*. I like my words; they're self-explanatory and, to my mind, much needed. Who'd believe that English is the only Indo-European language without an adjective to describe the inhabitants of the island of Corfu? Cutter Pinchbeck says we don't need *Corfunian*. In his priggish rejection letters he states that the people of Corfu are called Greeks, and that an etymolophile wouldn't be a lover of words, but a lover of the origin of words. He patronizingly says that *hiphopera* almost merited a lemma as an innovative, confluent melding of high and low culture; however, it didn't possess the "straight gully, niggerish perspicuity of this year's new entries, e.g., *badonkadonk*, *bling*, *bootylicious*, *dead presidents*, *hoodrat*, *peeps*, and *swol*," just to name a few slang ephemerals. And despite my having enclosed signed affidavits from my mother and a video of me, age twelve, winning twenty-five thousand dollars on *Name That Tune*, Cutter Pinchbeck doesn't believe that I, nor anyone of the hundred billion people who've trodden on earth in the past fifty thousand years, has ever had a phonographic memory—but I do. I remember everything I've ever heard. Every dropped nickel, raindrop drip-drop, sneaker squeak, and sheep bleat. Every jump rope chant, Miss Mary Mack Mack hand clap, and "eenie meanie chili beanie oop bop-bop bellini" method for choosing who's it. I remember every sappy R&B radio lyric and distorted Hendrix riff. Every Itzhak Perlman pluck and squishy backseat contorted make-out session. I can still hear every Hey you, You the man, and John Philip Sousa euphonium toot and every tree rustle and street-corner hustle. I remember every sound I've ever heard. It's like my entire life is a song I can't get out of my head.

"Ow." The Nigerian has burned himself. He's shaking his hand wildly and sucking air through his teeth. His date laughs, seizes his hand, and licks and nuzzles his seared fingers.

The jukebox ballad ends with a note that Ellington lays down with the gentleness of a child setting a wounded bird into a shoebox lined with tissue paper. A series of English words for "the day before yesterday" dies in the back of my throat—*penultidiem . . . prepretoday . . . yonyesterday . . .* —and like an unwitting Tourette's Syndrome utterance, a word for "the day before yesterday" flies from my mouth. "Retrothence!" The blonde and the Nigerian give me a strange look. I'm going to send that to Cutter Pinchbeck III at *Kensington-Merriwether. Retrothence* will look awfully nice on page 1147 of the Fourth College Edition, nestled between *retrospective* and *retroussé.*

"You still have some songs left."

The Nigerian is standing next to the jukebox.

"Put in 1007. You can play anything you want after that."

Rock 'n' roll saunters into the room. Overdubbed guitar riffs that don't come off as gimmicky, drums driving the song with the tough staccato love of a caring drill sergeant, and the bass, the bass is above the fray, suspended above the strings, synthesizers and percussion, brimming with a cocksure confidence, always threatening to show off but never doing it.

"Who is this?"

"The Magnum Opus."*

They're Southern California, sprawling, hazy, fickle, as underground as a rock group that sold twenty thousand records could

---

*Obscure but seminal L.A. garage band that in 1982 had one groundbreaking gig at the Roxy during which the lead singer, Manuel Ozuna, is reputed to have invented crowd surfing.

be. The critics hail groups like the Smashing Pumpkins and Pearl Jam as the purveyors of the new rock 'n' roll, choosing heroin vapidity over depth, haircuts over musicianship, head-to-toe white-boy pallor over a Mexican/black/American/*guapo*–politic band whose music has nothing to do with being Mexican, American, black, or handsome. High-pitched and just this side of screechy and that side of cogent, the vocals hydroplane over the melody.

"They're good," the Nigerian says.

"They are good," I wanted to say, "but two nights ago, not so far from where you're standing now, me and the greatest musician you've never heard of played two minutes and forty-seven seconds of musical perfection as timeless as the hydrogen atom and *Saturday Night Live*. A beat so perfect as to render musical labels null and void. A melody so transcendental that blackness has officially been declared passé. Finally, us colored folk will be looked upon with blithe indifference, not erotized pity or the disgust of Freudian projection. It's what we've claimed we always wanted, isn't it? To be judged 'not by the color of our skins, but by the content of our character'? Dude, but what we threw down was the content not of character, but *out* of character. It just happened to be of indeterminate blackness and funkier than a motherfucker."

CHAPTER 2

I MISS LOS ANGELES, the place where the sounds in my head started. I miss the midday smog; I liked the way my lungs pained after chasing my dog around the backyard fig and lemon trees, the dog, nearly as winded as I, licking the grit off my face, the sting from my eyes. I miss my day job at Trader Joe's, a convenience store for rich folks on gluten-free diets who, while I hand-pressed oranges into fresh-squeezed orange juice, would come up to me carrying two bottles of wine and ask which one would I recommend with light Indonesian fare, the Chianti or the Beaujolais? That was one of the good things about the job: You got to say "Beaujolais," "Gouda," and "Reblochon." I miss saying "Reblochon." I miss the landslides and the brush fires. For those of us who lived below the poverty line, which in Los Angeles is below five hundred feet above sea level, Mother Nature was the poor flatlanders' great equalizer. Lo, the guilt-free schadenfreude of watching a Coldwater Canyon dowager on the nightly news standing on the rooftop shingles of her ranch house armed with a garden hose, dodging embers and fighting back flames fanned by the high winds and my cynicism. I miss the Malibu mansions tumbling down rain-soaked mountainsides. Their owners tromping through the mud in Italian rain slickers, their beachfront dream homes now five-million-dollar piles of driftwood. In Los Angeles memorable nights are as countless as the Fatburger double-king-chili-cheese permutations. They're warm and prevailing as the Santa Ana winds that announce them and they play out like student films, scratchy, nonlinear, experimental, self-indulgent, and overexposed. Nights lubricated with stolen Volnay, Bordeaux, and magnums of Louis Roederer. Nights that dismissed themselves when the psilocybin-induced cartoon characters stopped frolicking on the shag carpet and climbed back into the television to become men with generic American drawls asking, "Has God touched you today?"

I miss those nights, but what I don't miss is the fear. In Los Angeles my fear was audible. *What up, cuz? Was happenin', blood? Pinche mayate, what are you doing in this neighborhood, ese? Hands behind your head, face on the ground! Are you sure you can afford to pay for this?* What with all the posturing, the slam dunk scowls, the hip-hop bravura, the What, me worry? middle-class nonchalance, and the condomless B-boy fucking on the down low, you'd never guess that we black men are afraid of many things, among them the police, water, and the math section of the Scholastic Aptitude Test; however, what we fear above all else is that out there among the 450 million other black men who inhabit this planet is an unapprehended habitual offender, a man twice as bad as Stagolee and half as sympathetic, a freeze-motherfucker-or-I'll-blow-your-head-off nigger on the lam who looks exactly like us.

Moving to Berlin reduced the fear of being mistaken for someone else to almost nothing. I stopped having the recurring nightmare of being at the post office and seeing a poster tacked to a bulletin board that read, WANTED FOR GRAND LARCENY, WHITE SLAVERY, AND CRIMES AGAINST HUMANITY. The profile and face-front mug shots didn't resemble me, but were me. Albeit a me I didn't know. A hard, slit-eyed, sneering me who went by an assortment of dead giveaway aliases, Pol Pot Johnson, Steve Mussolini, Mugabe von Quisling. Underneath the background information would be the rules of engagement and the amount of civic recompense. "This man is considered armed, ugly, and nuclear-meltdown dangerous. If you have any information concerning the whereabouts of this person, please notify the appropriate authorities immediately! Reward: $500,000 and the Eternal Gratitude of Your Government and Fellow Citizens."

But that fear of myself was who I was. It was all I and a lot of other little Los Angelenos had. I waited to be picked out of the crowd, actualized by white America, and if not by her, then a kiss from Velma Reinhardt, the big-bosomed, blonde-neighborhood vixen would do. However, as luck would have it, America beat Velma to the punch.

When I was fifteen I got a letter from the Los Angeles Unified School District notifying me that I was to report to the University of California Los Angeles for "special testing." I'd finally been identified, picked out of the crowd. This letter frightened my parents and me to no end, for there was a time not too long ago when colored men were purposely infected with syphilis, forced to ingest large doses of LSD, and timed in the forty-yard dash all under the guise of "special testing." His voice cracking, Daddy called the school board. "Yes, sir. I fully understand, sir." He muffled the receiver with his palm and whispered, "It's a math test. There'll be three other Negroes, two Chicanos, and an Eskimo boy there." Mother removed her eyeglasses and mouthed, "White boys too?"

"Yes," Father nodded. The dog scratched at the back door. My mother cried and turned her pages. I didn't think anyone could read E. L. Doctorow that fast.

I was one of those kids who liked to be first, and I made sure, without looking too rascally, that I was the first one in that classroom, pretending that I was the first black non-athletic-scholarship student to reintegrate UCLA since the death of affirmative action. I took a seat near the open windows overlooking the quadrangle and stuck my head out of the ivory tower, a nappy-headed Rapunzel. *White people's air more refreshing,* I thought to myself. *The wind brisker, more invigorating. The shade shadier. The squirrels squirrelier.* The proctor called my name—*Hey!*—then thumbed me to the back row, a row now occupied by two Sunday-suited black boys and a colored girl in what must have been her mother's cut-down wedding dress. The Eskimo kid, his bottom lip swollen with a tobacco chaw, was the last to arrive.

"Uukkarnit Kennedy?" the proctor asked.

Without skipping a beat Uukkarnit said in a deep, hickory-smoked, filtered drawl, "It sure ain't Ladies Love Cool James." Everyone laughed, as we West Coasters hated the sappy LL Cool J, much preferring Too Short's perverse rap limericks.

"Sit anywhere you like, Mr. Kennedy," he was told, and though the white section had plenty of open seats, Uukkarnit sat with us. He nodded hello in the chin-up Negro fashion. After coolly depositing a glob of brown drivel into his spit cup, he set it on the corner of the desk. His sitting with us was an act of solidarity. A late-twentieth-century equivalent to a lunch counter sit-in; and up to that point in my life, his placing that Styrofoam spittoon on that desk in full view of those white kids was the bravest thing I'd ever seen. Sometimes just making yourself at home is revolutionary.

The proctor walked up and down the aisles, placing a mechanical pencil and a sealed test booklet on each desk.

"If you find yourself in this classroom, it means that you've scored in the ninety-eighth percentile on the Tennessee Mathematical Proficiency Test for Non-Asian Eighth Graders. This booklet I'm placing in front of you is the Math Skills Assessment measure given to all incoming freshman math majors here at the University of California at Los Angeles. Do not open the booklet until you are told."

A nervous cough. From below, on the quad, the sounds of a coed touch football game. I leaned forward and asked Uukkarnit what his name meant. Without looking back he answered, "If you shave the polar bear, you'll find his skin is black."

"Is that true?"

"The meaning of the name or the shit about the black skin?"

"Both."

"The former is true; as for the latter, I've never been north of Santa Barbara, much less seen a shaved fucking polar bear."

The scores were posted outside the classroom in descending order. It was the first computer printout I'd ever seen. There was something affirming about seeing my name and score— FERGUSON W. SOWELL: 100/100—at the top of the list in what was then a futuristic telex font. I felt official. I was real. One by one we were summoned to a small office. When my turn came, the man behind the desk launched into a rapid-fire spiel about the Cold War and "finding suitable candidates for training in the aeronautical and nuclear sciences." When he said "suitable," he slowed down, finally stopping altogether mid–sales pitch. My inherent unsuitability having dawned on him, he had nothing more to say to me other than, "You may keep the mechanical pencil."

The white students were placed in an advanced mathematics class at the university; we Negro boys, and the lone girl, were given instruments and sent to the Wilmer Jessop Academy of Music. I never saw Uukkarnit again.

I won't say I didn't learn anything at Jessop Academy, but they never taught Why? Why was I playing? Why was music so powerful? What can I do with music? Can it heal? Can it kill? They never taught me who Wilmer Jessop was, either, now that I think about it. I learned more about music from watching Spencer Tracy on Turner Classic Movies than from any composition class. Pick a movie, any movie—*Boys Town*, *Bad Day at Black Rock*—when Spencer Tracy enters a room, he stares hard at the floor, looking for his acting mark. He ambles up to it, squints at it, jabs his toe at it, casually places his hands on his hips, lifts that broad beatific face of his, then acts his motherfucking ass off. I tried to teach myself to play like Spencer Tracy acts. Incorporating "looking for my mark" into my trumpet solos, playing with the knowledge that the search for identity and a sense of place is both process and result, and the trick is to fool the audience into thinking you know exactly where you're going. That math test score was the first time I spotted my mark on the stage. I knew where to stand. I existed, and would go on to further differentiate myself from the rest of black maledom with an SAT math score that to this day I carry in my back pocket, so when anyone asks for my papers I can show them my test results and declare, "I don't know what other nigger did what to whom, but it couldn't be me. Look, 800 Math."

Back then I harbored dreams of being the insouciant jazzman, figuring my given name, Ferguson W. Sowell, guaranteed that in a few years my pipe-smoking visage would be on the cover of a string of eponymous Blue Note albums. I had a desk drawer stuffed with scraps of paper bearing these unreleased titles: *Sowell Brother, Sowell Survivor, O Sowell Mio, Sowell'd Out, Summer Sowellstice*. I did have some talent; my phonographic memory allowed me to replicate any piece of music perfectly. But I never knew what I was playing. No matter how many times my music teacher reminded me that the tunes sounded like their titles, I couldn't tell one Thelonious Monk composition from another.

"*Bum baba bum. Bum baba bum,*" he'd scat. "*Bum ba bum ba bum bababa bum.* What song is that, Mr. Sowell?"

" 'Epistrophy'?"

" 'Blue Monk,' you tone-deaf ignoramus!"

I was "phased out" of the jazz program at Jessop Academy and became the only student enrolled in "Audiovisual Studies," the music-school equivalent of special education. I spent most of my time preparing for a future career as a roadie by setting up drum sets, tuning instruments, and wheeling projectors and sound equipment from classroom to classroom. During my free time I locked myself in the storeroom and fucked around with the computers and the turntables. For graduation I was expected to hand in a thesis paper explaining how to properly mic up a drummer who sings background vocals, but instead handed in a version of Handel's *Messiah* composed entirely of elements from the Beastie Boys' *Licensed to Ill* album. My baroque/brat-rap/mash-up oratorio became that year's valedictorian speech. After graduation I decided to give up the trumpet, enroll in junior college, and become a DJ.

DJing was so much easier. Too easy, really. Play "Knee Deep" at the wedding reception and even the groom's grandmother would ease out onto the dance floor to shake her brittle hips and swing her pendulous tits.

Look, I'll be the first to admit it, I'm not the most technically gifted disc jockey ever to put needle to wax. Acute left-handedness, a fear of crowds, and what I consider to be my healthy hatred of self make for a catchy stage name, DJ Darky—That Right-Brained, Self-Absorbed Agoraphobic Boy, and not your prototypical beat-juggling, speed-mixing, whirling dervish yelling, "Art form! Art form!" after every body contortion and scratch. Much of what little scratching I do is accidental, so I compensate for a lack of skills and Negritude with a surfeit of good taste and a record collection that I like to think is to DJing what the Louvre is to painting.

I envy the Louvre's curator. Whoever it is, they have it better than I do. No beating the bushes for the next impressionistic phenom. *There's this kid Monet you have to see. His brushwork is impeccable.* No flipping through portfolios, listening to mix tapes, hoping your heavy sigh conveys intrigue, not exasperation. No one ever asks what you think about Jeff Koons. Twice a year the curator takes a slow, temperature-controlled elevator ride to the basement, greets the armed Algerian guard in the burgundy polyester blazer with a patronizing wave, and asks him to pick a letter, any letter, and blows the dust off the Degas and the Delacroix. *We'll show theez onez, no?*

All the important decisions were made for him back in 1793 when the Louvre opened its gilded doors and said, *Enculez le chic,* fuck cool. At the end of the eighteenth century, neoclassicism was pop culture. Goya was a graffiti artist. Lithography was computer graphics. Mozart rocked the house sporting a Suzy-Q hair perm that'd make any time-traveling L.A. gangster rapper worth his curling iron and shower cap ask where he could cop one of them wigs, sans the powder? When Zerezo transformed the bolero, a Spanish folk dance, into French ballet, he might as well have been Crazy Legs or Rock Steady teaching break dancing to the urban doyennes, their hair in buns and their other buns in the air.

. . . *and roller-skate, roller-skate . . . and demi-plié, demi-plié.*

I've never seen the Mona Lisa, and from what I hear it's overrated. But what isn't? Da Vinci got lucky. Every genius does, especially the prolific ones. I feel the same way about Leonardo as I do about Tupac and Edgar Allan Poe. Two composers whose baggy-eyed, drug-induced prolificacy, in much the same way the millionth monkey on the millionth typewriter types Shakespeare, resulted in a few random pieces of brilliance among reams of rhyming, repetitious, woe-is-me claptrap. "The Raven," "How Do

U Want It?," "The Tell-Tale Heart," "Dear Mama," "California Love,"—each is a masterpiece, but when's the last time a prep school taskmaster called upon a cardigan sweater for a recitation of "Tamerlane," "To F——s S. O——d" or "The Conqueror Worm"? And on that most sacred of holidays, Tupac's birthday, every urban-contemporary radio station in the world knows not to play "Honk If U Luv Honkies," "Thugs, Slugs and Butt Plugs," and "Real Niggaz Get Manicures." To me the Mona Lisa is little more than a Renaissance *Playboy* centerfold. Blemishes and Mediterranean hirsuteness airbrushed out, she has been retouched to the point of meaningless perfection. However, I understand the painting's value: the allure of a piece of art that not everyone adores, but that no one hates. My record collection lacked a Mona Lisa, an apolitical, simple yet subtly complex piece of music that no one could dismiss. A beat that when you hear it at a party makes you think you're special even though you're dressed, speaking, drinking, dancing, and thinking exactly like everyone else. This beat that spoke directly to you and no one else. Telling you in no uncertain terms that you're alive.

I didn't know it then, but I was starting out on the quest for quintessential dopeness that would eventually lead me to Berlin.

Buddha had his first revelation under the bodhi tree. I had mine under the influence of Vicodin, Seconal, and what a cat named Twitchy told me were the last two quaaludes south of San Luis Obispo. *Here in this DJ booth my body may shrivel up; my skin, my bones, my flesh may dissolve; but my body will not move from this booth until I have attained Enlightenment, so difficult to obtain over the course of many caipirinhas.*

It was a fundraiser, a marathon rave where I played sixteen hours straight, spinning a depressant electronic-dance-music sutra

PAUL BEATTY

comprising two hundred records so similar in melody and bpm they might as well have been issued on one manhole-sized platter. I was still unenlightened and I was down to my last record, a techno single that had somehow snuck into my crate the way a crop-devouring beetle slips into the country in a sack of coffee beans. Techno is the only musical genre I find completely incomprehensible. I won't say it's noise. Noise at least has a source. I played the record; the incessant drumbeat tom-tommed throughout the club. My raga turned into a powwow. Hordes of shirtless strobe-lit frat boys bejeweled in glowing necklaces and bracelets zigzagged from medicine man to medicine man, war-whooping their cares away, while sweaty coeds danced in tiny Ojibwa circles.

Enlightened by the realization that playing records at weddings and raves wasn't the way to enlightenment, I'd reached the end of my meditative period. When DJ Blaze, my best friend and fellow member of the Beard Scratcher record collective, arrived with the crate of records I needed, he was two hours late. His eyes were glazed and reddened from indica bud. My indica bud.

"You sure you wanted *this* crate?" I nodded and motioned for him to hand me a record, any record. "These white boys going to lynch your ass. Not for reckless eyeballing, but for reckless rap." He handed me the next record in the crate, one that, despite our collective's vow to share all resources, was one I didn't want him to know I had. I placed it on the deck and cued it up. Back then playing New York hip-hop in an Inland Empire dance club jam-packed with white kids expecting industrial and synthpop was akin to Hernán Cortés landing on the beaches of Hispaniola. Each booming bass note was a starboard cannon blast fired over the heads of primitives and into the rain forest. "I hereby claim your heathen souls in the name of *the South Bronx, the South South Bronx!*" A shrapnel shower of tree bark, scratching, and slant rhyme rained down on the natives. No one danced. No one told me to stop, either.

Blaze craned his neck to look at the spinning record. The label had been peeled off but he thought maybe he could glean some information from the serial number scratched into the run-off or the width of the grooved portion. I can say what it was now, Stezo's "It's My Turn."

Funk not only moves, it can remove . . . it'll clear your chakras; I'll give it that. But it isn't enlightenment. None of it is. Jazz, classical, blues, dancehall, bhangra—it's all scattered chapters of the sonic Bhagavad Gita.

Blaze and I drove home windows down, cool air and cool FM jazz blasting in our faces. Clifford Brown swung through "Cherokee" and I thought of all things Indian: Buddha's pilgrimage, Jim Thorpe, Satyajit Ray, peyote, Tonto, lamb korma, extinction, overpopulation, cricket, Bob "Rapid Robert" Feller, and antique 350cc motorcycles.

Once back in my bedroom, I sought to dampen the techno echoes still reverberating in my head. To do this I consulted my Buddhas, both the oxidized green brass figurine that sat serenely inside my gohonzon and the moist, spinach-green buddha-bless sealed inside a sandwich baggie and buried at the bottom of my underwear drawer. That wasn't the night I decided to come to Germany, but the longest journey starts with a single toke.

The weed was good. A kind blend of medicinal from the alternative clinic and the remnants of the hydroponic I mooched off Alice in Chains. I sparked the joint and made the mandatory pothead vow: "From now on, man, everything's going to be different. Soon as I graduate from SMCC with an associate degree in library science, shit's going to be on. The world will be my card index."

The pot kicked in harder. Marijuana doesn't erase my auditory flashbacks but mitigates them in much the same manner that Fats Waller's left hand and infectious asides keep one from paying attention to the inane lyrics of those Tin Pan Alley ditties he was forced to sing.

That night, in addition to the techno, I was being tormented by my worst sonic memory. The sound of a brutal injury my endorphins prevented me from feeling but not from hearing. I'm eight. Playing Nerf hoop. Going one-on-one against the dog. I have a lane for the dunk but never get airborne. There's only the crack of my tibia snapping in half like a giant pair of takeout chopsticks, followed by the Velcro rip of one side of the broken bone tearing away from the muscle and shooting up my leg, knocking off my kneecap with a sixty-decibel pop that sounded like a schoolboy stepping on a empty milk carton. The dog. The dog is whining, yelping, and frantically scrambling, trying to get out from under my broken body.

I used to be a loudness maniac. I'd try to drown out my sound memories by standing next to jackhammer operators, cupping my ear when the fire engines roared by, or sticking my sand-covered head into the deafening, numbing sting of the board-walk showers at Venice Beach. Apart from two weeks of blissful tinnitus brought on by an eighty-thousand-watt Blue Öyster Cult concert at the Fabulous Forum, these noisy escapisms always proved to be short-lived. The ringing in my ears eventually subsided, a piece of boulevard sidewalk would catch me in the face or a pushy elderly couple would bogart my shower, then proceed to flap water from my stream onto their distended, sea-salt-caked pubes. Still, I'm one of the few who relish the wailing baby on a crowded plane.

The higher I got that night, the softer and mellower my fugue. In time, the more fragile and subtle sounds from my past began to dominate my thoughts: the cuteness of every puppy sneeze I ever heard, the freedom in the whir of a Tour de France peloton coasting downhill, the unlimited artistic possibility in the click of a four-color pen, the anticipation in a firecracker fuse's sizzle. I sifted through these sounds and tried to come up with the most comforting sound from my childhood, one that if I were on my deathbed would actually be the last thing I'd want to hear. I remembered how I used to sit in the den with Moms just so I could listen to her read the *New Yorker*. In those days the literary and paper quality of that magazine was much better than it is now. Those pages had an intellectual and textual heft to them. They felt like parchment, a parchment that no family ever had the temerity to throw away. Ma would turn through the Bellow and the pages rustled as though the story had been printed on numbered autumn leaves. I decided that if I could collapse all my memories into one sound, it would be the sound of those pages turning. Crisp. Mordant. Pipe-smoke urbane. I went to my turntables and tried to replicate it. That was when I first started mining the favorite sounds in my memory bank in the hope that one day I'd compose a soundtrack that'd loop inside my head over and over again. I, like many a mixmaster who's come before me—Count Basie, the biathlete's heart, and the inimitable Afrika Bambaataa—was looking for the perfect beat, the confluence of melody and groove that transcends mood and time. A beat that can be whistled, pounded on lunchroom tabletops, or blasted from shitty undermodulated car-stereo speakers and not lose its toe-tapping gravitas. A beat that would make all the ladies in the house say Hey! without prompting from a concert rapper in dire need of some stage presence. A beat that couldn't be commercialized and trivialized by Madison Avenue, reduced to thirty hard-sell/soft-sell seconds. A timeless beat, never to become an "oldie but a goodie" but always destined to be as fresh as French bread. The sonic Mona Lisa.

Above my decks hung an eight-by-ten color photo from a house party I had done a while back. In it I was positioned in some nondescript Mar Vista garage exactly as I was then, bent over a set of turntables, face barely visible, left shoulder awkwardly raised to my ear to hold the headphone in place. Fingertips freshly licked and resting lightly on the vinyl as if I were testing a hot iron's readiness. My Piru-red XXXL T-shirt with the words TRADER JOE'S/PRONTO MARKET silk-screened just above the breast pocket, billowing away from my scrawny body. Blaze in the background, in profile, Locs sunglasses, black wool beanie pulled down past his ears, frozen in mid–pop lock, a contorted Toltec testimonial to post-Hispanic Mesoamericana. Behind him, leaning against the garage wall among the gardening tools and surfboards, a multidysfunctional lineup of Westside hoods, homies, and honeys of all races, intellects, and loyalties to Laker basketball. I looked at the photograph and knew then that all I knew was sound, and that sound would be all that I'd ever know.

"That was incredible, dude."

It was Blaze. He was holding two cheap but intricate-looking pewter beer steins, two six-packs of beer, and singing the Löwenbräu commercial: "Here's to good friends/Tonight is kind of special/The beer will pour, must say something more somehow/Tonight let it be Löwenbräu."

"Is that Löwenbräu?"

"No, I'm just singing the song—my sister wouldn't send me some shit we could steal from Trader Joe's, this is the unpronounceable shit."

Apparently Blaze's older sister, Mariela, a tank mechanic stationed in Germany, had sent him a case of that strong leathery beer we loved so much. Beer that, no matter how much we drank, never left us with a hangover, only an urge to obey orders.

As the beer percolated in the steins, we clanked them together.

"To the Reinheitsgebot."

"Reinheitsgebot!"

"What was that radical stuff you were playing?"

"I'm trying to find the perfect beat."

"That was damn close, bro. Remember that offshore storm senior year when we went up to Zuma? Set after perfectly timed set of glassy eight footers, steep-ass take-offs, big barrels, remember that?"

"Yeah, even the sunset session was fucking excellent."

"If there had been five miles per hour less wind, it would have been absolutely perfect conditions."

"The wind made the shoulders just a tad too gnarly."

"Well, that's what your mix sounds like. It's easily the best beat I've ever heard and probably the best beat I'll ever hear, but it's five miles per hour too windy."

The beer and the weed complemented each other well. I was drunk and high at the same time. Close my left eye and I was high, shut my right and I was drunk.

High.

Drunk.

High.

Drunk.

I squinted through the mental fog and looked at the detail on the stein. The castles, elks, and mustachioed Kaisers came to life. A beer maiden, her hair in thick sausage curls, whispered my name.

Over the next few months I set about composing my perfect beat, whittling off a mile per hour of wind here and a couple of knots there. Eventually I succeeded in splicing together a two-minute-and-forty-seven-second amalgamation of samples, street recordings, and original phrases. It was with some trepidation that I played it for Blaze and the rest of the Beard Scratchers. The Beard Scratchers being the members of our record pool, and so named because of our capricious yet squandered intellectualism, the way we listened to jazz with our faces pinched in agony as if we were suffering from migraine headaches as much as from our scruffy and chronically itchy chins. Though the Beard Scratchers, like most DJs, were inveterate biters, incorrigible beat snatchers who would rip off any rhythm or melody not copyrighted in triplicate and claim it as their own, I wasn't worried about anyone stealing it. The beat was impossible to replicate. Too many layers, obscure riffs from pop bands that never popped, folk music from countries without folksiness, sea chanteys from landlocked nations, all overlapped with my favorite idiosyncratic sounds and pressed into a musical ore as unidentifiable as a fragment of flying saucer metal in a 1950s sci-fi film. I was worried, though, that it was too long to be a beat or break. That what I had composed was an interlude or, even worse, a song.

When the music ended, all the Beard Scratchers scratched their beards save for Elaine Dupree, aka DJ Uhuru, the only member of the collective for whom a beard was an impossibility. But Elaine wasn't even rubbing her chin: She was dialing a number on the phone.

"Who you calling?"

"Bitch Please."

Bitch Please was an aging, once-platinum-selling rapper who occasionally purchased beats from us whenever her latest career reinvention called for some sonic esotericism. She once said about me that when I spun, no matter how frenzied or attentive the crowd was, I always looked unsure of myself. Looked as if I smelled gas but didn't have anyone to ask if they smelled it too, much less the nerve to strike a match.

Elaine put the phone on speaker and held it up.

"Hello, this Bitch Please, the world's only rhinestone rockstar doll, baby baba. Please leave a message."

On the beep, Elaine motioned for me to hit the play button. The beat was only ten seconds in when Bitch Please answered the phone: "I don't know who this is, but I'll give you thirty thousand dollars cash for that track right now."

Elaine hung up.

Thirty thousand dollars was an absurd amount of money to pay for a beat, and after the poor sales of her latest release, *Bitch Please Raps the Cole Porter Songbook*, I doubted that her bank account held half that amount. Still, it was a meaningful gesture.

"So it is a beat?" I asked.

"A damn near perfect one at that, *presque parfait*, as the French would say," said DJ Umbra. "What's in it? Anatomize, yo, anatomize!"

I began to break down some of the more obvious samples, getting only as far as the de rigueur Mantronix, when Elaine interrupted me by blurting out, "Popsicle!"—the name of the only Swedish pop group worth blurting out. And it was without trepidation that DJ Skillanator followed with, "Foreigner, 'Feels Like the First Time,' opening lick, second and third chords transposed with the handclap from the Angels' 'My Boyfriend's Back,' interpolating on the downstroke."

DJ So So Deaf, a beat jockey who is in fact deaf, and who made a decent living playing bass-heavy music at dances and sock hops at schools and universities for the hearing impaired, began waving and gesticulating wildly in his slang B-boy sign language. His brother, DJ You Can Call Me Ray or You Can Call Me Jay but Ya Doesn't Have to Call Me Johnson, whose bailiwick was comedy albums and television theme songs from the seventies, interpreted. "So So Deaf says, 'Only Roger Daltrey's epiglottal scream from "Won't Get Fooled Again" can raise the hairs on his arm like that.' He loves how you flared it."

I touched my hand to my lips and kissed out a sign language thank-you to So So Deaf in return for his compliment. As the music played on, our thoughts returned to the beat *presque parfait*.

There were no more guesses and the Beard Scratchers leaned in, eager for just a taste of the beat's trace elements; and seeing the wide-eyed puppy-dog looks of inquisitiveness on their faces, I felt compelled to recite the only true truism I'd ever heard. "I should warn you before we begin," I said loudly and urgently, as if I were delivering a line from the final act of a Tennessee Williams play, "that I'm not going to necessarily tell you the truth."

The Beard Scratchers nodded.

DJ Close-n-Play asked, "Is that a quote from *Catcher in the Rye?*"

It was saxophonist Masayoshi Urabe's opening statement from his *Opprobrium* magazine interview, but I didn't want to get into "Who's he?" and "What's 'opprobrium' mean?," so I simply turned up the volume and said, "No, it's my motto," and went about naming my sources.

"That's 'Insider Tradin' on My Mind' by Penthouse Red," I whispered, "from his *Work Songs and Office Hollers of the Corporate Elite* sampler."

"Same cat who did 'My Trophy Wife (Makes Me Feel Like a Loser)'?" asked DJ You Can Call Me Ray, et cetera.

"No, you're thinking Greedy Steve McNeely."

I went on.

"Audio Two's 'Top Billin'' as rapped in the whistled language of the Nepalese Chepang."

"I knew it!" Umbra said, pounding his forehead in musicologist shame.

I continued my list: "Brando's creaking leather jacket in *The Wild One*, a shopping cart tumbling down the concrete banks of the L.A. River, Mothers of Invention, a stone skimming across Diamond Lake, the flutter of Paul Newman's eyelashes amplified ten thousand times, some smelly kid named Beck who was playing guitar in front of the Church of Scientology, early, early, early Ray Charles, Etta James, Sonic Youth, the Millennium

Falcon going into hyperdrive, Foghorn Leghorn, Foghat, Melvin Tormé, aka 'The Velvet Fog,' Issa Bagayogo, the sizzle of an Al's Sandwich Shop cheesesteak at the exact moment Ms. Tseng adds the onions . . ."

Blaze raised his hand. "That's enough," he said. "You're spoiling it. You're explaining rainbows, motherfucker."

He let the song play out, then continued. "You know what your beat reminds me of?"

"No," I answered, rewinding the tape.

"It reminds me of the code of Hammurabi, the Declaration of DJ Independence, the Constitution, or some shit."

Everyone else nodded in agreement, but I didn't understand the comparison.

"Look, dude, you've sampled your life, mixed those sounds with a funk precedent, and established a sixteen-bar system of government for the entire rhythm nation. Set the DJ up as the executive, the legislative, and the judicial branches. I mean, after listening to your beat, anything I've heard on the pop radio in the last five years feels like a violation of my civil rights."

We the true music lovers of the world, in order to form a more perfect groove . . .

Don't get me wrong, I appreciated Blaze's praise, but I didn't like my music being compared to a piece of paper and said so: "I think of it more as a timeless piece of art, you know, like the Mona Lisa of music. Your Constitution metaphor is too political. You're making it seem like my music is propaganda."

Pressing the play button, Blaze laughed, "Man, didn't anybody ever tell you that all art is propaganda? It doesn't matter whether you think it should be or it shouldn't be, it just is, and motherfucker, like or not, you're sitting on a funky Magna Carta. An unbelievably dope beat that's this close to being the supreme law of the land—but as it stands now is no more than a musicalized Equal Rights Amendment, a brilliant and necessary idea doomed to the dustbin of change."

The music quieted the room with a thumping irrefutability that was indeed just short of perfection. I turned it down.

"So what's it missing?" I asked.

Blaze leaned back in his chair and smoothed his goatee. "Like any important document, it needs to be ratified."

"Take my track to the thirteen original colonies and get people to vote on whether they like it or not?"

Elaine scratched at her jawline. "No, he's just saying you need that one special somebody to approve it," she said. "Think Mick Jagger ratifying Carly Simon's 'You're So Vain.' "

Umbra contemplatively tugged on his soul patch and tossed out another example: "Charlie Christian ratifying Benny Goodman's 'A Smo-o-o-oth One.' "

So So Deaf stopped playing with his pointy imperial beard long enough to sign, "Like Kool G Rap on Marley Marl's 'The Symphony.' "

"So who can ratify my beat?" I asked.

Blaze looked at me like I was stupid. "The Schwa," he said, crossing his heart and blowing a kiss to the sky. "Who else?" The rest of us bowed our heads in reverence. Who else indeed.

Charles Stone, aka the Schwa, is a little-known avant-garde jazz musician we Westside DJs had nicknamed the Schwa because his sound, like the indeterminate vowel, is unstressed, upside-down, and backward. Indefinable, but you know it when you hear it. For us the Schwa is the ultimate break beat. The boom bip. The *oo-ee oo ah ah ting tang walla walla bing bang*. The *om*. He's the part in Pagliacci where the fucking clown starts crying.

He had one minor hit record, a hard-bop rendition of "L'Internationale" that ironically charted briefly in the early stages of the Vietnam War. "L'Internationale" is on his seminal *Polemics* album. *Polemics*, recorded in 1964, is an engaging, thought-provoking, and shabbily produced masterpiece. Listening to that record is like sitting in on an impromptu graduate seminar taught by a favorite, slightly tipsy professor at the campus pub. Measure by measure the Schwa deconstructs nursery rhymes, advertising jingles, and the more sonorous of the world's anthems. Each tune, from "Ten Little Indians" to "The Battle Hymn of Andorra" to the Slinky song, is lovingly turned inside out and played in a style so free it makes entropy jealous. Sandwiched between the Nazi Party's "Horst Wessel Song" and Johnny Rebel's swampbilly classic "Some Niggers Never Die (They Just Smell That Way)," "Do-Re-Mi," the whitest song ever written, becomes more than simply a song I hate: The Schwa exposes that Alpine ditty for what it is, hate music.

But "L'Internationale" stands out. I'm the type who prefers to listen to one song a hundred times rather than a hundred different songs one time. And I listened to that song a thousand times straight, its majestic strains as quotidian to my day as breakfast cereal. It was a song that made me wish I'd come of age during the Spanish Civil War, shared a foxhole with George Orwell. It was a song that would've shamed Stalin and lionized Paul Robeson. In fact, I'm quite certain that if the song had gotten more radio play, America would've never stopped buying union.

Background information on the Schwa was scarce. I'd scoured the underground jazz magazines and reference books, and all I could find was a scant entry in *The Jazz Encyclopedia:*

Stone, Charles—b. 4/17/33, Los Angeles, California. A well-respected musician proficient in the improvisational techniques of the free-jazz movement of whom little is known.

And a heavily redacted copy of a brief FBI file:

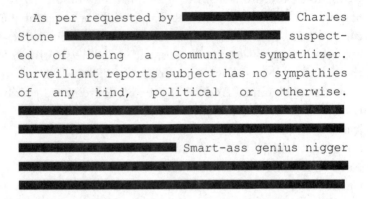

```
Dear Mr. Hoover,

  As per requested by ███████████ Charles
Stone ██████████████████████ suspect-
ed of being a Communist sympathizer.
Surveillant reports subject has no sympathies
of any kind, political or otherwise.
████████████████████████████████████
████████████████████████████████████
██████████████████████ Smart-ass genius nigger
████████████████████████████████████
████████████████████████████████████


Stay American, Baby!
Buddy Rich
```

There were also scattered concert reviews from the early fifties that praised the "physicality of his performance." It seemed the Schwa played with his body contorted in ghastly positions. Sometimes he stood onstage gyrating his pelvis or dislocating his shoulders for five minutes before producing any sounds. Most critics theorized that these corporeal contrivances were designed to illustrate that making music is more than a mental process, that a musician brings his body to a gig, not just his brain.

The Schwa's discography was slight: three albums and a smattering of monaural EPs that had seeped into circulation. The most recent being *Darker Side of the Moon*, a foray into fusion that featured a cover photo of a black man's backside and had the good fortune of being released at the same time as Pink Floyd's multiplatinum *Dark Side of the Moon*. Due to clerical errors and acid-rock fans tweaked on microdots, the record did a steady if not brisk mail-order business. But since then the Schwa had completely disappeared from the scene, an act that served only to endear him to me all the more. There's a special place in my heart for artists who inexplicably disappear at the top of their games. The list is a short one: Gigi Gryce, Louise Brooks, Rimbaud, D'Angelo, Francis Ford Coppola.* I admire these aesthetes for withdrawing into themselves knowing they have nothing further to say, and even less desire to hear what anyone has to say to them. That's why I've never read *Catcher in the Rye*: I don't want the novel to ruin a good reclusion.

Elaine broke my trance. "Man, it'd be almost worth finding the Schwa just to get him to play over your beat."

"I'll make the first pledge," Blaze said, throwing sixty dollars on the floor. "Seriously, you need to find him. The chance for true perfection doesn't come along every day."

The phone rang. "It's Bitch Please," Elaine announced sotto voce, her hand over the receiver. "She says she'll pay fifty thousand dollars for the beat."

---

*Every film post–*Apocalypse Now* has been directed by a lookalike hired by the movie industry to keep the dream alive.

CHAPTER 3

Back in los angeles I used to score porn films. Still do when money's tight. Not much difference between the American and German smut, except that German pornographers don't see the three Ps, pubic hair, plot, and perky breasts, as anachronisms. In the beginning I took the job seriously. Most cats just handed in any old piece of music they weren't able to sell. They could care less about the music matching the mood. I actually watch the schlock. Sometimes I'll go so far as to compose different themes for each character. For a while I even tried working as a soundman, thinking that would give me some insight into the X-rated mise-en-scène. However, my latent prudishness was exposed when to my open-mouthed and wide-eyed surprise I discovered 1) females ejaculate, 2) they're capable of expelling said ejaculate over long distances, 3) it's salty, and 4) it stings like hell! Despite my rubber-gloved, hands-on approach to scoring porn films, the only thing I learned was why the great film composers like Michel Legrand and Lalo Schifrin stayed away from the set.

After dropping *le beat presque parfait*, I'd composed the soundtrack for a blue movie called *Splendor in the Ass*. A score that Rick Chess, a director with whom I'd worked before, deemed "too musical." I explained to him how the overlap of the progression and the extended glissando matched the sex act's natural music. The rhythmic clapping of the stud's testicles against the star's buttocks accentuated the trombone runs. Her "fuck-me-you-motherfucker-harder-goddammit" guttural scatting was contrapuntal to the lower-register xylophone. Rick started to ask what *mise-en-scène* meant, getting only as far as the *mise* before grabbing me by the elbow and ushering me into the bestiality department. He removed a videotape from a manila envelope and popped it into the editing machine. A bespectacled man, his pants dropped to his ankles, was fucking a chicken. Rick twisted a knob. The music came up. A sound so beautiful it should have been incongruous with the image on the monitor, but it was instead transformative. The man was making love to the chicken, and the chicken was enjoying it. I recognized the musician immediately. It could have only been the Schwa.

Rick Chess fiddled with the hydraulics of his computer chair, raising and lowering his seat in rhythm to the music.

"This is quality footage, but it's unusable. The music is too good. Now the shit is an art film. Some sick fuck in a peep booth on Santa Monica Boulevard doesn't want to jerk off to art—he wants filth."

"Who is this?" I asked Rick.

He looked at me crazily. "How'm I supposed to know? Came in the mail as an audition tape."

He tossed me the envelope. The return address read, "Schallplattenunterhalter Dunkelmann, Slumberland Bar, Goltzstraße 24, 10781 Berlin, Germany."

"Can I have this?" I asked.

Rick nodded. "Sure, keep it. I want you to use this as an example of what not to do, because you're reverting to your old ways." He stuck his hand into his receding, greasy hairline and kept it there. "I want the hack back. I want the DJ Darky who provided nondescript background music for *Lawrence of a Labia* and *12 Angry Menses*, conveyed the apolitical intrigue in *All the President's Semen*. I don't want the high-concept genius."

"Yeah, sure."

Nonplussed in the proper *Kensington-Merriwether* usage of the word, I was only half listening to Rick's harangue. I couldn't believe that distinctive legato that swirled inside my head was coming from the Schwa. I'm not the "it all happens for a reason, God has a plan, everything will work out like an HBO television show" type. Before Rick Chess played that video, the only serendipitous occurrence in my life was that I misspelled "serendipity" during a local spelling bee and thankfully wasn't aboard the bus carrying the area's best spellers to the city finals when it plunged off the Sepulveda Overpass.

This was no happy accident. I turned my attention back to the video. Serenaded by an exquisitely delicate diminuendo, the stud and the hen reached a cackling, groaning, mutual orgasm.

Chess elbowed me in the ribs. "Who came first, the chicken or the egghead?"

When I got home I took a good long look at the envelope. I didn't have to be Easy Rawlins to figure out the Schwa didn't send the tape. The use of *esszet ligatur* in "Goltzstraße." The crosshatched 7s. The handwriting just looked too German.

I called up West German information and over a staticky connection asked for Schallplattenunterhalter Dunkelmann's phone number in West Berlin.

The operator couldn't stop laughing.

"You making fun with me. This must be that American television show . . ." I could hear her flipping through her dictionary. ". . . *Straightforward Kamera*."

She meant *Candid Camera,* but at $3.75 a minute I wasn't in the mood to correct her.

"So there's no Schallplattenunterhalter Dunkelmann in the Berlin directory?"

"*Nein.* We have an Andreas Dunkelmann auf der Lausitzer-strasse. A Dieter Dunkelmann on Derfflingerstrasse. A Hugo on . . ."

"What about the Slumberland Bar?"

"Please, hold for that number."

"Hallo, Slumberland," the bartender, a woman with a sultry Mae West rasp, yelled into the phone, trying to make herself heard over music and the raucous din. I remember thinking the place sounded dangerous. I asked for Dunkelmann.

"There are many *dunkel* men here. Who do you want to speak with?" she asked, sounding a bit leery. I felt like I was making an international crank call.

"I'd like to speak to Schallplattenunterhalter Dunkelmann."

The bartender paused for a moment. "You want to speak with maybe a DJ Black Man or a DJ Dark Person?"

Suddenly the cryptogram became obvious. "Schallplattenun-terhalter Dunkelmann" was an approximation of my nom de musique, DJ Darky. The bartender explained to me that in German, *Dunkelmann* means "obscurant" or, more literally, "dark man," and that *Schallplattenunterhalter* was an East German term for "disk jockey." East Germany being a place where the global predominance of English had yet to suck the fun out of the language's tongue-twisting archaism.

The phone call sealed it: I had to go to Germany. Obviously someone there had heard my music and appreciated it enough to think I was worthy of finding the Schwa. What I couldn't figure out was why all the subterfuge. Why not just tell me where he was?

Music history is rife with no-brainer collaborations that

should've but never happened. Charlie Parker and Arnold Schoenberg. The Osmonds and the Jackson Five. The Archies and Josie and the Pussycats, and though I didn't even have the name recognition of Valerie Smith, Josie's tambourine-shaking sidekick, such a missed opportunity would not befall the Schwa and Schallplattenunterhalter Dunkelmann. If I could figure out a way to raise the funds to get my ass and my record collection to Germany, history would have its perfect beat.

Of course, I wasn't about to sell my beat to Bitch Please or any other track-starved rapper, so I started saving my cash and begging every German Institute and art organization I could find for grant money and a visa. But after discovering that DJs and porno composers don't qualify as musicians or artists, I took another tack. I became a jukebox sommelier.

CHAPTER 4

THE JUKEBOX-SOMMELIER IDEA came to me not long after hearing the chicken-fucking song, during a night out at Sunny Glens, a dive bar on Robertson Boulevard populated by Hamilton High alums who'd graduated in the bottom third of the previous twenty graduating classes. Bridgette Lopez and I were on one of our rare public dates. Some days I thought I could marry Bridgette. She was a forty-five-year-old divorcée who, during my Sunday-night gigs at La Marina in Playa Del Rey, sat next to the DJ booth, her pudgy legs crossed at the knees and looking like two porpoises trapped in fishnet stockings. She'd ply me with cosmopolitans and five-dollar bills, scratch a long ex-chola burgundy fingernail down my forearm, and request a song or sex act. More often than not I granted both her requests, and by the end of the evening we'd be singing sweet doo-wop oohs and coos and making slow jam vows to love each other always and forever. Apart from having to listen to Heatwave ad infinitum the rest of my days, a life with Bridgette wouldn't have been too bad.

She stuffed quarters into the pool table and I bought drinks. I had to shout to make myself heard over the loud, keening, post–*Diver Down* Van Halen guitar riffs coming out from the rainbow Wurlitzer. "What you drinking, *pendeja?*" I yelled. Bridgette loved it when I talked dirty to her.

"*Dame una vaso de vino, mayate.*" And I loved when she called me nigger in her woeful Spanish.

"Red or white, *puta?*"

"*Rojo, cabrón.*"

"Red wine," I screamed into the bartender's ear. He shook his head and slammed down two bottles of bum wine, neither of them red or white. I told him to pour the green even though he was pushing the orange.

Whenever I think of Bridgette I think of the sound of her pool breaks. They were molecular and sounded like an introduction to an organic chemistry textbook. I loved to tape-record them. The cue ball flying toward the pyramid of painted ivory neutrinos as if it'd been shot out of a particle accelerator.

Bridgette sank two solids off a clean, wonderfully cold-blooded-sounding break, and as she lined up her next shot, she took her first sip of Chateau du Ghetto. "Who the fuck is the sommelier here—Big Daddy Kane?" she said with a thick tongue and cough-medicine face.

We both laughed, and spent the rest of the evening shooting pool, wondering if green wine was supposed to be served chilled or at alleyway temperature, and cracking corny rotgut jokes.

"When the bartender said, 'Would you like the house wine,' I didn't know he meant *crackhouse* wine."

At some point we tired of the classic rock 'n' roll thumping from the jukebox. There's only so much Eric Clapton–bluesy Negro mimicry a person can take, and I made a halfhearted comment about reprogramming the jukebox. "I could be a jukebox sommelier." I'd never said *sommelier* before and I liked how the word sounded coming from my mouth. I looked for an excuse to say it again, but Bridgette beat me to the punch.

"You *could* be a jukebox sommelier," she suggested in all seriousness. "Nobody ever gives enough thought to what's on the jukebox. It's always the same selection, fifty greatest hits CDs, a mediocre Motown anthology, the essential Billy Joel, a mix tape of Top 40 singles from two years ago, two Los Lobos CDs and that fucking Bob Marley album."

"*Legend.*"

"That's it, *Legend.* My God, the bar scene has made me hate that fucking record. Drunk white boys singing 'Get Up, Stand Up.'"

I grabbed a chunk of Bridgette's ass and eased her out the door.

"You want to go back to my place to hear some good music?" I asked her.

"Not if by good music you mean that classical crap you played for me last time."

"Come on, you got used to it."

"That's the problem, you listen to that shit long enough, you start thinking you're rich and white. And rich and white is no way to go through life if you happen to be neither."

Later that night Bridgette Lopez became the first of a not-so-select group of women to hear the chicken-fucking song. Back then the ultimate sexual maneuver was to sprinkle cocaine on one's engorged penis just before penetration. I've never done it but the rumored pleasures are boundless, the shared orgasms supposedly more intense and lasting than championship chess. Listening to the chicken-fucking song with her that night was like sprinkling cocaine on my heart.

To this day I don't abide artificial intrusions in my sex play. I prefer natural light and abhor toys, pills, and negligees. My only coital enhancement is the chicken-fucking song. I drape a towel over the TV, put the tape into the VCR, and play it for paramours and other sundry pieces of ass with the bad luck to end up in my arms. The music adds a Romeo-and-Juliet double-suicide poignancy to the otherwise loveless and in my life almost perfunctory one-night stand. Suddenly everything I say becomes something Khalil Gibran wishes he'd said. Every kiss and caress has the all-or-nothing, give-me-intimacy-or-give-me-death honesty of a Sylvia Plath poem. In my mind, my lumpy full-sized bed becomes the beach in *From Here to Eternity* and I'm Sergeant First Class Burt Lancaster fucking a voluptuous Rhode Island Red on a wet, sandy Hawaiian beach, the tattered sheets crashing over us in waves of cotton and rayon.

The morning after with Bridgette Lopez set the tone for all the rest that would follow. It was arduous and awkward, a runny-egged breakfast of stilted conversation and averted eyes. There is something about the song that embarrasses and shames you like catching yourself picking your nose in public.

The last thing Bridgette ever said to me was, "I'm serious, do the jukebox-sommelier thing." So I did. I wrote a letter to the Slumberland Bar in Berlin requesting a position as a jukebox sommelier, enclosing a résumé and an unlabeled mix tape. Two weeks later I received a small packet in the mail containing the paperwork for a work visa, a one-way plane ticket, a beer coaster, and a brief letter that stated my salary and equated the finding of my tape to the excavation of King Tut's tomb.

PART 2

DEUTSCHLAND ÜBER ALLES

CHAPTER 1

I ARRIVED IN BERLIN on a hazy mid-autumn afternoon, emerging from the coach-class bramble wrinkled, hungry, cold, and funky smelling, but happy as a runaway slave.

The cab ride to the hostel was in a Mercedes-Benz. Apart from a nervous three-block joyride in a Cadillac Seville, it was my first trip in a luxury car. I sank deep into that leather seat, thinking that if I hadn't reached the promised land, Germany was at least a land of maybes and we'll sees.

West Berlin was like a city populated entirely by Quaker abolitionists. Everyone was so nice—to a point. When I showed up to lease my first apartment, the landlord knocked seventy-five deutschmarks off the rent for reparations but wouldn't shake my hand to close the deal. Over time the friendly small talk with the newspaper vendor devolved from "How do you like Germany? Do you plan on staying?" to subtle get-the-fuck-out-of-my-country-nigger musings like, "Wow, I can't believe you've been here three months already? When are you going back to America?" When I went to local jazz clubs like the Quasimodo or the A Train, patrons at the bar would buy me drinks as an excuse to pick my brain about jazz and American racism. This was a typical conversation.

"Thanks for the beer."

"*Kein Problem.* I bet you're glad not having to drink that shit American beer. Blah, so bad."

"Yeah, you motherfuckers are on to something with these pilsners . . ."

Then Willi, Karl-Ludwig, and Bruno would defer to the American expat who'd take a stultifyingly mediocre saxophone solo that would inexplicably bring the house down. At the bar my newfound friend would put his arm around me and say, "You know, jazz improvisation comes from the slaves having to improvise in order to survive. Too bad every idiom of black music, be it jazz or rhythm and blues, or whatever, has declined in its Negroidery and purpose. It's become whitified."

Now I know why Harriet Tubman faked those blackout epileptic seizures: It was the only way she could get those damn abolitionists to stop patronizing her.

I quickly learned not to respond to jazzophile opinions that, judging from their use of words like *Negroidery* and *whitified,* had been stolen from the latest Wynton Marsalis magazine interview. I held then, and still do, that it's ridiculous to think that slavery had anything to do with jazz improvisation. In order to survive, slaves didn't improvise, they capitulated. The ones who stood their ground and fought back died. Making a holiday meal from pig innards isn't improvisation; it's common sense to throw whatever's left into the fucking pot. If anybody was improvising, it was the free black population. And if anybody was "whitified," it was the suit 'n' tie–wearing Marsalis. Like Negroes hadn't seen a white face until they saw the slave catcher. As if all the fucking race mixing in Spain, Egypt, ancient Rome, and Ethiopia never happened. But I knew no Berlin jazz aficionados wanted to hear me denigrate their romantic notions of white oppression being the progenitor of black musical genius. I didn't even want to hear myself say these things. So I'd politely nod in agreement and say, "Have you ever heard of Charles Stone?"

My visa didn't allow me to start work until November, so I spent the next two weeks contemplating the irony that though I'd be working at the Slumberland, I hadn't slept since I got to Berlin. Slumberland. The name itself was foreboding enough to keep me out. It brought back all the childhood traumas, the sleepless nights staring at the lightning-bolt-blue night-light while pondering the relationship between reality, the dream state, and death. My father, the embittered literature Ph.D. who worked for the county naming the streets within walled communities that sprouted up on the Californian hillsides like concrete weeds, did nothing to ease my fear of the dark and dying. He'd look under the bed and in the closet, and speaking in the effete horror-movie accent of a Transylvanian ghoul, he'd name the monsters and demons lurking in the shadows. "Hello, Chimera. Good evening, Medusa. Glad to see you're well, Mary Shelley's Frankenstein monster, not the peace-loving miscreation who read Milton, Goethe, and Plutarch, but the vengeful brute from the second half of the book who killed innocent children without compunction." With my eyes bulging from their sockets and my heart beating so hard I could hear it, he'd tuck me in with one of Shakespeare's innumerable quotations about restless slumber. "To sleep, perchance to dream—ay, there's the rub," Father would say, bussing me on the forehead and finishing the quote just before the click of the shutting door, "For in that sleep of death what dreams may come when we have shuffled off this mortal coil."

I was dizzily homesick. My attempts at re-creating my California lifestyle were amusing but ultimately ineffective. The citrus smell that wafted from the orange rinds I placed on the radiator made me sneeze constantly. The small colony of black ants

Mother airmailed to me, so I could force march them across my windowsill, died when they were unable to digest the glutinous gummi bears I fed them. I rented a car and got five traffic tickets in one day for making right on red after right on red. I'd regurgitate Laker games I'd heard Chick Hearn call, play by play, commercial break by commercial break:

Magic frontcourt ... Magic yo-yoing up and down ... over to Jamaal ... four on the clock ... that's good. Lakers by twelve and folks, this one's in the refrigerator. The door's closed, the light's off, the eggs are cooling, the butter's getting hard, and the Jell-O's jiggling. We'll be back for Lakers wrap-up after a word from our sponsor ... Here's Cal Worthington and his dog, Spot! If your axle is a-saggin', go see Cal. Maybe you need a station wagon, go see Cal. If your wife has started naggin' and your tailpipe is a-draggin', go see Cal! Go see Cal! Go see Cal! Did you know I could put you in a used car or used truck for just twenty-five dollars down ... It's Worthington Ford in Long Beach, open every day till midnight, we'll see you here! Bring the kids!

In addition to missing the Westside, the Lakers' fast break, and the incessant Cal Worthington commercials, I missed black people, which was strange for me. But somehow I longed for the sounds of urban working-class blackness. The heavily aspirated T's and P's. The Sunday-morning supermarket shushing of a woman too tired to do her hair, much less lift her heels, as she scuffles down the aisle as if she's wearing cross-country skis and not a pair of furry baby-blue bedroom slippers. I missed the quiet of my room after Father had put me to sleep, perchance to dream. Sometimes on a sleepless night I could almost hear Brian Mooney proudly idling his '64 El Camino lowrider in the driveway across the street. Other times I could hear my frustrated father in the other room rambling like a mindless maniac, trying to come up with the last ten of the two hundred "Spanish-sounding" street names he needed for a new city called Santa

Clarita, names that had to reflect the area's Mexican heritage and
yet have enough of an "upscale ring" to convey to any Mexicans
foolhardy enough to move to the Santa Clarita hinterlands that
they weren't wanted. Having come up with such gems as Via
Palacio, Arroyo Park Drive, and Rancho Adobe Drive, Pops
would reach his wits' end.

"Son?"

"Yeah?"

"You up? I know you're awake."

"And?"

"You hang out with lots of Mexicans? Gimme some Spanish
street names."

"Toreador Lane."

"Won't do. Connotes animal cruelty. Give me another."

"Calle Street."

"Redundant. Come on, I'm serious."

But unfortunately for him, I never was.

"How about We Need Faster Service at Tito's Tacos Drive?
Viva La Raza Boulevard. Badges? We Don't Need No Stinking
Badges Circle. Reconquista Califas Ahora Terrace. Margarita,
You Thieving Pendeja, I Know You Stole the Ten-Dollar Bill
I Left on the Kitchen Counter, You're Fired, and to Think We
Treated You Like Family Road."

I was so lonely those early Berlin nights, I missed my own father calling me a dumb nigger. So lonely that I missed black
people, which is to say I missed people who can't take a joke,
people to whom I was supposed to relate but couldn't, if that
makes any sense.

Those first few weeks in Berlin the closest I'd come to kinship
with another life-form was with the newly imported emperor
penguins at the zoo.

Emperor penguins, like the American Negro, are notoriously
fickle creatures, and the city had gone to great lengths to ensure

they would feel at home. But instead of re-creating the snow, rock, and water formations of the Antarctic tundra, they removed twenty-five square meters of actual polar cap, transported it intact to Berlin, set it down in the space once occupied by the dromedaries, and covered it with a climate-controlled biodome. All for about what it would have cost to enforce the environmental laws that were supposed to protect the endangered birds in the first place.

The penguin exhibit opened to great fanfare; however, the supposedly sprightly birds refused to perform. People came in droves to see their aquatic grace, but no amount of pleading toddlers or zoological trickery could coax them into the water. I visited my Antarctic familiars every day. Setting my tape recorder in the corner of the exhibit hall and taping the dismay of the visitors who'd paid good money to see the winsome waterfowl.

Like Miles Davis in concert, for the most part the penguins stood stock-still, their backs to the audience. Every few minutes a curious bird would cause a commotion by skating his webbed feet across the ice to the water's edge. The zoo patrons would rush the railing, lifting the children onto their shoulders and their box cameras to their eyes, then with a squawk the penguin would invariably waddle fearfully back to the pack.

The crowd would turn ugly. They'd pound and spit on glass, cursing the reluctant birds: "Now I know why these things are nearly extinct—these snooty fuckers think they're too good to get wet!"

At least the penguins had one another. I'd return home alone. Collapse on the couch and listen to my recordings of the day's events. Reveling in penguin defiance in the face of the curious stares and the stereotyped expectations of the outside world. One day on an overcast autumn afternoon, while on my way to the zoo, I chased down a lone ray of sunshine through the tree-lined streets of Charlottenburg. When I caught up to the sun ray, it shone directly upon the Amerikahaus and nothing else. The Amerikahaus is an ivy-covered building that sits in the middle of a residential street like a cultural trading post and offers fellowships and cultural indoctrination instead of beaver pelts and fire water. Inside the glass-enclosed vestibule, next to the flagpole, stood a black security guard, wiping his hands on Old Glory as if it were a restroom towel dispenser.

In those days, seeing a black face in Berlin was almost as rare as a black field goal kicker in the NFL. And I stared. Stared unabashedly at my fellow human penguin. The tall African-American watchman belonged to the long legacy of freak show blackness including the Venus Hottentot; Ota Benga, the Congolese pygmy displayed as the missing link in the Bronx Zoo; Kevin Powell and Heather B, the first two African-Americans on MTV's *The Real World*; and myself. When the guard spotted me peering at him through the glass, he cheerily waved me inside. I opened the door to his cage. His face was warm, thick, and brown as a wool sock in an L.L.Bean catalog. The creases in his gray uniform were sharp and fell down each pant leg to a pair of polished black combat boots. A set of official-looking keys jangled from a thick steel chain. He didn't carry a weapon; he disarmed intruders with his smile. I eased in close enough to read the writing on the ID tag; it read, simply, SECURITY.

"Can I get an L.A. *Times* inside?"

"Yeah," he said. "Usually it's a few days late, though."

"That's cool." It'd been weeks since my voice had deepened into the What's happenin'? baritone I reserved for addressing black men whom I didn't know.

"How long you been on *this side*, brother? How you like it?" he asked, though before I could answer and lodge my complaints about the coarseness of the toilet paper and bath towels and the puzzling absence of air conditioners and wall-to-wall carpeting, he looked around to see if anyone was listening, then whispered in my ear, "Germany is the black man's heaven."

"What?"

"These people know how to take care of you. They treat you like a king. Your wish is their command."

I stepped away from him cautiously. He was dead serious. I excused myself, and as I backed out of the door he called out after me, "You just have to let them love you."

A week later, to ease the societal transition of the emperor penguins, the Berlin Zoo brought in a gaggle of the more gregarious rockhopper penguin, and soon the once-uptight emperor penguins were splashing and barrel rolling through the frigid waters of this cold-ass city as if they had heard and heeded the security guard's advice. *You just have to let them love you.*

And God, I needed to be loved.

CHAPTER 2

SLUMBERLAND. NO MATTER how tightly I cupped my hands around my eyes, I couldn't see inside the bar. A hazy red light filtered through the always-drawn bamboo blinds. The window vibrated with the murmur of loud conversation and reggae music. Judging from the rhythm of the shaking window, I guessed that the song was one of my favorite ballads, Aswad's "On and On," a deeply respectful cover of Stephen Bishop's easy-listening hit.

Down in Jamaica . . .

I walked into the bar. And indeed, "On and On" was on; I was more than pleased with myself. I felt like a superhero who'd just discovered his powers. The ability to identify a song from the way its backbeat vibrated a windowpane wasn't going to save the world from alien invasion or a runaway meteor, but I could envision winning some bar bets.

For Berlin, the pub was crowded. There were only two open seats, a stool at the bar and an empty chair at an otherwise occupied table. The Slumberland was a repressed white supremacist's fantasy. At almost every table sat one or two black men sandwiched by fawning white women. At a strategically located center table, four grinning white men sat voyeuristically watching the bloodlines of their race putrefy. I'd never been in a place more devoid of platonic love. The air was thick with the smell of musk oil, patchouli, and sweat. I had to breathe by taking big fish gulps of air.

The desert-yellow walls were decorated with colorful paintings advertising various African businesses, barbershops that shaved petroglyphs into Cameroonian heads, Namibian eateries, and Senegalese fix-it shops. A white woman coming from the bathroom slithered past and winked at me. I froze like an Eisenhower-era virgin on his first trip to a Tijuana cathouse. No one had ever winked at me before. I didn't think it was something real people did, and this was a blatant Betty Boop c'mere-big-boy wink come to life. I pretended to be preoccupied with the artwork and turned to the painting nearest me. It was a hand-painted graphic for a Ghanaian herbal center that sold various cure-alls. An asthmatic boy clutched his chest. A bald man, suffering from a painful condition called "kokoo," squatted on the ground with his back to the viewer, hot brownish-red diarrhea spewing from his watercolor butt like lava. In another section of the painting the word POWER was underlined by a veiny, rock-hard penis attached to a well-muscled torso whose owner, apparently, no longer suffered from erectile dysfunction.

I sat at the bar and introduced myself to the bartender as the new jukebox sommelier. Doris shook my hand, poured me a scotch the size of which you'd find only in a John Ford western, and told me that the owner, Thomas Femmerling, wasn't sure when to expect me, but would be happy to see me when he got back from the Canary Islands.

"If he has to listen to 'Get Up, Stand Up' one more time . . ."

There was no mistaking that wonderfully alluring husky voice. Doris was the same woman who answered the phone when I first placed that long-distance call to the Slumberland.

I took out the envelope the chicken-fucking song came in and asked if she knew anything about it; maybe the writing was familiar.

Doris examined it and beckoned me to look at the postmark. "This was mailed from *East* Berlin."

"So?"

"An East German can't just mail a package to America. That's high treason. Whoever mailed it probably works for the government or the Stasi. What was in the envelope?"

"A videotape of a man having sex with a chicken."

"That's very German," she said.

I'd soon come to learn that to a German, anything involving sexual perversion, punctuality, obsessive-compulsiveness, and oblique references to the deep-rooted national malaise was "very German." Of course, for me it wasn't these concepts or behaviors that were very German, but rather it was the reflex to characterize such things as "very German" that was very German.

I asked Doris if she knew Charles Stone. She shrugged and asked me to describe him. I got out, "Black . . . musician . . . older gentleman," before I realized I was describing half the bar's clientele, and that I didn't even know what the Schwa looked like.

Stone wasn't a self-promoter; he never appeared on his album covers, gave interviews, or posed for publicity head shots.

Doris licked a fingertip and lifted a tiny grain of coal-black detritus from my glass.

"Hey, don't worry," she said, rolling the almost-microscopic piece of dreck between her fingers. "If he's a black man, he'll come through here sooner or later. They all do. Look at you."

For a second I panicked. What if he isn't black, I thought. Not that it mattered; in fact, my respect for Wolfman Jack, Johnny Otis, and 3rd Bass's Pete Nice and MC Serch increased when I found out they were white. A part of me hoped the Schwa was white; maybe then he'd be more congenial, less embittered than those Slumberland Negroes.

I spun around on my stool and looked down my broad black nose at those men. There but for the grace of my record collection go I, I thought to myself.

This was Berlin before the Wall came down. State-supported hedonism. Every one-night stand a propaganda poster for democratic freedom and third-world empowerment. In my mind I made a vow that I'd never be like those sex warriors who subsisted only on their exoticness. These men of the diaspora who smiled meekly while libertine frauleins debated as to who was the "true black": the haughty African with his tribal scars, gender chauvinism, and piercing eyes, or the cocksure black American, he of the emotional scars, political chauvinism, and physical grace. This was a time when if a white women saw a black man she wanted, she'd step to him and dangle her car keys in his face. The customary response on the part of the buck was to take those keys in hand and drive her home.

Next to me a middle-aged *Grossmutter* jabbed her tongue down the throat of a handsome African half her age and twice her height. I made my "I smell gas" face and braved my way into the main room, mumbling the minstrel wisdom of Bert Williams under my breath.

> *When life seems full of clouds and rain,*
> *And I am filled with naught but pain,*
> *Who soothes my thumping, bumping brain?*
> *Nobody.*

Though I'm purportedly black—and, in these days of racial egalitarianism, a somebody—I'd never felt more white, more like a nobody. DJ Appropriate but Never Compensate. I was amanuensis Joel Chandler Harris ambling through the streets of Nigger Town looking for folklore to steal. I was righteous Mezz Mezzrow mining the mother lode of soul, selling gage on 125th Street, tapping my feet to Satchmo's blackest beats. I was Alan Lomax slogging tape recorder and plantation dreams through the swamp-grass miasma looking to colorize the blues on the cheap. I was 3rd Bass's MC Serch making my own version of the gas face. A rhyme-tight, tornado-white, Hebrew Israelite, stepping down from the soapbox and into the boom box to spit his shibboleth.

I missed cats like Serch and Mezz. I found their lyrical introspection and unabashed nigger love comforting. Unlike Republicans of color and the Slumberland's barroom lovers, they were race traitors with everything to lose. Their verses and riffs had both John Brown's passion and his Harpers Ferry praxis. They feinted and weaved with the dazzling whiteness of Pete Maravich's ball handling, the exactitude of Jerry West's jump shooting. I hoped against hope that the Schwa was a white man who hung out with white people.

> When winter comes with snow and sleet,
> And me with hunger and cold feet,
> Who says, "Here's two bits, go and eat?"
> Nobody.

Besides not knowing what the Schwa looked like, it occurred to me that I had no idea if he was dead or alive. Considering the timelessness of his music, the chicken-fucking song could've been twenty years or twenty minutes old.

Maybe someone whom I'd wronged in my past was dangling the Schwa in my face. Luring me into some Hitchcockian trap.

The kind where I chase my proverbial tail looking for proof that I'd seen what I'd seen, heard what I'd heard.

Here I'd sold my car. Signed a lease to sublet an apartment for five years, and the Schwa could be here at the Slumberland bar or in the slumberland of eternal sleep. Cary Grant always lives in the Hitchcock movies. Neither I nor the Schwa was Cary Grant.

Americans die in this city. Fleeing political and parental oppression, they come to Berlin claiming to be maligned and marginalized by a racist America too insecure to "get" them. Most find something less than moderate success and end up dying pitiful, meaningless, alcoholic deaths in small two-room flats, to be found by friends laid out in their own excrement, their livers bloated, their artwork unsold and dusty.

> *I ain't never done nothin' to nobody.*
> *I ain't never got nothin' from nobody, no*
>   *time.*
> *And until I get somethin' from somebody,*
>   *sometime,*
> *I don't intend to do nothin' for nobody, no*
>   *time.*

Slumberland. The room pulsed with sexual congeniality. My vow against lustful miscegenation was quickly forgotten. I longed for someone to squeeze my thigh, pinch my ass. Ain't I a man? Seated underneath a fully grown banana tree, two women at a corner table stared in my direction so hard I had to double-check that I didn't have a ticket in my hand and that there wasn't an electric sign over their heads that said, NOW SERVING NUMBER 86.

Slumberland. I was past the point of no return, asleep, dreaming and dead all at the same time. My feet grew heavy; with each step into the room I seemed to be sinking deeper and deeper into the floor. I looked down. The floor of the entire bar was covered, six inches deep, in pristine, white beach sand.

The redhead gawked unapologetically like a bewildered child looking at a disfigured passerby. The brunette's gaze was one of an unrepentant sinner simultaneously demanding from her lord both satisfaction and salvation. I was about to choose the brunette—at least she wasn't licking her lips—when Doris grabbed me by the elbow.

"You okay?"

"Yeah, why?"

"For the past ten minutes you've been standing here in the middle of the room like a statue. Everyone's looking at you like you're crazy."

Gently, like a psychiatric orderly leading a patient back to the dayroom, Doris returned me back to the bar and sat me down.

A jaunty Afro-pop song fluttered her deep-set eyes and pursed her whisper-thin lips with appreciation. Fela Kuti will do that to you. Now it was my turn to stare. Her eyes were the same soft macadamia nut brown as her hair. The laugh lines in her face accented the high cheekbones and the square, almost brutish jaw.

"What's your favorite band?" she asked by way of readjusting me to my surroundings.

"When People Were Shorter and Lived Near the Water," I said. "Well, they're not my favorite band. They're my favorite name for a band."

"That is a good name, but did you ever notice that nine out ten times, bands with good names suck?"

I liked Doris from the moment her tongue touched the roof of her mouth. She was very pleasant sounding. Her slight lisp gave her sibilant fricatives a nice breathiness, so that her S's and zeds sounded like the breeze wafting over the Venice Beach sand.

"What's your favorite band name?" I asked.

"The Dead Kennedys," she shot back, and for the next few minutes we volleyed excellent band names back and forth.

"The Soul Stirrers?"

"10,000 Maniacs."

"Ultramagnetic MCs."

"Dereliction of Duty."

"The Stray Cats."

"The Main Ingredient."

"The Mean Uncles."

"Little Anthony and the Imperials."

"The Nattering Nabobs of Negativity."

"The Original Five Blind Boys of Alabama."

"The Butthole Surfers."

"Peep Show Mop Men."

"Sturm und Drang."

"The Big Red Machine."

"Ready for the World."

"The Cure."

"One of the great mysteries of the universe is why bands with really good names rarely make it."

Doris took off her apron and took the seat next to me, abruptly ending her shift. I ordered something called a Neger off the drink menu. My German at this point was limited to a few insults and numbers under a thousand, but *Neger* looked suspiciously like *nigger*, and when the waitress delivered a murky concoction of wheat beer and Coca-Cola, two shades darker than me, I had to bite my tongue to keep from laughing.

I loved the blatancy of the German racial effrontery of the late eighties. Black German cabaret singers, with names like Roberto Blanco and Susanne Snow, sang on late-night variety shows accompanied by blackface pianists. The highway billboards featured dark-skinned women teasingly licking chocolate confections. The wall clocks in the popular blues joint Café Harlem read:

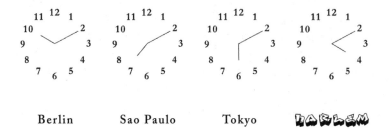

Berlin   Sao Paulo   Tokyo   Harlem

My Neger was cold and surprisingly tasty, but I had to know. "So what exactly does *Neger* mean in German?"

"It means 'black person,'" said a woman eavesdropping in to our conversation.

"No, it doesn't, it means 'nigger,'" corrected Doris. "Don't try to sugarcover it."

The conversation turned to my reasons for coming to Germany. Doris listened patiently, and without a hint of shame explained to me that she either "knew bible-ly" or knew someone who "knew bible-ly" every black man who'd set foot in the Slumberland in the past two years, and that she had never heard of or met any Charles Stone.

A customer dropped a coin on the bar. That metallic oscillation between sudden loudness and nothing is a beautiful sound. I imagine that from far enough away, our galaxy sounds like a fifty-cent piece dropped onto an ice cream parlor tabletop. I wrote my phone number on a pasteboard coaster and flicked it and a fifty-pfennig coin over to Doris. She put the coaster in her bag and asked what the money was for. I told her to use it to call the number I'd given her.

"But you're not home."

"No shit."

She picked up the red house phone, dropped the coin in, and made the call. The white guys from the center table passed by me on their way out. One placed his hand on my shoulder and said, "You're from a good family. A very good family, I can tell."

He meant it as a compliment, but the implication was that most black families were not good. I was inclined to agree with him, because so far as I knew all families were fucked-up.

Doris returned from the phone call shooing the guy away like a fly.

"'For the nigger it niggereth every day.' What kind of answering machine message is that?" she asked.

I told her it was the Schwa introducing one of his songs, that it was a play on a Shakespeare quote: "For the rain it raineth everyday." "We're drinking these Negers, I heard the coin drop on the table. I don't know, I thought maybe you'd recognize the voice."

"So that was this Schwa man's voice?"

"Yeah."

"Well, I've never heard it before, and at the end of this niggereth stuff, the music, if that's the Schwa too, you really need to find this man."

I don't know how many Negers I drank that night, but I had as much fun ordering the beer as drinking it. "Gimme two niggers!" I'd yell out to the waitress. "How much for two niggers? I'll have a gin and tonic, the lady will have a large nigger."

Eight hours later I awoke to Doris in the front room watching television with her eyes closed. She was swathed in a terry-cloth bathrobe I never wore and rewinding the chicken-fucking video. I turned up the radiator and I sat next to her. The VCR whirred and jolted to a clunky stop. She pressed play.

"How long you been up?"

"I don't know, an hour maybe? You listen to this song and you get lost in time."

Doris curled into the fetal position and put her head in my lap. After every phrase the Schwa played, she'd mutter something about the harmonics, coloration, and Stravinsky. Five minutes went by before she'd stopped shaking her head in disbelief and making faces whenever my stomach rumbled.

"I did it," Doris said, speaking into my belly button.

"Did what?"

"On television I once heard an American homewife tell her UFO encounter. She spoke the usual bullshit—'bright object in the sky,' 'incredible speed,'—but then she said the spaceship flashed a color she'd never seen before, and speeded off. Ever since then I've tried to imagine a color I've never seen before. And now I just did it. It was the music."

She opened her eyes. They were a color I'd seen before.

"But if we find him, no one will purchase the music."

"Why not?"

"It's too good. Too much."

"Come on, people are starving for this music."

"Exactly, but when you have hungered for a long time, if you eat too much, you die."

Doris sank her teeth into my nipple. I turned up the volume to a deafening loudness that no doubt violated the Berlin laws against Sunday-morning noise. No one complained.

CHAPTER 3

I PUT THE SEARCH for the Schwa on hold while Doris and I had a one-night stand that lasted the month and a half the owner of the Slumberland was on vacation. We never truly got to know each other. Past a weakness for screwball comedies, the only thing we really had in common was our appreciation of the Schwa.

At our most intimate we'd play lazy games of backgammon and listen to his records. As soon as the music ended we'd fight. My Calvinist tendencies and her gloomy German stoicism clashing like two kindergartners playing musical chairs and attempting to squeeze their behinds into the last remaining plastic seat. We'd argue bitterly over the frequency of my showers and her refusal to turn her thermostat above sixty degrees in the dead of winter.

Doris, of course, blames our breakup on the frequency and length of my showers. In her eyes I'm a religious fanatic who every morning takes a hot-water baptismal to the gods Proctor and Gamble. My "obsession" with cleanliness symbolizes two hundred and fifty years of American sanctimony. If my fingernails are clean, my soul is pure and lemony fresh. I'm 100 percent Puritan. A squeaky-clean American.

Doris: You crazy, uptight Americans. Do you know what we call "skinny-dipping" in Germany?
Me: No.
Doris: Swimming!

On our last night as a couple Doris sat on the floor of her spacious, impeccably furnished, penthouse igloo, bundled up in three layers of thrift-shop sweaters, settling an argument we had earlier in the day about Chico Marx's piano virtuosity by making a list of piano players in descending order of greatness, while I washed the dishes and stared at the plastic frog with a thermometer for a spine suctioned to the kitchen window.

I could never explain Doris's thermal frugality. I knew it'd been passed down from her parents, who, having been raised in the moldy-potato austerity of postwar Germany, made sure that she had a healthy respect for creature comforts like heat, clothes, salt, and toothpaste. She wasn't cheap. She'd often splurge on pricey nonessentials that she then treated like foster children. She put regular gas in her BMW 7 Series sedan and her silk blouses in the washing machine. She drank expensive wine out of paper cups. Used African artifacts as doorstops and had a state-of-the-art central heating system installed, one capable of warming the bathroom floor and the towel racks but whose thermostat was as off-limits as a North Korean nuclear plant.

"Doris, it's eight degrees in here. Do you know what that is in Fahrenheit?"

"About fifty degrees."

"Fifty-one-point-eight degrees to be exact, which is the temperature at which black men lose their fucking minds. In 1967 when my Uncle Billy turned down a scholarship to UCLA and volunteered to go to Vietnam, it was eight degrees Celsius. On that clear, blue, carry-me-back-to-Ol'-Virginny morning when Nat 'Crazy Like a Fox' Turner looked directly into a solar eclipse and decided there and then to kill every white person in the world—it was eight degrees Celsius. In *Rocky II*, when Apollo Creed agrees to give Rocky Balboa a rematch in Phila-fucking-delphia, Rocky's hometown, it was eight degrees Celsius, fifty-two fucking degrees."

Doris and the cackles of the chicken-fucking song snuck up on me from behind. She burrowed her head between my shoulder blades and ran her hands under my shirt. She hadn't bathed in three days, but she was warm.

"And you, black man," she asked, tweezing my nipples with her nails, "how will you lose your mind on this fifty-two-degree night? Perhaps you go so crazy and finally give me oral sex, yes?"

"I would, but you smell."

She unbuttoned her sweaters and yanked her shirt over her head. An earthy, almost steamy pungency closed my throat.

"Do I smell bad?" she asked.

I cupped my hand and passed it through the air like a chef wafting the vapors of the soup du jour toward his nostrils.

"You smell, but you don't smell bad. Sort of like a basket of rotten fruit."

We both paused to listen to a jaunty movement in the chicken-fucking song. Doris took the first page of her list, wiped her hairy underarms with it, and handed it to me. I held it gingerly because a single strand of black underarm hair, long enough to bisect pianist number nine, Wolfgang Amadeus Mozart, like an editor's strikethrough, was epoxied to the page with a natural adhesive of perspiration and grit.

"Smell it," she commanded.

I pressed the tip of my nose to Mozart and inhaled. The page smelled of nutmeg and paraffin with a hint of fresh bacon grease. I searched the rest of the page for Chico Marx. He wasn't on it. I had him just behind Fats Waller and ahead of Chopin. Doris removed her bra and slid page two along the sweaty folds of her breasts. The dampness smudged Debussy, Jerry Lee Lewis, and Dave Brubeck. It was a damn good compendium. It smelled like a mothballed down jacket on the first cold day of winter. And still no Chico Marx. It went on like that for five minutes. She'd peel off a page, lick it, rub it over her scalp, run it between her toes, her pubes, the backs of her knees. Each page smelled different. Each body part and erogenous zone imparting its own aroma, every piano player and keyboardist emanating his or her own unique, musty funk. Mary Williams, Nat King Cole, and Doris's right elbow smelled like hijiki salad, Grandma's immutably stuck-to-the-wrapper butterscotch candies, and boiled *Kutteln*. Ray Manzarek, Thelonious Monk, and her inner thigh were redolent of burning rubber and a flat diet soda. Stevie Wonder, Glenn Gould, and the back of her neck reeked of day-old pizza, a blue urinal cake, and Laurel Canyon eucalyptus trees. Doris slid the last sheet of paper down the crack of her ass, and there, at the bottom of the page, sandwiched between her twelve-year-old nephew Andreas and Schroeder, the piano-playing Beethoven fanatic from the Charlie Brown cartoons, was Chico Marx, smelling like ass and "unscented" two-ply toilet paper; nevertheless I had a raging hard-on.

The Schwa was in full swing and suddenly I understood why Doris, a woman who loved music unconditionally, kept her flat so cold. The cold heightened your senses. I not only heard it, I felt, saw, and tasted the music. My ears were suddenly bionic, and if I concentrated and made the *didudidudidudid* Bionic Woman sound effect, I could hear the stud's distended nut sack slapping against the bird's shiny belly plumage. I could hear the Schwa's breathing. See iridescent polka dots of sound float from the speakers and pop suddenly in midair like music-filled soap bubbles. The cold electrified my skin like a charged prison fence; the glistening notes that landed on my skin sparked and fizzled.

I swirled the song in my mouth, isolating its sweet complexities as if it were a vintage Château d'Yquem stolen off the shelves of Trader Joe's and downed between mouthfuls of chili-cheese fries. I couldn't smell the song. Doris and her body odor were hanging onto my neck and biting my lip. There's something beautifully Taoist about two people kissing when one partner is naked and the other clothed.

"Do I smell?" she asked.

I nodded. We kissed again.

"Good," she said.

We fucked. Intermittently and passionately, in time we both stank. Our spooned bodies stuck to the linoleum floor and each other with cold sweat. With her back toward me, Doris propped herself up on her elbow. Pages two and five of her list were stuck to her shoulder blades like deformed angel wings.

"You know if someone got up after making love to me and showered like they do in your American movies, I'd fucking kill them."

I pulled off her crumpled wings. She had Liberace, Neil Sedaka, Prince, and Brian Eno ranked ahead of Tom Waits and Art Tatum. The chicken-fucking song had ended. There was only the hum of the refrigerator and the swinging tick-tock of the Kit-Cat clock's tail. We were doomed to start fighting. *Liberace?* It would be our last argument. The inevitable clash of puritanical Americanism and German pragmatics. I should have known from the start it could have never worked. We both were fond of hip-hop, but she was strictly Queensbridge, a proponent of MC Shan, Marley Marl, and Roxanne Shanté. I was down with BDP, Boogie Down Productions. KRS-One, Bronx-sworn Capulet to her Queensbridge Montague.

Doris grabbed my penis and pulled me in closer to her and, without turning around, asked, "Why?"

"Why what?"

"Why in American movies do they make so much noise when they kiss?"

I shrugged and slipped my frozen feet in between her fleshy calves.

"Is it the more smacking, the more saliva, the louder the kiss, the more in love? Is that what it is?"

Liberace. Prince. Schroeder. MC Shan. Fuck.

"Ferguson?"

"What?"

"Do you love me?"

I took her question seriously, but I felt like Schroeder at his toy piano, exasperated by Lucy Van Pelt's persistence and the dreamy glaze in her black pinprick eyes.

Do you love me?

I'd never been in love. I'd always thought love was like reading *Leaves of Grass* in a crowded Westside park on a sunny Tuesday afternoon, having to suppress the urge with each giddy turn of the page to share your joy with the surrounding world. By "sharing" I don't mean quoting Whitman's rhythm-machine poetics to a group of strangers waiting for auditions to be posted at the Screen Actors Guild, but wanting to stand up and scream, "I'm reading Walt Whitman, you joyless, shallow, walking-the-dog-by-carrying-the-dog, casting-couch-wrinkles-imprinted-in-your-ass, associate-producer's-pubic-hairs-on-your-tongue, designer-perambulator-pushing-the-baby-you-and-your-Bel-Air-trophy-wife-had-by-inserting-someone-else's-sperm-bank-jizz-in-a-surrogate-mother's-uterus-because-you-and-your-sugar-daddy-were-too-busy-with-your-nonexistent-careers-to-fuck, no-day-job-having California Aryan assholes! I'm reading Whitman! Fuck your purebred, pedigreed Russian wolfhound! Fuck your WASP infant with the Hebrew name and the West Indian nanny! Fuck your Norwegian au pair who's not as hot-looking as you thought she'd be! I'm reading Whitman, expanding my mind and melding with the universe! What have you done today? It's ten in the morning, do you know where your coke dealer is? Have you looked at the leaves of grass? No? I didn't think so!" That's what I thought love would be like. Reading Whitman and fighting the urge not to express your aesthetic superiority.

Doris turned to face me, her cheeks calcified with tearstains.

"Do you love me, Ferguson?"

"No."

She released my penis and clambered over me, placing her forehead to my temple. A tear ran down her cheek and onto mine. I didn't bother to wipe it off.

Why? She asked over and over. Why, if I didn't love her, why was I with her? I told her the truth. Probably the first time I'd ever been completely truthful in my life. *I was lonely.* She raised her hand and I flinched, expecting to ward off a blow; instead she stroked my face as softly as she ever had. "That's a reasonable answer," she cooed. No voodoo curses were cast. No demanding the return of shit I'd thrown away without telling her. No vengeful postings of my nude photo, phone number, and salacious fisting fantasies on gay dating Web sites. Doris simply returned the chicken-fucking song, asked if I wanted to go to the movies on Thursday, and if she could help me find the Schwa.

The security guard at the Amerikahaus was right. Berlin is heaven.

CHAPTER 4

O N MY FIRST DAY of work, Thomas Femmerling, the owner of the Slumberland, did two things: He gave me a set of keys to the bar, then he showed me how to properly pour a pilsner.

"It takes exactly seven minutes for *ein gutes Pils*," he said, handing me an effervescent glass of beer with a head so thick it could support a silver piece. "And I figure if it takes that long to pour a good beer, it'll take at least seven or eight months to program a good jukebox, so take your time, DJ man. Take your sweet time." Then he plucked his coin from my beer and left me to my duties.

Bars in general are depressing places, but especially at eight thirty on a serene Monday morning. And there I was, alone and unbreakfasted, drinking a seven-minute beer, unable to block out the disconcerting chatter of children skipping merrily to school.

The Slumberland juke was a brand-new Wurlitzer SL-900. Unplugged, it sat dark and lifeless against the far wall. I immediately sympathized with the machine, for it reminded me of myself some years ago: a newborn black child come into the world obsolete and passé. The SL-900's curse was that it played 45s and not the digital compact discs that were then just starting to take over the market share. Only two weeks old and the juke was already an antique. Still, it remained impressive and intimidating, and I approached the noble machine with the reverent caution that a game warden uses on the sedated grizzly bear.

"There, boy. Settle down, everything's going to be all right."

I opened the lid and counted fifty record slots. Room enough for one hundred songs, approximately thirteen hours of continuous music. That meant I had to come up with a playlist of fifty songs so compatible with one another that any one jam had to be able to seamlessly follow, precede, complement, supplement, and riff off any other jam. I also had to take into account fifty additional B-sides. Songs whose strains might be less familiar but, if mistakenly punched into the jukebox, wouldn't bring the mack-daddy maneuvers of the Slumberland's miscegenation menagerie to a screeching halt, and might even hip a funk-drunk listener to some classic James Brown besides "Papa's Got a Brand New Bag." I needed songs that would make the bar's black male clientele feel important, knowledgeable, and, yes, superior. Songs whose intricacies and subtext they could explain to the fräuleins without feeling like racial quislings to the Negress mothers and wives left back home to toil over the Serengeti and Amana ranges. I needed songs that spoke to the white woman's inner nigger. The nigger who had so much in common with these defeated and delusional men, the bipolar white nigger woman in all of us who needs to be worshipped, whistled at, and sometimes beaten.

I've always maintained that one could make the case for the white woman being the most maligned personage on the planet. Like Pandora and Eve, white women have been built up as paragons of virtue and beauty only to be unjustly blamed for the world's ills when they decide to come down off the pedestal to exercise their sense of entitlement and act human.

Yes, the Slumberland jukebox would be stuffed with perennial pop songs, bebop sui generis, and Memphis soul. It would be a fifty-pfennig musical library capable of dispensing stereophonic hope and salvation to the downtrodden from Harlem to Wiesbaden. It would help a haughty German woman come down off her high horse and put a discouraged, diasporic black man on his.

This wouldn't be like making a mix tape for a schoolyard crush filled with slow jams, conscious rap, James Taylor, saccharine jazz, and rainstorm interludes. I had to program that jukebox so it'd be me DJing on autopilot. Turn it into an electronic doppelgänger flashing its rainbow lights, blowing its plastic bubbles and my trademark shit. "Goddamn, get off your ass and jam" eclecticism. All I needed was that one record that would get the party started. Make the ladies say, "Ho," the homosexuals say, "Hey," and the skeptics say, "Fuck it."

I sipped my beer, the second-best beer I'd ever had,* and asked the question I imagined all great artists ask themselves before engaging in the creative process: "Is there a God?" I weighed the arguments pro (Hawaiian surf, Welch's grape juice, koala bears, worn-in Levi's, the northern lights, the Volvo station wagon, women with braces, the Canadian Rockies, Godard, Nerf footballs, Shirley Chisholm's smile, free checking, and Woody Allen) and con (flies, Alabama, religion, chihuahuas, chihuahua owners, my mother's cooking, airplane turbulence, LL Cool J, Mondays, how boring heaven must fucking be, and Woody Allen), not so much to prove or disprove the existence of a powerless almighty, but to engage my increasingly tipsy thought process with so much conscious prattle that an idea might strike me when I

---

*The first being a Budweiser tall boy I'd snuck into a Mothers Against Drunk Driving fundraiser.

wasn't looking. After about twenty minutes of this I'd come as close as anyone with an associate's degree in library sciences has come to disproving the existence of God,* but was no closer to programming the jukebox. Such is the way of the amateur atheologian and the professional jukebox sommelier.

Squweeek.

There was a cautious, almost shy squeak coming from outside the bar. *Squweeek.*

I lifted the bamboo window shade to investigate and, to our mutual surprise, revealed a startled schoolboy writing on the dew-covered windows with his fingertip. He blinked once, smiled, then resumed his condensation graffito. Though he wasn't finished, it was obvious he was writing, "Ausländer raus!"—*Foreigners Out!*—on the pane. No one ever writes, "Ausländer, Bleibt! Wir brauchen, mögen und schätzen die kulturelle Vielfalt, die ihr uns durch eure Anwesenheit schenkt." *Foreigners Stay! We need, enjoy, and respect the cultural diversity your presence provides us.* Ausländer raus is a phrase most commonly associated with racist skinheads after German reunification; it was in fact popular in West Germany long before Ronald Reagan wreathed Nazi graves at Bitburg and demanded that Gorbachev tear down the Berlin Wall. However, it wasn't the boy's xenophobia that intrigued me: It was the sonorous screeches his finger made as he wrote on the glass. It reminded me of a sound that I couldn't quite place, and I went outside to get a better listen.

---

* 1. If God exists, then he/she/it/whatever is like mad perfect.
2. If God exists, then he/she/it is the creator of the universe.
3. And if God is perfect, the universe should be perfect.
4. But the universe ain't perfect, as evidenced by this specious-ass logic argument and the pathetic state of contemporary everything.
5. Matter of fact, if God exists, then there would be no need for if/then statements.
6. Unless, of course, the if/then statement is God.

Just as the kid was putting the finishing touches on his public ignorance, he saw me coming and tried to run away. He was weighed down by his haversack, so I easily ran him down and marched him back to the window. He went obediently to erase his work, but I stopped him.

"Nein. Nein," I said, waving my finger in his panic-stricken face. "Bitte ende." *Please finish.* I held his hand to the glass and he timidly completed his opine, the squeaking letters loud and pitched in a distinct minor blues key I recognized as C minor but whose timbre and color I still couldn't place. When the little xenophobe made the long downward stroke of the exclamation point, it hit me. The squeaks sounded exactly like Oliver Nelson's tenor in "Stolen Moments." I had my first tune for the jukebox.

"Stolen Moments" is Oliver Nelson's signature tune, a song I find to be the ultimate mood setter; it's a classic jazz aperitif. Oftentimes, when I play hardcore underground hip-hop or punk gigs, after three or four especially rambunctious tunes the mosh pits begin to resemble the skirmish lines of a Bronze Age battlefield, the warehouse windows start to shake, the record needle starts to skip, the women have that "I'm down with the pogrom" whatever-motherfucker look in their eyes, and I know the party is one more Wu Tang killa bee sting or Bad Brains power chord from turning into Attica, I play fifteen to twenty seconds of "Stolen Moments" to ease the tension, keep the peace. Its incongruous beauty brings about the wry existential lugubriousness of the Christmas Eve carol coming from the enemy encampment on the other side of the fog-covered river in a hackneyed war movie. "Stolen Moments" is that type of intrusion, a lull in the fighting, a time to finish that drink and forgive and forget. The people know I'm providing a respite from the real by granting them a temporary gubernatorial death-row reprieve before I hit them with the next piercing Mobb Deep fuck-you falsetto,

Bounty Killer lick shot, or soul-splitting, pre-sellout, angst-ridden, Biohazard scream.

I knew immediately that "Stolen Moments" would be the Slumberland's signature tune; a smooth midtempo song, it would provide a sticky, almost humid, languorous background to an already sexually charged atmosphere. If a female failed to become aroused by a Tanzanian peacock unfurling his tail feathers, it'd bring out the pavonine sheen of his olive-green polyester slacks, burgundy silk shirt, and tan patent leather shoes. When the middle-aged West Berlin lioness slinks about the place flicking her feather cut and stalking her prey, Dolphy's flute would gently lift both her sagging breasts and spirits, Paul Chambers's bass would enhance her rear end with some downtown Detroit rotundity, and Bill Evans's piano would unaccent her English, put words in her mouth that she didn't know she knew and make her immune to egotistical black-male bullshit. Maybe one day Doris, while stocking bar, would hear the song and forgive me for stealing her moments. I know the song has yet to be written that would allow me to forgive myself.

The schoolboy dotted the exclamation point, and I thanked him. "*Ausländer raus!*" never sounded so beautiful. I went back inside to finish my beer and watch the sun erase his slur.

CHAPTER 5

GERMAN BARS DON'T have happy hours. They have hubris hours. There is no designated time for hubris hour. It happens unexpectedly and without warning. The bartender doesn't ring a bell at five P.M., announce that for the next two hours drinks are two for one, and that sage advice and unmitigated superciliousness are on the house. In fact, the only way I can tell when it's hubris hour is by the look on Lars Papenfuss's face.

Lars Papenfuss is Doris's new boyfriend and my best friend. We met about two weeks after the unveiling of the jukebox. He's a freelance journalist. A master spy who uses his cover as a pop-culture critic to prop up dictatorial movements like "trip-hop," "jungle," "Dogme 95," and "graffiti art" instead of puppet third-world governments. He's assassinated more visionaries than the CIA, but when we first met he was eager to come in out of the cold.

"Why are looking at me like that?" he asked.

"Because you look funny."

"How do I look?"

"You look proud."

"Then indeed I do look funny."

I'd seen that self-satisfied smirk on a German face only once before. CitySports Bar was open until the wee hours of the morning so the Charlottenburg locals could watch Graciano Rocchigiani fight for the light-heavyweight title in Las Vegas. These storied German boxers never fight outside of Germany and are rarely even German, but "Rocky," as his countrymen lovingly called him, wasn't an adopted Pole or gargantuan Ukrainian, and that night the native Berliner beat a potbellied black man senseless in the Las Vegas heat. In the sixth round when the referee's count reached ten and the American slumped into the arms of his cornermen, the fight fan next to me, Heiko Zollner from Wilmersdorf, swelled with a smug patriotism that his German guilt wouldn't allow him to express. He wanted to say, "I'm proud to be German" but he couldn't, it's illegal. Even the slightly less salacious "I'm happy to be German" would've compelled him to turn himself in to the authorities, whereupon he would've been sentenced to six months probation and a hefty fine and required to recite the first fifteen lines of the kaddish in Hebrew or French kiss a leper.

After the fight Heiko and I drunkenly reenacted the bout over a frothy pitcher of beer. With the orange peels we'd stuffed into our mouths serving as mouthpieces, our hands cut through the stream rising from a stainless steel bin of freshly hard-boiled eggs. When we finally tired, Heiko, no longer able to contain his German pride over Rocky's victory, raised a goldenrod mug of Bitburger beer brewed and poured to print-ad perfection. He pounded on the table. "Wie glücklich bin ich doch über dieses wunderschöne Bier heute morgen zum Frühstück," he exclaimed. *How fortunate I am to be able to partake in this beautiful glass of beer for my morning repast.* That was all the displaced praise his champion and country would get.

* * *

Lars looked just like Heiko did that night. His face lit up with that same hubris-hour smirk. He ordered a round of drinks and stuck out a hairy hand. He was there to interview me. I'd seen him around. Sitting at a corner table by himself, drinking his wine and observing. Every now and then he'd walk over to the jukebox, put his hands on the glass, and peer into the machine like a mechanic listening to an engine.

He'd done a lot of record promotion disguised as objective music journalism for a record company headquartered in Berlin. Doris was tending bar at a meet-and-greet for an American boy band when he asked her to make him something different and if she'd heard any good music lately. She mixed him an Adios Motherfucker,* then offhandedly mentioned the Slumberland jukebox. Told him the bar's patrons were so impressed by the jukebox selection that two or three times a night the place would go quiet for minutes at a time, that it wasn't a rare occurrence for newcomers to get shushed for talking over Charles Brown's "Drifting Blues" or for the crowd to applaud some particularly adroit Jackie McLean solo.

Intrigued, Lars had shown up once or twice the week prior to research his story by standing in the machine's opalescent glow and pressing his nose against the glass.

I consented to the interview so long as he promised that he wouldn't print my name or the name of the bar in the article, and, most important, that he wouldn't tell any of his fellow hacks about the place. Nothing ruins a good thing like its discovery by aging rock 'n' roll critics looking for a scene.

---

*Adios Motherfucker: A popular and potent ghetto cocktail introduced to Berlin by Slumberland's American clientele. Warning: This drink is strictly for professionals. Never drink it alone. Psilocybic. Liquid antimatter. Never mind about operating heavy machinery; you'll have trouble lighting a cigarette. Good thing, too, 'cause it's highly flammable.

While Lars fumbled with his old-fashioned cassette recorder, I took out my minirecorder and placed it on the bar, answering the why-the-fuck-don't-you-trust-me look on his face by explaining that I always tape random sounds and wanted to record the sound of the record button being pressed, telling him how I wasted the summer between fifth and sixth grades trying to press the record button fast enough to record the sound of its being pressed.

Lars laughed and said, "There's some Einsteinian relativity to that somehow."

I liked him immediately. I liked the word "Einsteinian." I liked him enough to be jealous of how he managed to pull off wearing a turtleneck sweater. Whenever I wore one I moved about stiffly, craning my neck as if I'd been in a car accident and the turtleneck was less a masculine-magazine fashion statement than a way of hiding my neck brace. Doris sat down to join us.

I pressed record.

Lars pressed record.

I turned off my tape recorder and said, "Before we begin, I'd like to tell you that not everything I say to you will be the truth."

He asked whether the jukebox had changed the bar's notorious reputation as a meat market. I shrugged modestly, and Doris elbowed me in the side, forcing me to tell him the Carly Simon story.

The day after the new jukebox had been plugged in I stumbled upon a woman giving a guy head in the bathroom. Such Weimaresque displays of public affection, although common at raucous Berlin bars like the Kumpelnest and Café M, were unheard of at the race-mixing joints. For us Slumberlanders the sexual electricity was all about the pretense of taboo and stigma. If blacks and whites kissed in public it would take the fun out of the game. Sour the forbidden fruit *gemütlichkeit*, so to speak. Yet there they were, he leaning back against the sink, she squatting in front of him, her stringy blonde head plunging in and out of his nappy, ashen crotch, her hands grabbing onto the faucets for support, his hands wrapped around her neck for psychological and physical leverage. They were both crying and singing in tandem to Carly Simon's "You're So Vain," the lachrymal ballad that dripped from the bathroom speaker. It was the most romantic and disgusting scene I'd ever witnessed. The scene played out like a page stricken from a long-lost *Othello* folio.

Act V, Scene I
OTHELLO
Lo, sweet Desdemona, many a knave and nobleman hath warned me, "Thou canst not maketh a ho into a housewife." And yet, sainted wife, my dagger knows no other scabbard.

140

If they saw me, they continued to sing, and I continued to look and listen. He was in astonishingly good voice, a princely Ugandan alto with a hint of Jagger's pseudo-cockney accent. She, on the other hand, was understandably garbled. I can still hear their orgiastic duet.

"Yeah," I answered blithely, "the Slumberland's the same, but different."

We talked freely and openly for hours, the interview finally ending with Lars inquiring in that strange fractured syntax that most people adopt whenever discussing anything niggeresque, "How come they ain't no hip-hop on the jukebox?"

"There isn't?"

"No."

"I guess it's because rap doesn't sound right in a bookstore, bar, coffee shop, or television commercial."

"Less authentic?"

"It's more about the acoustics. What makes hip-hop special is its spatial intimacy with the listener. Rap is a claustrophobic music that sounds best on headphones jammed deep into your ear canals, in a cinder block dorm room or a car packed dashboard to trunk with your friends, the music so loud that the rearview mirror pops to the beat, the weed bounces up and down on the Zig-Zag, the factory-installed bass speakers fight for their lives as the bass threatens to blow them and your eardrums out. You can't play the music loud enough in here to give it any import. Maybe when hip-hop dies, and it will die, then it'll be fit for public consumption. Can you imagine listening to "Rebel Without a Pause" at low, unobtrusive Muzak volume, sipping a hot, cream-free double espresso and wondering, 'Is this what Public Enemy meant by black power?' "

Lars turned off his tape recorder. As if on cue, the finger snaps to Peggy Lee's "Fever" strutted into the bar, black-cat cool and followed by a finicky, purring vocal that slinked into your lap and demanded attention. On the other side of the bar a portly woman leaned over a dreadlocked American to put her drink order in to the bartender and her angora-covered breasts in his face. Her order placed, she tucked her hair behind her ear and started snapping her fingers to the beat. She wasn't giving me fever, but the woman sitting next to the dread got hot and told her to step back.

Lars watched the scene curiously, drumming his pen on the bar, when he slowly turned his head in my direction and said, "Charles Stone"

I don't how to punctuate that quote. There is no way to classify its purpose, for it was spoken without one. It came across more as an involuntary Tourette's utterance than anything else. What could possess him to name-drop the Schwa, my paper-thin and increasingly futile raison d'être, for no apparent raison?

"Charles Stone"

This time the words hung in the air, swinging like a shopkeeper's nominal shingle in an ominous Dickensian London breeze. Their only defining characteristic, other than the unaccented phonation, was the tone, a tone that had a tinge of the spy's trench coat trepidation when broaching a potential contact with the opening fragment of a cryptic code phrase.

"Charles Stone"

I didn't know the proper response. During D-Day, Allied soldiers crawled and cowered in the French hedgerows doing their best to avoid being victims of friendly fire by shouting, "Thunder!" at one another and anything else that moved. The only way friendlies such as the groundhogs, the clouds, and scared-shitless draftees wouldn't be fired upon was to answer the "Thunder!" with a prompt "Flash!"—preferably spoken in a strong Texas dialect.

I was afraid to say anything. I looked to Doris for help, but she excused herself to fix a cola dispenser that had run out of CO_2. Maybe "Charles Stone" was the music critic's "Halt! Who goes there?" We all have our dinner-party litmus tests. Standardized oral pop quizzes that we give to the moderately attractive person with the mouth stuffed with deviled eggs in order to find out if they're worth spending the next half hour with, much less the rest of one's life. My litmus test of compatibility is "Tom Cruise." I hate people who hate Tom Cruise, cultural automatons who at the mention of his name reflexively bridle and say the diminutive thespian and Theta level Scientologist is "crazy" and "a terrible actor." They hate him because he's easy to hate. They think that despising Tom Cruise's lack of personality and supposed lack of talent is somehow a blow against the bland American Anschluss of the rest of the planet. Tom Cruise may indeed be the Christopher Columbus of the twentieth century, sent off by the kings of Hollywood to prove the new world of International Box Office isn't flat and to find a direct route into the Asian market, but the decline of everything isn't his fault; he's just a cinematic explorer and a

damn fine actor. And hating him doesn't make you seditious—
it makes you complicit.

Maybe Lars Papenfuss was waiting for me to say the wrong
thing so he could deem me unworthy of German recognition
and the social-democratic largesse that came with it, then take
me out back and shoot me.

"Charles Stone."

That one had a period on it. A punctuation of suspicion put
there because my eyebrows kept folding to crazy angles as I tried
to hold a dumbfounded look on my face.

"Charles Stone."

I ignored him. Focused my attention on the Dreadlock-
American and the two women. He had them both entranced.
Every caesura in his story followed by a sigh and an earnest, "See,
I'm from the ghetto . . ." He playfully slipped pretzels onto the
ring fingers of both women and asked them for their hands in
marriage. Answering with yesses that didn't come off as face-
tiously as originally intended, they laughed and kissed him on the
cheek. I had something to do with that. A few years down the
line when one, possibly both of these women are catching dread's
kids at the bottom of the slide and answering the "What was
daddy like?" question, I'll gaze nostalgically through the park
fence at their happy, caramel-colored, schnitzel-eating kids and
say to myself, "Me and Peggy Lee had something to do with that."

Peggy Lee's "Fever" subsided, and during the record change a
tense silence filled the bar. The dread jump-started his conversation with the usually patented "See, I'm from the ghetto . . . ,"
only this time he was silenced by both women. They leaned
backward off their stools, ears cocked toward the main room.
They wanted to hear what was coming on next. The panting
hound dog leitmotif to George Clinton's "Atomic Dog" bounced
jauntily into the room, lifting me and at least half the other
drunks out of our seats and onto the sand-covered floor. There

we shape-shifted and transmogrified from one funkified pose to another. The funk and nothing but the funk running over us like a hot iron, flattening and steaming the Slumberland universe into a single wrinkle-free dimension. Pressed into the walls, our limbs raised and bent at odd, acute, and not-so-cute angles, we looked like dancing figures circumscribing an ancient Babylonian vase. An earthenware urn telling a story of modern antiquity, glazed and fire-hardened civil servants riding and shimmying what they thought was the downbeat, illegal aliens flying fancy free for the first time in their destitute lives, finally feeling like the African royalty they so often claim to be.

I'd always thought music writers, like gangsters, were too cool to dance; yet there was Lars doing a very credible strobe. Stopping and starting his body rock with such rapidity it looked as if he were moving underneath the flickering brightness of a strobe light. He pop locked over to me and touched me on the arm.

"Charles Stone."

This time I knew what to say.

"Tom Cruise, motherfucker."

During the next few weeks Lars and I bonded over Osamu Dazai, a thirty-year-old bottle of Poit Dhubh malt whiskey, the welterweight fearlessness of Oscar De La Hoya, and the cleverness of contemporary American everything at the expense of passion. He claimed to be the only person alive who'd actually read Thomas Pynchon's twenty-five-pound opus *Gravity's Rainbow* without having yawned even once, and I believed and respected him for it. "A wonderful piece of children's literature," he said. "If only it were five hundred pages longer and a little less transparent." For him reading the book to completion was like fighting a meaningless war and living to tell about it. Vietnam, Desert Storm—I'm against the wars but support the soldiers. He'd invite me over to his flat just so I could watch him finish his review of the latest

American "me novels." He'd toss the galley copy into the trash and say, "I'm against the author, but support the reader," then tell me how he gave up fiction because whenever he submitted a gritty, realistic manuscript the publishers would say, "We like it, but we want more plot," or if he submitted a tight, linear narrative, they'd say, "We like it, but we want more realism." Jealous of everyone and anyone's success, I gathered up the nerve to show Lars my novel, a work in perpetual progress composed entirely of opening sentences, the best of which he thought was, " 'We will be cruising at an altitude of zero feet, our estimated time of arrival is never, and the temperature in hell is bloody hot with searing winds out of the southwest. Sit back and relax and ignore the seat belt sign. Thank you for flying Kamikaze Airways,' the pilot announced into the loudspeaker, his shoulders shaking with what the psychiatrists call 'inappropriate laughter.' "

Defiant in my determination to complete my quest solo, I avoided any talk or discussion about Charles Stone until one autumn day when Lars, Doris, and I drove back from Jam, an outdoor party held on the banks of the Spree. Horace Silver's "Señor Blues" crackled from the tinny dashboard speakers. It's a wonderful driving song, and his sun-faded red Alfa Romeo convertible scuttled through Berlin leaking oil and bop pianissimo. At a stoplight Lars lowered the volume.

"What's it like listening to jazz with no white people around?" he asked, apropos of nothing except that Horace Silver and me were both black and he wasn't.

I recall my face in the side-view mirror. Forlorn. Fed up. Homesick. I wish I hadn't been so offended by Lars's curiosity. I wish that, like he and most other cultural critics, I believed in the mystique and exclusivity of Negro expression.

"You know what happens when you listen to jazz when there's only black people around?"

Lars stiffened excitedly in his seat, his hands tightening

around the steering wheel. I cleared my throat of sarcasm and hocked a spit wad of derision into the street.

"Well, if there's just the right amount of barbecue sauce on the ribs and mentholated smoke in the air, we pass around the 'jungle juice,' a fruity, tribal, hallucinogenic Kool-Aid-based beverage, and wait for Coltrane, Clifford Brown, or some other goateed shaman to hit that perfect flatted fifth, sending us all into a collective trance state that awakens the dormant recombinant gris-gris gene in our mitochondrial DNA, thereby catapulting us into the fifth dimension where we surrey down to a stoned soul picnic, rejoicing in the cessation of the racist phenomenological world and attainment of Negro nirvana that for me, ironically, is absent any other Negroes."

"Fuck you."

"You asked. Next time I'll tell you about how whenever two black quarterbacks face each other in a football game, black America gets a collective migraine because we don't know which team to cheer for."

At least Lars was curious about the appeal of jazz to black folk; for most observers, such ponderation is akin to contemplating why gorillas like bananas. The attractiveness of jazz to the nonblack is well documented in publicly funded documentaries where experts speak of jazz in the past tense. They look authoritatively into the camera and ingratiate themselves with the Man by saying things like, "White people were hearing something in jazz that says something deeply about their experience. I'm not sure that it would have been this way if we were not a country of immigrants . . . so many people felt kind of displaced . . . I think that was part of its amazing appeal, was how it spoke to feeling out of sort and out of joint and maladjusted."*

---

*Gerald Early, Ph.D., *Ken Burns Jazz*. I remember the entire series word for word and note for note, but what I remember most is that no one ever mentioned Sun Ra. Not once.

What hogwash. Does my fondness for classical music make me well adjusted? Besides, people who are really fucked up don't turn to jazz; they turn to heroin, opium, whiskey, and Vonnegut.

Lars turned up the radio. A bouncy yet vacuous tune that I couldn't quite place replaced the Horace Silver. The music didn't fill the air so much as pass through it. The song tried hard to be jazz, to be noble, to be American. The band wasn't playing jazz so much as it was playing the history of jazz. I said something I rarely say about any piece of music.

"I have no idea who this is."

Lars started to laugh, but a look of concern quickly reconfigured his face.

"You don't know?"

"No."

"You're not fucking with me?"

"No," I insisted, staring down the radio dial as if that would give me a clue.

The trumpet player's recording levels were set a shade higher than the rest of the band, so I figured he was the leader. He lit into a bewailing tremolo. His technique was exquisite. The tone had the crisp dryness of a nice house sake, but there was a sterility to his phrasing that left me feeling empty and used.

Lars looked at his watch and, taking his hands off the wheel, pretended to write an obituary on the palm of his hand.

"Tonight, at five fifty-seven P.M. on a warm October evening, the American Negro was officially declared dead. His passing will be mourned by all who've enjoyed his musical precocity."

"This time, fuck *you*."

Lars drove with his knees better than I did with my hands. He'd eased the car into a fairly sharp turn, merging into traffic with a smile and peace sign for the Renault he'd almost side-swiped. The song and Lars forged intrepidly on.

"When I reviewed this record, the best description I could come up with was 'nondescript.' I was listening to it and completely forgot it was on. You know, when I review a good jazz album my neighbors' kids come running into the flat, hands over their ears, screaming, 'Was ist das Herr Lars? Was ist das?' begging to know the name of the strange sounds coming from my living room. This time they stayed at home. Frau Junker, the elderly woman who lives across the hall, was the only one listening. In the middle of a solo she rang my bell, and when I opened the door, she says, 'It's a shame about the black man. I miss them,' and returns to her business."

Lars wouldn't take the wheel. Pissed off that blackness was dead, he sat there with his arms folded and a Fritz Lang monocle squint on his face.

"Wynton Marsalis," I said suddenly, pounding the dashboard in disgust. "That's who this is."

I should have known sooner; the tempo's self-important braggadocio was a dead giveaway. Marsalis, New Orleans born and New York praised, is jazz's most famous living musician. He's been around for years, but until that night I'd never heard one note of his astringent horn in public. I'd never seen one of his CDs in a poolroom jukebox or seen a spry, elderly, know-it-all black man hanging out in front of the supermarket, snapping his fingers and whistling one of his melodies to pass the time. He's a middle-aged child prodigy to whom everyone gives plaudits, but no one plays.

The tune, like most contrivances of the black telegentsia, seemed lost, a corny cacophonic search among the ruins of a romanticized African history for a self-affirming excuse to love being black. However, Wynton's pretentious narcissistic nigrescence couldn't fool me.* The pentatonic scaling and the repetition of the ninth through twelfth bars belied an underlying skittishness, and the song flitted aimlessly about like a flock of canaries that have flown into a room and can't find their way out. If I had had a sack of breadcrumbs and sprinkled them on the car floor, his cawing notes would've fluttered from his trumpet one by one, landed at my feet, and begged for attention. The thunderclap of an Art Blakey rim shot would've scattered the song into nothingness, leaving nothing but muted airs and some unresolved psychosexual issues with Mother Africa.

I hate Wynton Marsalis in the same manner Rommel hated Hitler. Whenever I hear Marsalis's trumpet playing I feel like the Desert Fox forced to come to grips with the consequences of totalitarianism after the war has been all but lost. At least Rommel had Wagner. All I've got is Wynton. His musical Valkyries arrive not on winged steeds but astride caged birds.

Wynton Marsalis reminds me that I was born wearing the wrong uniform. That I'm a Negro-Nazi who, being only a DJ and not a general, politician, or movie director, is at best a functionary or house-party gauleiter. At the tribunal I will not claim that during the culture wars I was deceived by my superiors and had no knowledge of the camps. I will plead guilty to the charge of crimes against humanity. Admit that I was a deceiver. A trickster whose greatest transgressions were kick-starting the strip-club putsch of 1989 by giving voice to the earliest in Afro-fascist rap (Young MC, JJ Fad, and DJ Jazzy Jeff and the Fresh Prince) and knowing of the existence of the death camps: the University of California at Berkeley, the Nuyorican Poets Cafe, the Lyricist Lounge, Naropa, Def Jam and Bad Boy

*Once, in a fit of neologic haughtiness, I submitted *nigriscence* to my main lexicographer Cutter Pinchbeck at *Kensington-Merriwether,* who wrote back, "S'up wit chu, N-Word? *Nigrescence* is already an N-word."

Records, the Abyssinian Baptist Church, and that Auschwitz of free thought, Jazz at Lincoln Center.

The song labored on, Wynton's band, like the critics, playing in the past tense. I began to feel a wave of black conformity wash over me and I felt the need to remind myself that oppression didn't start with Kunta Kinte and that the trains probably ran on time before Hitler. A yawn that I didn't bother to stifle left my lips.

Modern jazz, like the modern man, was devoid of funk, devoid of mystery. Maybe what Wynton's band needed was a maladjusted white cat, a Bix, Benny Goodman, Gerry Mulligan, Adam Yauch, or an F. Scott Fitzgerald to give it some fervor. That way they could stop playing with a sense of entitlement and start playing with the daring birthed by vicariousness—but these days there's never a Gene Krupa around when you need one.

The existentialists say the flap of a butterfly's wings in the jungles of Mauritania can cause a hurricane in the plains of Kansas, but a high C from Wynton Marsalis's trumpet doesn't even change your mood, much less your mind. And I don't know whether or not Marsalis's music is an allegory for race, American democracy, or black fascism, but I do know the Schwa's music is anarchy. It's Somalia. It's the Department of Motor Vehicles. It's Albert Einstein's hair.

When we arrived back at my place I took out the chicken-fucking song and wiggled it in Doris's face, indicating that I wanted to play it. Doris shook her head. That was our song. Our little free-jazz secret. I popped it into the VCR anyway. Lars was perusing the stacks of books that rose from the floor of my dingy apartment like paperback stalagmites. He opened a tattered Nabokov. Appropriate because the Schwa plays like Nabokov writes. I'm convinced that Nabokov wrote his novels around words like *agglutinate, siliceous, gardyloo, ophidian, triskelions.* That he took an ESL course at a local night school and the teacher wrote those words on the blackboard and said, "Today's assignment is to take these words and use them in a first novel the *New York Times* will call 'Riveting, truly a classic for the ages.'" Surely the Schwa's process is similar, because every ten measures or so there's a snippet, a riff within a riff that makes you realize that the previous nine measures were just an excuse to play a tricolor chord that bursts open in the middle of the song like a firework exploding in a clear night sky.

Lars sat on the arm of the couch grinning at Nabokov's prosody. He was as relaxed as a boxer who thinks he's far enough ahead on the card in the fight for cultural hegemony to let his hipster guard down and coast to an easy victory. He wasn't paying that overhand left whistling in the distance any mind, and when the Schwa's avant-garde jazz trochaics hit him, the smile on his face changed from mirthful to the be-mused toothy grin of a boxer who's been seriously hurt by a punch but doesn't want his opponent to know he can hear his own brains sloshing inside his skull. The genuflecting glaze in his eyes gave him away. Lars knew straightaway who it was. He considered himself Europe's foremost authority on Charles Stone, and here his best friend was playing a heretofore unknown Stone gem, and he was hurt. Throw-in-the-towel hurt.

I wouldn't turn off the music. The Nabokov fell face open into his lap. It might have been from muscle fatigue, though I suspect it was to hide an erection. The stud on the screen continued to pound the chicken doggy style, if that's at all possible. The music continued on as if the Schwa were in the room using the book as sheet music . . . *shadography, Lacedaemonian sensation, ocelate* . . . Lars began to cry. Hearing that unknown recording of the Schwa affected him the same as if I'd told him Steve Biko, Bud Powell, Janis Joplin, Patrick Lumumba, and Bob Marley had survived the *Rolling Stone* rhetoric and were running glass-bottomed boat excursions off the Florida Keys. He buried his head into a sofa cushion, not in shame but to muffle his sobbing so that it didn't interfere with the music. When the song ended he fired the Nabokov at my head.

"How can you live with yourself?" he yelled. "You *verdammte* DJs with your secrecy, your white labels and hush-hush-close-the-door-we're-the-only-ones-with-cocaine-and-a-Japanese-import-on-vinyl-cooler-than-thou attitude. You know I worship this guy. How dare you sit on the greatest jazz piece recorded since 1969, unveiling it only to select guests like it's a stolen fucking Picasso. You people think that because you own the recording you own the music."

"You people?" I asked, slipping behind my turntables.

"*Entschuldigen Sie.* DJs aren't people, they're parasites."

Lars picked up a Zora Neale Hurston and a Eugene O'Neill and fired a double-barreled scattershot blast at Doris.

"And fuck you too! Keeping this from me! You guys are probably fucking behind my back too!"

I switched on the sampler and calmly dropped the needle on the record. The first booming thump of my almost-perfect beat caved in Lars's chest. When the hook kicked in it was as if Doctor Funkenstein had tapped his spinal cord with a rubber hammer. The autonomic reflexes took over. The crispy highs caused his neck to snap and jerk back and forth. The pounding lows dropped his ass halfway to the floor, rolled his shoulders, and turned his pelvis into a gyroscope of grinding sensuality. Meanwhile his pronated hands hovered mummylike in front of his chest and surfed the midrange. I finished my groove and

Lars bit down hard on his bottom lip. I knew what he wanted to say. He wanted to say, "Damn, nigger, so that's what it feels like to be black."

Instead he opened the windows, letting the very last of the cool daylight air blow into the room like a runaway child come home. "Now I know why you came to Germany," he said. "You want to get Stone to lay down an original groove over your track."

Lars ejected the tape and flipped it around, looking for clues as to where it came from. He was too much of an ethical journalist to ask me to divulge my sources. Not that I had any.

"It came in the mail."

I handed him the envelope the chicken-fucking song had come in, making sure he noticed the return address and the East Berlin postmark. He held it gently, as if it were an old museum piece. "Wow, it feels good to know that Charles Stone might be out there."

"There" meant the 350 square miles of divided Berlin expanse that existed in Lars's head. From my window, "there" was the oak-tree-lined intersection of Schlüterstrasse and Mommenstrasse, an overpriced Italian restaurant, a furrier, and, almost directly underneath us, two stories down, Blixa Bargeld, the infamous leader of the industrial band Einstürzende Neubauten, sitting on the fender of his sports car. Dressed head to toe in Berlin black, his legs crossed at the ankles, he'd take a long pull on his cigarette, hack into his fingerless leather glove, then crane his neck down the block. He too was waiting for somebody to come out of the growing darkness.

"That's dusk you feel," I said to Lars.

"No, it's more than that," he replied. "This city, this country has been dead for a long, long time, and if somebody like Charles Stone is out there somewhere, it means the cultural soil is no longer fallow. Picasso blossomed in Paris and the city flowered along with him. Gauguin in Tahiti. Kerouac in Mexico. Erich von Stroheim in Hollywood. DJ Darky and Charles Stone in Berlin."

"The Schwa—back home we call him the Schwa."

A flat-chested Chinese woman who played up her exotic communist appeal and downplayed her beauty with an X-Acto-knife-sharp bowl cut, kung fu slippers, square plastic Jiang Zemin glasses, a Red Army jacket with matching floppy Long March hat, and a bootleg Dead Boys concert T-shirt sidled up to Blixa and without asking coyly shared his cigarette.

"We haven't had a great thinker since Heidegger, a great artist since Riefenstahl. Don't get me wrong, you're a great fucking DJ, but DJs aren't artists or thinkers. They can't be Picasso or Kerouac. But they can be one of those thankless unknowns that came before them. Influenced them. Threatened them. Fed them. Maybe you're Dean Moriarty, Alice B. Toklas, Fab Five Freddy, or Allen Ginsberg's 'negro streets at dawn.'"

I watched Blixa and his girlfriend kiss, and with every vicarious grope I cared less and less about the Schwa and my perfect beat. I'd rather look for love, but blind, crippled, and crazy, I'd slept with damn near every woman in West Berlin, so I was running out of options.

On our way to the Slumberland we walked past the intertwined Blixa and his Red Guard. He stopped nuzzling his Sino-sylph long enough to stare me down. He'd heard the beat. It had fallen from my window and landed on his head like a Newtonian apple. The curious rhythm bruising his auditory cortex and, I suppose, his ego. Still ringing fuzzily inside his head. Just as Sir Isaac knew the laws of gravity couldn't be ignored when the apple struck him, Blixa instinctively knew that the George Clintonian Law of Universal Funk must also be paid obeisance. For every funky object in the universe attracts every other hip-hi-de-ho object with a soulsonic force directed along the bass line of centers for the two objects that is proportional to the product of the masses of their asses and inversely proportional to the bustin' out of L7 square of the racial separation between the two objects.

$$F = G\,\frac{m_1 m_2}{r^2}$$

where: F is the Funk, G is the Groove constant, m_1 is the mass of the first ass, m_2 is the mass of the second ass, and r is the great racial divide.

We left Blixa to his own calculations, and four hours later it was hubris hour at the Slumberland, Lars's proud face beaming at the new multiculti Germany around him and still pontificating on the coming rebirth of both his city and the black man.

"Think about it, fifty years ago we tried to kill culture, and now without trying we're going to resurrect it."

In the middle of the bar a Watusi climbed on a table and danced the Watusi. I thanked the gods there were no tribes called the Mashed Potato, the Electric Slide, or the Funky Chicken. West Berlin, Lars drunkenly insisted, would prove to be the modern-day equivalent to the Olduvai Gorge. It would be the birthplace of the neo-protohuman, the new black man.

There was one sitting across the table from me. A premature protohuman baby with whom Lars and Doris had periodic threesomes named Tyrus Maverick. Tyrus was a self-described "performance artist slash poet slash playwright slash filmmaker slash activist" and, as I liked to add, "slash asshole" who still owes me three hundred dollars. He hailed from Southern California, claiming Compton though he'd spent the greater part of his boyhood in Hawthorne. He'd tried to pal up citing our common Sureño palm tree and In-N-Out burger vato loco heritage, and I was friendly at first until I went to a reading of his play *Iceland Is Hot!*

Tyrus had the annoying habit of tapping me on the arm whenever he had something to say. "Hey, man"—*tap, tap*—"I think Doris still likes you. She's always carrying on about how you the only black man she'd ever known who during a dinner date didn't insist on sitting in the seat facing the door like a wanted criminal."

Tyrus was good for one thing, though: He kept up with contemporary African-American male literature. That night he was reading a trade-paperback tome entitled *Want Some, Get Some. Bad Enough, Take Some.* Like everything else he read, it invariably bore a series of blurbs comparing the author's biting satire to Ralph Ellison and Richard Wright, a comparison that I never understood because Richard Wright isn't funny.

"Can I borrow that when you're finished? I'd like to read it."

"No doubt. This cat's a hell of a writer. Damn near as funny as Richard Wright."

I loved reading these books. The black tweed-jacketed eruditeness mixed with street-corner irreverence, the honesty about racial turpitude coupled with the dishonesty about its manifestation. Like the authors, the protagonists are always brilliant, underappreciated men in search of white approval and, therefore, self-affirmation. I know these cats. These are

---

Iceland Is Hot! tells the story of an African-American volcanologist who travels to Iceland to practice his craft, but fails to be taken seriously by the volcanological community there because of his inability to correctly pronounce *fjord*. Once ostracized, he correctly predicts the eruption of Mount Hekla and becomes a celebrated scientist, only to die of frostbite when he falls into a snowbank after being accidentally shot by his illegitimate son, Halldór, founder of the Reykjavik Crips, in a vicious sleigh-by shooting.

the dudes from the neighborhood who got white-boy SAT scores, attended small Midwestern liberal arts colleges, and married frumpy white girls with hairy legs who douche with rainwater. Yet the female love interest who grounds their protagonists to their fragile blackness while they trek through the absurdist, mine-laden landscape that is America is always a demure, brown-skinned female with a refined intelligence, no personality, and no problems, the kind of woman guys like the ones who inhabit these novels would never be attracted to. I needed a real woman exactly like the fictional ones that always showed up in Part III of those novels. Where was my Melba? My Wanda? My African queen without the African features?

When I looked up from my musing, a full-chested, auburn-haired woman splattered with freckles from her cheekbones to her clavicle was seated at our table, jingling her car keys in my face. Lars slipped his pompous-looking mug over her shoulder and raised an eyebrow. Doris's bumptious face suddenly appeared over the other shoulder. Together they looked like a smug, three-headed Aryan hydra.

"I know you're thinking about giving up looking for the Schwa," Doris said. "Don't."

The middle head smiled broadly, licked her lips, and this time jangled her keys so that the BMW logo on her rubber-tipped ignition key was prominently displayed.

Lars raised the other eyebrow. He was drunk, drunker than I'd ever seen him, which was saying a lot.

"Hey, man," I said to him, "you never told me, why so proud tonight?"

He leaned in, speaking very softly. "Don't tell anyone, but tonight, tonight I'm proud of the holocaust. Not the killing per se, but the efficiency. The drive. The single-minded devotion to a task. Is that so wrong?"

At that moment I needed a black woman in my life like never before. However, my venture into the mysteries of black carnality would have to wait, because the middle hydra head had taken my hand and placed it on her left breast. I kneaded the doughy appendage. It felt like strudel. And I love strudel.

PART 3

THE SOULS OF BLACK VOLK

CHAPTER 1

M Y FAVORITE BERLIN DAYS are those rare late afternoons when I go outside full of an unflappable faith in mankind that only a double espresso and a clean T-shirt can muster, only to find the streets deserted. It's like entering the set of a postapocalyptic 1959 film. The traffic is nonexistent and all the shops are closed. I'll wonder if I've slept through the air raid sirens. Missed the mandatory evacuation pending the invasion from outer space. On the way to the newspaper kiosk I'll hear a plaintive yelp, then I'll sprint around the corner expecting to see a fifty-foot-tall, one-eyed, iridescent green robot zapping a stray dog with a ray gun. Is that a dust cloud churning down Kantstrasse, or some comet-borne, incurable, and highly communicable virus that liquefies innards and turns eyeballs to smoke? In the tiny chain-link confines of Albertus Magnus Park the rusted swings will creak, their meager ridership consisting of only the breeze and me. Eventually a hump-bearing dowager will sit in the next swing over, kick her varicose-veined, knee-high-stocking legs back and forth, and complain about the cold and the *verdammte türkisch-polnische Neger-Ausländer Kanaken*. Then I'll know my fears of the apocalypse were unfounded and that it's only some national holiday no one bothered to inform me about before their visit to Oma und Opa. Maybe it'll be May Day or Three Kings Day or International Women's Day or My God What Were We Thinking When We Voted for Hitler? (Twice!) Please Forgive Us—It's Been Fifty Years Already! Day.

For fun I'll ask the muttering old woman how she feels about the *Neger-Neger* (Nigger-Niggers) like myself and she'll say, "Love them. Slept with a couple after the war. Nice boys. Polite. Big *Schwänze,* small minds, and even tinier ears. Maybe that's why they're so stupid, they don't hear everything." Oh, I love those Berlin days, empty streets, yowling dogs, and swinging on the swings with kindly, racist, octogenarian sex addicts. So it stands to reason that I hate undeclared and impromptu holidays like the fateful one when I'd flung myself into the streets with my usual hangover Weltschmerz and dirty-underwear petulance, and found the sidewalks packed stoop to curb with giddy, overly inquisitive Germans drinking Coca-Cola and noshing bananas and all moving in the same direction. As they passed me by, each one took a long moment to stare at me like a child on a field trip to the *Völkerschau*—people zoo. One boy, ignoring his mother's don't-feed-the-animals admonition, offered me a Coke and a smile. Both of which I gladly accepted.

At first I wasn't quite certain they were German. They spoke German. They looked German, albeit with even tighter pants and uglier shoes, but there was something different about them. I figured maybe the Austrian national soccer team was in town or there was a *kartoffelpuffer* famine in Luxembourg. What was really eye-catching about the horde was how incredibly un-eye-catching they were. Not to say they were unappealing. On the whole they weren't any uglier than any other mass assemblage since Bon Jovi's last concert date. Yet even the most stunning physical specimens among them carried themselves without the slightest hint of pretension. The people seemed to be a lot like their clothes. They were a sturdy wash-and-wear group who favored comfort and practicality over style and flash. For them it wasn't the clothes that made the man. It was the person who made the clothes.

A towering blonde Calliope exited the perfumery pressing cardboard samples to her Linda Evangelista nose and blissfully inhaled for all she was worth. Somehow, against all odds, that breathtakingly beautiful woman with the statuesque figure and the tweaked oblique eyebrow countenance of a *Vogue* covergirl wasn't vaingloriously strutting the catwalks of Paris, twirling a Givenchy bag and scanning the frigid fashionistas for her heroin dealer, but clomping the streets in the most ungainly pair of dog-shit-brown flats, digging wax out of her ears, and wiping the viscous find on the sleeves of her denim jacket. And she gawked at me like I was the monkey masturbating in the trees.

An impossibly ordinary-looking man interrupted the stare down.

"How much does such an automobile cost?" he asked me in English, running a hand admiringly over the fender of a parked Mercedes-Benz sedan.

"I don't know. Fifty, sixty thousand?"

He looked familiar but I couldn't place him. Returning to the Benz, he peered into the car with his hands cupped around his eyes, drooling at the leather interior and dashboard gadgetry.

"*Scheisse,* that's ten years' pay plus bribes, plus five . . ." he mumbled something that sounded like "assassination bonuses," then with a giddy, almost criminal look on his face spat out a dare disguised as an innocent question: "Ever ride in one?"

"Once."

"Smooth?"

"Like I was flying in a dream, maybe better."

"I knew it."

"Can I ask you something?"

"*Bitte.*"

PAUL BEATTY

"Where did all these people come from? Was there a soccer game?"

The bland man stopped looking at the various pipe-cleaner-sized metal rods he'd removed from his jacket pocket.

"You haven't heard?"

"Heard what?"

"The Wall fell."

I boldly stepped into the second-most embarrassing moment of my life and asked, "What wall?"*

Thus confirming every stereotype of American ignorance about world affairs and geography. I, of course, knew of the Berlin Wall and its storied history, but as so often happens to black Americans abroad and domestically, I found myself trapped in a culturally biased break in the race-time continuum. Just as the bright but underprivileged inner-city child will correctly and for all the wrong reasons answer "b" to the following PSAT puzzler:

> Mademoiselle Chiffon took a soothing sip of oolong tea and smiled mournfully at the strains of chamber music coming from the conservatory. Her genteel mind flashed to the carefree days she'd spent summering in the Tuscan hills before the war. *Oh, Gaston,* she thought to herself, *am I forever doomed to hear your voice only in a string quartet's violins?* Silently, she cursed Bartók and returned the teapot to the _____ while absentmindedly fingering her warm _____ _____.

> a. sink, first-edition Molière
> b. saucer, ~~tea cozy~~, *wet coochie*

---

*The most embarrassing moment of my life came in college when Alizah Silverman caught me in the student union stuffing my face with McDonald's and reading *The Fountainhead* minutes before I was supposed to march in a demonstration against corporate globalism.

c. table, Chinese exercise balls

d. cupboard, baroque lute

I too nearly fell victim to the ignorance resultant from a lack of exposure. Like the tea cozy to the ghetto child, the Berlin Wall was not a part of my lexicon. I'd never seen it. When the indescribable man mentioned "the Wall," any number of walls flashed through my mind. The Great Wall of China. The Wailing Wall. Pink Floyd's classic album. The blue wall of silence the LAPD erected at the disciplinary hearing held for officers Barbella and Stevenson after they'd beat me and Blaze's ass in the ninth grade for suspicion of stealing a car while we were at the bus stop waiting patiently for a bus.

The Mercedes's door popped open with a satisfying click.

"Typical," the faceless man said before sticking his mundane mug underneath the steering column and fiddling with the wires.

"You Americans own the world but never bother to venture into your own backyard. That's the attitude that allowed us to steal the basketball final in the '76 Olympics from under your noses, use Leo Strauss to infiltrate the Republican Party with his madcap philosophy of cruelty parading as humanism, convince you that VHS was superior to Betamax, and lure you into the Vietnam, Korean, and cola wars. New Coke? That was Vita Cola, the swill we East Germans have been drinking for forty years. No doubt your president will take credit for the fall of the Wall as signaling the end of Communism, but it's all part of the master plan. It's a misdirection maneuver somewhat analogous to your trick plays in American football, a geopolitical Statue of Liberty or fumblerooski, if you will. Soon, my dense Afro-American friend, you'll be casting invisible digital votes in the name of democracy. Enslaving the vast majority of your work-force with a negligible minimum wage in the name of liberty.

Charging mobile-phone users to *make* and *receive* calls in the name of free enterprise. Training the very same religious zealots of the desert who'll . . ."

The robust revving of the eight-cylinder engine drowned out the rest of his prognostication and my question about what in hell was a mobile phone.

"Come," he said, patting the passenger seat. "Come see the breach in the Wall through which the four horsemen of the American apocalypse will ride."

"Are you some kind of spy or just a well-informed car thief?" I asked, closing the door behind me.

"I'm a spy, though by tomorrow I might be a war criminal."

"Me too."

Traveling in four-door, heated-leather-seat luxury, we drove slowly through the masses. The man with the run-of-the-mill face told me he was stealing the Benz to replace his Trabant, a piece-of-shit socialist sedan that could be completely assembled and disassembled with a crescent wrench.

"How do you double the value of your Trabant?" he riddled me rhetorically. "Fill it with gas!"

When we reached the Wall, I turned down his offer of a tour of the bowels of the evil empire. I'm one of those folks who poses for photos standing next to the sign that says, YOU ARE NOW ENTERING SUCH AND SUCH STATE, then sleeps through the windy drive through the majestic Grand Tetons.

Otis Redding's distinct rhythm 'n' blues profundo bellowed from the car speakers. I couldn't figure out if the refrain to "(Sittin' on) The Dock of the Bay" was prophetic or not because it seemed as if everything was changing and yet remained the same.

Two East German border guards, hats askew and tunics unbuttoned, sat at their post taking alternating slugs and pulls from a Jack Daniel's bottle and an American cigarette. The first day-trip sojourners into Western imperialism were just starting to return to their homes. Exhausted families of four and only four walked past the guards, the parents dragging their sluggish, candy-smeared, toy-laden, lumpen proletarian progeny behind them. I half expected to hear an announcement saying, "Disneyland, excuse me, West Germany is now closed. Mickey, Pluto, Helmut, NATO, Japan, the United States of America, and the rest of the G7 thank you for your patronage and servitude. Get home safely."

The invisible man pressed a button and unlocked my door. "The one thing I regret is that we created the Beatles," he said apologetically, "then killed Otis Redding."

"We?"

"Yes, 'we.' The dirty Reds killed Otis Redding. Mystery solved, okay. Look, the Beatles had been on top four years in a row, doing the job we gave them, which was to lull the West into a sitar secular stupor, and here comes this majestic black man with a haunting voice knocking them off the charts. We couldn't have a Negro on top of the pop charts in 1968 blurring the racial hegemony. Bad for propaganda. Everybody—Moscow, Washington, Capitol Records—everybody agreed on that. Otis Redding and Martin Luther King both had to go. Made a two-for-one deal with the FBI."

"C'mon, he died in a plane crash."

"Ever notice the talentless, the harmless ones, never die young? Vanilla Ice, Lawrence Welk, the Disco Duck. You know how the monks scour the countryside and choose a small child to be the Dalai Lama? In Memphis there's a bratty little boy named Justin Timberlake who's been chosen to be the next King of Pop. He'll live to be a hundred. It's all part of the plan to keep you people docile."

Unable to bear any more achingly plausible conspiracy theories, I moved to leave the car before I was exposed to the pointy, bloodletting half of the Stasi's shield-and-sword motto. I was too late. The man of a thousand and one faces, each one more bland and forgettable than the one before it, had a Walther PPK pointed at his temple. He held back tears. His face convulsed, yet his hand remained steady. He whistled along with the classic outro of "(Sittin' on) The Dock of the Bay," backed up by the sounds of the crashing surf and the giddy laughter of East Berliners returning home from their first day of freedom.

When the song faded out he said, "Before I shoot myself, Schallplattenunterhalter Dunkelmann, isn't there something you want to know?"

"'Schallplattenunterhalter Dunkelmann?' It was you who sent the chicken-fucking tape?"

"It was."

"How did you know I was looking for Charles Stone? And if you knew I was looking for him, why didn't you just call and tell me where he was? Why fuck with me like that?"

"I fucked with you like that because I'm an East German secret agent and I'm trained to fuck with people like that. I don't say, 'Good morning, how are you feeling?,' which is the American way of fucking with you, as if you people really care how someone is feeling. I fuck your mind."

"So why me?"

"Well, Herr Darky, I first heard your music at a very exclusive stag party I attended. We were watching a film you might be familiar with, a pornographic western called *High Poon*."

"Some of my best work."

"Indeed, personages no less than Heiner Müller, Valeri Borzov, Nicolae Ceaușescu, and Deng Xiaoping commented on how wonderful your score was. It was your work during that final scene that brought home the film's point that the gang bang is the truest form of existentialism."

"Thank you."

"After that I became your biggest fan, which meant that I

showed my appreciation not only by smuggling in your films and mix tapes, but I bugged your phone and intercepted your communiqués."

"Communiqués? I didn't know black people had communiqués."

"When I found out you were corresponding with DJs around the world as to Charles Stone's whereabouts, I decided to help you find him."

"And you sent the video."

"I couldn't just contact you. No way to justify that to the higher-ups. See, we knew this day was coming, and a few of us lower-echelon guys at the agency who are huge Charles Stone fans were afraid that his unreleased masters would be burned along with the rest of the nefarious evidence. We couldn't take the chance that this great man and his music would be lost to time and capitalism. So we arranged with the pornographers to use his music in their films as a way to preserve it."

"There's more music?"

"I'll send you a coprophagia short entitled *Eat Shit and Live!* His playing on that one is so unworldly that when someone puts a spoonful of shit in their mouth, you'd swear they were eating caviar."

"So the Schwa's alive?"

"Very much so. I don't know where he is, but you'll find him. That's why I put the Slumberland's address on the envelope. He'll come through there—all you soul brothers do."

"So why shoot yourself?"

"That was my dick in the chicken."

"Fire at will, motherfucker."

The chickenfucker laughed and lowered his gun. I scrambled out.

"One more thing," he said, starting the engine. "In time you will meet a woman named Klaudia von Robinson."

"Von Robinson?"

"It's not part of the master plan, but marry her anyway."

Blaring its horn, the Benz parted the crowd and drove through the gate. The Spy Who Loved Chickens flashed his ID and the guards scrambled to their wobbly feet and bowed and scraped and saluted and raised the tailgate all at the same time. I wondered what the Schwa had to do with East German scat porn and the collapse of Communism.

The parade of returnees was thicker now. So was the crowd watching them return to the other side of the Iron Curtain. A large middle-aged man wearing a tweed blazer with suede patches peeling from the elbows, faded from liquor, three fingers of perestroika, and a jigger of glasnost, spotted my black face in the overwhelmingly white crowd. He stumbled up to me and ensnarled me in a big bear hug. When he released me, he threw up his arms and shouted, "Ich bin frei!" *I am free!* Then, cribbing from Kennedy's famous speech, he whispered in my ear, "Ich bin ein Negro. Ich bin frei jetzt."

The claim was heartfelt. For him, being black and free was a boast, not a conundrum or an oxymoron. I, however, believed him more black than free. I thought of something my father would say whenever he'd come across a hard-luck colored person in a witness box, cardboard box, or coffin box before his time. He'd say, "Lincoln freed the slaves like Henry Ford freed the horses."

I suppose being East German was a lot like being black—the constant sloganeering, the protest songs, no electricity or long-distance telephone service—so I gave the East German Negro a hearty soul shake and a black power salute and wished him luck with the minimum-security emancipation he'd no doubt serve in the new German republic.

Full of the wonders of brotherhood, I approached the only other black face on the street. It was the security guard from the

Amerikahaus, still in uniform and standing stolidly among the revelers. Eager to discuss the geopolitical ramifications of the breakup of the Soviet Bloc with a fellow member of the reified oppressed, I asked him what he thought about the goings-on.

"What do I think?" he sneered. "More white pussy. That's what I think."

The black man's burden had never been heavier than it was at that moment. And I was more convinced than ever that the only thing that mattered was good music. Everything else was dead weight.

I took out my minirecorder and taped the sounds of freedom. Cars horns blared. A woman slammed a pickax into the Wall, grew tired, and then began to spit at the bricks. Chanting. Clapping. People said, "Wunderbar!" whenever a reporter shoved a microphone in their faces. Cameras clicked. Singing. Flashbulbs popped. A beer-hammered young man, too inebriated to lift his head, vomited his first Big Mac onto his first pair of Air Jordans. His boys teased him about wasting a month's pay on sneakers that didn't even last him a day. All in all, freedom sounded a lot like a Kiss concert.

CHAPTER 2

A FTER THE BERLIN WALL fell I never told anyone about my encounter with the chickenfucker and his internecine plans for my future. Despite his prognostications concerning the Schwa and a Klaudia von Robinson, nothing really much changed for me, except that I spent an inordinate amount of time watching syndicated broadcasts of *The All-New Mickey Mouse Club*. Every afternoon at one o'clock I'd flip on the TV and grouse to the unlucky woman who'd accompanied me home the previous evening that the little blond cutie-pie cabal of Justin, Christina, and Britney was evil incarnate. When the trio would be introduced for their next number I'd whine, "They might as well say, 'P. W. Botha, Imelda Marcos, and Eva Braun will now sing "Love Me Tender."'"

When I wasn't decrying the future of pop music, I was at the Slumberland. Liter of beer in hand, I'd wander from table to table drunkenly prophesizing about a reunited Fatherland's return to world supremacy. If not militarily, then cinematically, and if not that, a resumption of dominance on the soccer pitch at the very least. Unlike the chickenfucker's predictions, none of my divinations have come to pass, of course, but it's still early yet.

* * *

Klaudia von Robinson was the first of his presages to come true. I met her at a party I DJed at the Torpedo Käfer, a quaint six-table bar, two burly speed-metal musicians short of being trendy, in an East Berlin neighborhood two Thai restaurants short of being gentrified. My pay was forty deutschmarks and a fold of shitty discotheque blow left over from the seventies. I did the lines in the bathroom, half expecting to see Ziggy Stardust come stumbling out of a toilet stall, rubbing his gums for a freeze, complaining to anyone who'd listen that the coke was more stepped-on than Sacco and Vanzetti's civil rights.

I don't remember how long the Wall had been down, but I remember bringing more records to that gig than usual. Other than the time I took a photo at Checkpoint Charlie wearing a fur Russian Red Army hat, earflaps down, to send to my mother, I don't think I'd yet visited East Berlin with any sense of purpose. I had no idea what to play, and the cab driver waited patiently as I filled his backseat and trunk with milk crate after milk crate of records.

In order to fulfill my part in the resurrection of the black man, Lars determined to keep me alive by using his many connections to get me DJ and jukebox-sommelier gigs. I'd worked most of the clubs in West Berlin and had long since stopped measuring time in days of the week. Tomorrow was the day after South African pop night at Abraxas. Yesterday was Jazz Brunch at the Paris Café, pre-1935 Dixieland played by all-white bands with an allowance for any colored nostalgia about the Confederacy or lazy Negroes and rivers. The day before that it was Celia Cruz and more Celia Cruz at the Boogaloo. What music do the economically and politically subsumed listen to? Do they want punk rebellion or blue-jean conformity? Do they want to forget or remember? Do they want to dance or fight? I got in the taxi thinking compromise: the Pogues, Sham 69, the Buzzcocks, and some Wasted Youth and Neighborhood Watch demos, two Southern California bands I followed from backyard to backyard in the early eighties.

The cabbie didn't know the eastern half of the city very well, but as he slowed in front of a frosted plate glass window on a dark cobblestone street, he pointed to an electric chalkboard hanging on the front door. The question of what to play was answered in Day-Glo orange.

To-nite
BLACK MUSIC!

That narrowed it down.

"No worries," I said to myself, "I'm prepared. I'll spin the black classicists—Marion Anderson, Samuel Coleridge-Taylor, André Watts, Kathleen Battle, some Malinké fourteenth-century circumcision chants, maybe a bit of that Negro klezmer all those bored jazz musicians are playing." I did the cocaine in the water closet and knew immediately something was off. The bar was too crowded. The tables full. Every stool occupied. I checked my watch. I wasn't late. People weren't even due to trickle in for at least another hour or so. As I set up my console under the sneak peeks and unblinking stares, it dawned on me that I and not my music was the entertainment, the atmosphere. That night I spun mostly the unsung American and German funkateers: Shuggie Otis, Chocolate Milk, Xhol, Manfred Krug, and Veronika Fischer, throwing in a dash of sing-along grooves here and there for the uninitiated—the Bar-Kays, AWB, Slave, Gil Scott-Heron.

"Excuse me, Herr DJ Darky."

Klaudia von Robinson wore a strapless designer dress that shimmered and clung to her rolls of baby fat like wet sealskin. I acknowledged her with a papal you-may-approach-the-DJ-booth nod. She had big, brown, mackerel begging eyes and wore her hair pulled back in a scalp-tingling tight chignon. It'd been years since I'd talked to a black woman, even longer since I'd touched one. At least I assumed Frau von Robinson was black. I couldn't tell, her buttery-soft skin was the color of ten-million-year-old amber and nearly as transparent. Hers was an epic epidermis that seemed to have fossilized around her reluctant smile, wary heart, and the dragonfly tattoo on her shoulder. She wasn't black, she was gold. The aboriginal gold of a Solomon Islander's sun-kissed shock of an afro. The gold of my Auntie Marie's incisor. The gold of the Pythagorean golden ratio. How I longed to say to her, "Baby, in the words of Pythagoras, Euclid, and Kepler, you are as fine as 1.618033989."

Behind Klaudia stood her younger sister, Fatima, a stunningly beautiful woman whose own African heritage oozed "dream on, motherfucker" from her sloe-eyed Ethiopian features and her full, permanently puckered lips. She had been, as the Germans say, hit harder by the "nigger stick" than her sister. I suspected that they had different fathers. Princess Fatima daintily proffered a peola-brown hand, face down as if she were introducing herself to a prostrating underling. I shook her hand weakly. It was cold and bony. There was something sad and restive about her. She wore her blackness like the heroine in that Chekhov play who, when asked why she always wears black, replies, "I'm in mourning for my life, I'm unhappy." Fatima reminded me of myself. Omniphobic—scared of everything. *Omniphobic.* That's a good one. I'll have to submit it to *Kensington-Merriwether* and see what Cutter Pinchbeck has to say about it.

Klaudia, smug and even more stuck-up, never bothered to introduce herself. She just presumptuously pressed a finger to my chest as if my sternum were a doorbell.

"Do you have Sixto Rodriguez?"

"'Sugar Man'?"
"'Sugar Man.'"
I nodded. Great song. Probably do wonders for my cocaine headache. One often hears that Germans don't have any taste. True, though it's not that they are connoisseurs of schmaltz, it's that they appreciate everything. When a German shows good taste, I've learned not to be surprised. Here subjectivity and objectivity have a way of canceling each other out like common cultural denominators, so out of necessity they've invented a new nonqualitative state of perception, an all-appreciative "neutertivity," if you will. Everything's good. Nothing is bad. And if it is bad, it doesn't matter because somebody likes it.

I flipped through my crates and lifted out the Sixto Rodriguez album. Took me three years to find that record. This was before the Internet. When record collecting meant excursions to the suburban rec rooms of cracked-out, disbarred, no-longer-rich-as-hell affirmative-action uncles. Getting to the Ray Barrettos, *Artur Rubenstein and the NBC Orchestra Plays Rachmaninoff Concerto No. 2*s, and Booker T. and the MGs before they ended up at the bottom of an empty kidney-shaped pool covered with silt, rusted lawn chairs, and barbecue grills. I had to send all the way to Auckland for Sixto. Sixty dollars plus eight for shipping and handling.

Eyes hidden behind the darkest pair of shades I'd ever seen, Sixto peered out at me through the glare of the shrink-wrap. Quintessentially seventies, he sits on some wooden stairs in front of a small A-frame ghetto brick house. His polyester bell-bottoms, white shirtsleeves rolled to his elbows, feather-cut movie-Indian silky black hair complete with David Cassidy flip—there's no doubt in my mind he's the absentee father of someone about my age.

Sixto's plaintive wail pulsed in and out of the half-calypso and half-mariachi guitar lick and the cheesy, warbled sci-fi sound effects. *Sugar Man won't you hurry* . . . A simple 3/4 time bass line and a three-note muted horn announced the chorus. *Su-gar-man* . . . *Su-gar-man* . . . The Torpedo Käfer, not loud to begin with, went totally silent. Oblivious that he's singing over what sounds like the climactic battle scene in Orson Welles's *War of the Worlds*, Sixto continued on undaunted, calling out to his drug dealer like a sick dog howling at its last full moon. *Su-gar-man* . . . Klaudia slow danced with herself, eyes closed, hands tucked into her underarms, softly singing the chorus. Like me under the tanning lamp, she left the door slightly ajar. Providing me a peek, *me* being the closest embodiment of dopehead stereophonic pathos. A patron raised an eyebrow and a *bierflasche* in my direction. *Su-gar-man* . . .

Somehow Sixto slipped through the cracks of the album cover stairs he sits on and missed out on soul-man immortality. I'm not one of those DJs who thinks every underappreciated crooner should be deified in the same breath as Curtis Mayfield and Sly Stone. But it's a shame he wasn't at least a one-hit wonder. No reason this song shouldn't be on some compilation album, generating enough residuals to at least paint the A-frame, keep the child-support checks from bouncing. *Su-gar-man* . . . *Su-gar-man* . . . *Su-gar-man* . . . Powerful stuff. Not the Mona Lisa, but seminal.

The bartender set a bubbling pilsner on the table. I'd been playing about two hours straight and wanted to enjoy it uninterrupted, so I removed my headphones and put on the longest record I had with me, "Lizard" by King Crimson, twenty-three minutes and twenty-six seconds. Despite the shift from black to blacklike music, no one protested. The foam mustache made my upper lip tingle, and I didn't wipe it off until I noticed Klaudia was still standing there, circling her index finger over the record as if she were making it spin through telekinesis.

"Why are your turntables . . . *oberseite unten?*"

"What?"

She turned to the bartender. "Wie sagt man 'Oberseite unten' auf English?"

"Upside-down."

"*Genau*. Why are your turntables upside-down?"

"I'm left-handed. This way it's easier for me to move all the things I have to move—the tone arm, these switches, knobs—they're less in the way."

"And that's the main important thing—to have things less in the way or so?"

"Yeah, I guess."

"As a DJ you try to tell a story? Achieve a certain linearity, no?"

"No, I just play what I feel like hearing."

"No, you don't. You play what you think we should hear."

One day I'm going to call those folks at the Berlitz School of Language, tell them I want money back, that there is no such thing as conversational German, only argumentative German. She had a beautiful voice. The timbre of the German female voice is pitch-perfect. Every time I go to kiss one I'm afraid I'm going to catch something. They all sound like Marlene Dietrich with a head cold. The rasp denotes a woman who's able to take care of herself and, if need be, me too (in a film noir, femme fatale sense). I've come to realize that the high-pitched American-female "Oh my God!" squeal is a ploy for attention. A soprano subterfuge for a weakness sometimes feigned, sometimes ingrained, but always annoying.

"But you tell a story with what you play."

"What story is that?"

"A love story."

"It's soul music. It's like new-wave French cinema, it's always about love."

"But tell me why are the turntables *Obersiete unten?*"

It wasn't that she wooed me; it was that she was the first person to ever ask me twice.

The left-handed explanation is partially true. To compensate for a right hand so useless that it could barely place a record on the spindle, I've experimented with every configuration of gadgetry and form. Both decks on one side, no cross fader, hamster style, reverse hamster, S-shaped and straight tone arms—but even after my right hand became dexterous enough to perform the perfunctory party skills such as stabs, cuts, and scratches, I still felt unsettled behind the tables. Standing behind my decks was like sleeping in somebody else's bed.

The closest my work gets to ritual is the cleaning of the records. Hands gloved in thin white cotton, I treat the rare acetate 78s and the reissue-vinyl LPs with equal amounts of welcome-to-the-Waldorf-Astoria doorman respect. I follow the instructions on the cleaning fluid as prescribed. Removing static, crackle, and pop-producing dust particles and/or oily contaminants by handling the discs by the edges and labeled surfaces only.

I was cleaning an especially dirty record, something I never played, Earl Klugh, maybe, when it dawned on me why I was so uncomfortable behind the turntables: The records spin in the wrong direction. They turn clockwise when every other naturally occurring vortex, from spiral galaxies to hurricanes to flushing toilets to red-white-and-blue Harlem Globetrotter basketballs, spins counterclockwise. Looking at the Earl Klugh album, the dust particles clinging to the shiny black vinyl like stars to the desert sky, I realized that in my hand I held a dusty twelve-inch microcosm of the Milky Way. The LP is a grooved mini-whirlpool down which the needle spirals to produce sound. In the case of Earl Klugh, saccharine crap, but sound nonetheless. So I turned my turntables upside down. Now my records spin counterclockwise in concert with the spinning universe itself.

My explanation impressed Klaudia. She placed a heavy hand on my shoulder. It seemed to be pressing down on me, forcing me into place as if I were a misshapen puzzle piece. In the new jigsaw Germany, where does this strange one go? Her fingers, nails unpainted, cuticles chewed raw, dug into my shoulders.

King Crimson still had another three quarters of an inch of playing time left. I started to give some thought to the next song. When I play in front of a crowd, I don't sample. I play the entire recording. Live sampling is like taking a quote out of context.

I wavered between Brick's "Dazz," "Children of the Sun" by Mandrill, and readdressing my narcosis subtext with "Riding High" by Faze-O. Klaudia's hand slid off my shoulder. But she didn't go away. I settled for "Children of the Sun." For a plump woman she had a long neck, and I wanted to run the palm of my hand against the grain of blonde fuzz on its nape. I suppose she wanted me to ask her name. But I didn't want to know it. I wanted to know why the dogs in this city didn't bark, and that was about it.

I drained my beer, mixed in the chimes from "Children of the Sun" a shade behind the pounding downbeat of King Crimson's Mellotron, and realized there was something I did want to know.

"Do you know where I can see the sunset?"

"The sun is hard to find here. Does that go on your nerves?"

"Well, if you think of a place . . ."

Klaudia stuck out her hand and finally introduced herself. I gave her my card, making a point of handing one to her boyfriend, Horst, a bald-headed, rugger-nosed translator who looked like an IRA terrorist who moonlighted as a mountain crag between car bombings and kneecappings. He introduced himself by slipping a beer in my hand and an arm around Klaudia's waist. Maybe her sidelong glances were just that, sidelong.

Two days later, she called.

"Hallo? Please, may I speak to DJ Darky?"

She wasn't frumpy enough for me, too ladylike and, even at a Rubenesque 165 pounds, too skinny. I've always been slightly disappointed that German women ran thin. I expected buxom prison guards with flabby arms, fullback thighs, and mean streaks as wide as their broad, flat, Aryan asses.

"I was in a record shop when I found a song I thought you might like, an old GDR propaganda tune from the early sixties, 'Affenschande (Amerika stopft Affen in die Satelliten).' Would you like to know the English?"

I speak German but sometimes it's best never to let them know I *spreche* the *Sprache*. It's safer that way.

"In English the title is something like, 'Crying Shame (America Stuffs Apes in the Satellites)' or so."

"That's funny."

"Yes, it is. I also thought of a place where we can see the sunset as well. Shall I give you the record then?"

On the evening of my first Berlin sunset, only the thriftiest East Berliners hadn't spent the complimentary one-hundred-deutschmark note they received as Bundestag howdy-dos to the Free World. When we met that night at the base of the Fernsehturm, Klaudia von Robinson still had hers. *Fernsehturm* is the first German word any Berlin émigré learns. Built to commemorate the launching of the Sputnik satellite, the Fernsehturm is a forty-story television antenna that resembles a Soviet-era ICBM. Since the late fifties every guest worker, asylum seeker, and honorably discharged black American male with a predilection for white women has pointed at the city's tallest structure and asked, What the fuck is that?

Standing at the base of the TV tower, Klaudia turned the bill over in her hands, contemplating the strange-looking money the way Jack must have contemplated his magic beans. The elevator doors opened. The bean stalk sprouted. We entered wondering what magical adventures lay ahead. Inside the elevator a placard written in German, Russian, and English said the elevator would ascend two hundred meters in thirty seconds.

The Fernsehturm has always frightened me. It looks operational. I'm convinced the tower is the Communist Trojan Horse wheeled up to the Brandenburg Gate as a gift and that, somewhere deep in the backwoods of Saxony, in an underground bunker hundreds of feet beneath the Hungarian oak, firethorn bushes, and black bears, a top-secret cadre of East German scientists still fights the Cold War, memorizing the day's launch codes over breakfast. *Swie-Zulu-Foxtrot-sieben-sieben-Whiskey-fünf. Mach mit, Kamerad. Mach mit.*

Klaudia, sensing my nervousness, pointed to the face on her banknote.

"Who's Clara Schumann?"

"She was a pianist, composer."

"Where was she born?"

"Leipzig, I think. She was running with Brahms and them, so I'm guessing she was born in 1820 something. Maybe a little earlier."

"Ha, an Ossie, on the West's money."

"In 1820 it wasn't East Germany, it was *eastern* Germany. Wait, it wasn't even Germany, it was Prussia or some shit."

"Ja, das stimmt."

"Who was on the one-hundred deutschmark in the GDR?"

"Karl Marx."

At two hundred meters we stepped into the Telecafé, the revolving restaurant about two-thirds up the tower. Revolving restaurants are the world's slow-spinning sociocultural centrifuges. The g-force they exert is slight, but enough to separate modernity from kitsch, communism from capitalism, love from lust. The hostess seated us at a cozy linen-covered table across from the wait station. The busboy jammed his hand into the forks, then the knives, then the spoons. The sound of the parting silverware was beautiful. I tried to fight the urge to tape it, thinking that recording random sounds would be rude on a first date. But the sound won. It always does.

Klaudia too respected sound. Quietly, she waited for the waiter to finish rummaging through the cutlery, then I switched the machine off.

"Kannst du wechseln?" she asked, waving her cherished bill in my face.

I handed her change for the hundred. She fanned open the bills, then jammed the mélange of greenish-yellow fives, purply-blue tens, and one blue-green twenty and olive-brown fifty into an empty water glass and slid the ersatz flower arrangement between the dinner candles.

The restaurant kept spinning. A sharply dressed trio of West German carpetbaggers circled the observation deck and stopped within spitting distance of me to point out their next land grab. Not knowing whom of us was nonradioactive chaff and who was pure uranium-235, I waited for the café's centrifugal force to put some distance between us. I hate people with more money than me, which means I hate mostly everybody. The shortest speculator leaned rudely over our table. He said the green expanse out in the distance was the Pankow district. Speaking of amortization rates and marble staircases, his language was a patois of German banking terms and Beverly Hills real estate jargon. As he appraised the distant luxury villas occupied, according to him, by members of a soon-to-be-defunct politburo, his oversized tie fluttered off his potbelly and swung in front of my face like a Hermès pendulum. Without thinking, I reached out to touch it. I'd never felt anything so soft. It was a softness that made me question if I had made the right choices in life. I pressed the end of the tie against my cheek. The silk danced down the side of my face; its threads teasingly tangoed with my chin stubble, then freed themselves with mocking pops and haughty static crackles. Feeling the sexual tension, fat boy snatched his tie away and tucked it behind his belt buckle. He raised his hand to his forehead and made a motion as if he were turning the dial to a combination safe, the German sign for crazy. Ashamed of myself, I scooted away from the aisle and leaned against the window. The restaurant kept spinning. The carpetbaggers were hurled on their way, muttering about occupancy rates and the inevitability of the European Union. Outside the window Berlin, a panorama of stratified steel and concrete urbanity, drifted past. It was one of those Bashō, frog-jumping-into-the-pond, timeless-haiku, apple-on-the-head-theory-of-gravity Newtonian moments. But my mind, corporate-tax-return blank, could only spell epiphany. *E-p-i-p-h-a-n-y.*

The restaurant kept spinning. Klaudia flipped open her pocket-sized German-English dictionary. Her plucked eyebrows were cinched so tightly they formed the McDonald's arches above the bridge of her nose. I doubted she was looking up *epiphany*. I don't think I'd said it aloud. Apparently she had something to say to me and was searching for exactly the right words. I couldn't imagine what those words were. And I wasn't about to try.

The restaurant kept spinning. Klaudia slammed shut her little green *Wörterbuch*. She'd found the words she'd been looking for. Her thin lips opened. Revealing a sexy gap in her teeth the size of a Little League strike zone. The restaurant kept spinning. What could she possibly have to say to me?

"Ferguson, I think I fall a little bit in love with you."

I looked past her and, touching Klaudia's cheek through the glass partition like a pathetic prison lifer, was the sinking Berlin sun. Her fingertip traced the edges of my lips. These Germans, they either want to fuck you or kill you. Sometimes both.

The twilight was uniquely uninspiring. The sun looked wobbly and slumped toward the horizon like a carsick child sinking deeper and deeper into the backseat. Its last act of consciousness, this solar hurl of refracted light, the colors of which were so putrid they scattered the birds and the clouds, and left the moon to clean up the mess.

CHAPTER 3

G ERMANY CHANGED. After the Wall fell it reminded me of
the Reconstruction period of American history, complete
with scalawags, carpetbaggers, lynch mobs, and the woefully
lynched. The country had every manifestation of the post-1865
Union save Negro senators and decent peanut butter. Turn on
the television and there'd be minstrel shows—tuxedoed *Schaus-
pieler* in blackface acting out *Showboat* and literally whistling
Dixie. There were the requisite whining editorials warning the
public that assimilation was a dream, that the inherently lazy and
shiftless East Germans would never be productive citizens.
There were East Germans passing for West Germans. Hiding
their accents and fashion sense behind a faux-Bavarian stoicism
and glacier hat, and making sure that whenever someone said
the words *Helmut Kohl* they responded with "that fat bastard." It
wasn't even unusual to see Confederate flags stickered to car
bumpers and flying proudly from car antennas. The stars and
bars were a racist's surrogate for the illegal swastika, though if
you confronted somebody about it they'd claim it represented an
appreciation of rockabilly music, especially that of Carl Perkins.
My adoptive fatherland was still an introspective country, but

it was a new era; instead of gazing at its navel, the country stared at its big, historical, hairy balls. There was a real sense of joy and accomplishment. This time we were going to do things right. I say "we" because for a moment there I was starting to feel German. Though you never hear of a black person "going native" (that shameful fall from grace is reserved for whites), I had gone, if not native, then at least temporarily Teutonic for one special day. If you can find any footage of the inaugural love parade, that's me in the ten-inch platform sneakers drinking peach schnapps, sporting a blown-out pink afro and only a pair of black leather chaps, showing my glossy black ass and leading my band of wild white aboriginals down the Ku'damm like a sunburned Kurtz in a parallel universe.

Like Conrad's Belgian Congo, Germany in the early days of reunification was a land where light was dark and dark was darker. In tribute to this confusing state of flux I'd gotten into the habit of opening up my gigs with the Undertones hit "Teenage Kicks." The band had broken up seemingly at the height of its success, and in the trades I had once read a quote from Feargal Sharkey, the lead singer: "The last couple of years in the Undertones, for all of us, was very difficult. The conversations generally tried to revolve around, Can you turn that up a bit, or Can you turn that down a bit?" That statement summed up exactly how I felt about the world at that time. And my world was the new Germany—same as it ever was. The vast uninhabited no-man's-land was reforested into a rich-man's-land concrete tract of apartment complexes, shopping centers, and office buildings. Actors who when the Wall fell had begged and pleaded to play beleaguered Jews in small-scale indie films now longed to play misunderstood Nazis in big-budget features. If you stopped in a Munich train station and asked the mean-looking woman at the information desk how to get to the Dachau Concentration Camp, she'd snarl, "It's not a camp, it's a *memorial!*" The government legislated spelling-reform laws in a covert attempt to institute a uniform thought process. The country that spells together stays together, and it's no coincidence that as the ß disappeared, social welfare and a few unlucky people of color also vanished.

Initially, Doris and Lars were elated about the fall of the Wall. Their daytime excursions into East Berlin were like traveling to see an extended family of stepsisters and -brothers who had been sired by the same philandering father. They marveled at the bullet-ridden buildings, the ghastly mullet haircuts. Cherished their first sips of the famed Radeberger beer they had heard so much about. But just as the relationship with "Daddy's other kids" begins to tire over yet another you-look-just-like-Uncle-Steve conversation, Doris and Lars's affinity for their poor relations to the east began to sour. They began to view the East Germans, or Ossies, as fundamentally different from themselves. Lazy, unmotivated, and ungrateful. Every day they had a new joke about their backward countrymen:

Q: Why do East German policemen travel in threes?
A: One to read, one to write, and one to keep an eye on the two intellectuals.

The haughtiness they showed toward their Ossie brethren somehow led them to be less shy about expressing their frustrations with the burden of being German.

Once, on a drizzly May morning, Doris, Lars, and I were at an outdoor café sharing an English-language newspaper, when Doris made an outburst that almost caused me to choke on my bratwurst.

"I hate this old Jew!" she shouted, backhanding the World section.

The "old Jew" was David Levin, the paper's Berlin correspondent. I rather liked and identified with his conflicted personal accounts of the new Germany. Doris felt them too biased and bitter, and apparently too Jewish and too old.

Hearing the word *Jew* uttered in public used to be a rare occurrence. If a German used it around you it was a sign of affection. It meant that they were comfortable with you—and you too comfortable with them. Sometimes Klaudia would say it when she felt embittered about the second-class treatment Afro-Germans received. If she was feeling particularly aggrieved she'd take a good look around, ensuring that no Jews or Jewish ghosts were within earshot, and hiss, "maybe if I was *Jewish* . . . ," never finishing the thought.

Both Doris and Klaudia felt a certain entitlement to the word. Klaudia's sense of dispensation came from a "Hey, doesn't anybody care, they sterilized us and sent us to the camps too?" outlook. Doris's prerogative stemmed simply from the word being in the dictionary. If it was in the dictionary she was allowed to say it, wasn't she?

"Old Jew?" I said, peering over my sports section while Lars wisely played deaf.

"The fucking guy never says anything positive about our country."

Sometimes I'll be on the train, standing in an out-of-the-way corner looking at the commuters, skin-pierced punks, and college kids all sitting ramrod straight in their seats, eyes front, hands folded in their laps, elbows tucked into their sides, and my prejudice and genocidal fears get the best of me. I think that one day a buzzer will ring and these people will all stand in unison, snap to attention with a heel click and a bellicose "Jawohl!," and order me to take the *next* train. I know that this buzzer can sound in any country, at any time. And that some will stand in good faith and others will stand in fear, and that a select few will stand taller than the rest by fighting back, harboring, leafleting, dying, and trying. But still.

"It's the sins of the fathers, not the sins of the grandfathers—why should we Germans suffer forever?" Doris said, though as a devout pantheist she should know better than to think there's a statute of limitations on genocidal guilt, much less suffering.

What's funny is that if that buzzer ever does go off, I know I'd run to her. I'd skulk my way to Kruezberg, sprinting from shadow to shadow, until I ended up in her arms. And she'd sell her barely used possessions and find a way to spirit me out of the country. Any other persecutees would be shit out of luck because I wouldn't share a single can of soured herring with their asses.

Ladling spoonfuls of sugar into her coffee, she summarized the article aloud, thinking that once I heard the unnecessarily mean-spirited screed, I'd see her anger as justified.

"Mr. Levin says that in the short time he's lived in Germany he's noticed that Germans rarely speak in the first-person singular. He claims it's a symptom of groupthink. That talking to one German is like talking to eighty million German Siamese twins all conjoined at the mind. Ask someone what his opinion is, and the first word out of our mouths is *we*."

"You do that all the time."

"No *we* don't!"

The way she bandied about *Jew* made me miss the Wall. Before reunification no one called me *Neger* to my face or said *Jew* as a pejorative. Now young boys jump out of parked cars and, in a pitiful imitation of the syndicated American cop shows they watch on television, point finger guns at my head and demand that I "freeze." On the train a doughy white boy in the car ahead will catch my eye through the window and slide his finger across his throat. I'll visit a sick friend in the hospital and the man in the bed next to her will call me "Smokey."

I'm not the only one who misses the Wall; some Germans miss it too. The Wessies miss how special living on an island in the middle of a landmass made them feel. With no mandatory military service, West Berlin was a state-supported counterculture, a Jamestown without the Indians, Woodstock without the rain. East Berlin, on the other hand, was Wounded Knee without the news coverage, Wattstax without the soul music, and yet there are Ossies who miss the Wall. They miss the slow pace, the leisurely work hours, the obsession with free expression and not money, the lack of choice and the commensurate beauty of being able to go into a restaurant for dinner and not have to make nine imperialist decisions about your first course.

"Soup or salad?"

"Salad."

"Green, spinach, Caesar, or arugula?"

"Spinach."

"Italian, thousand island, French, blue cheese, or vinaigrette?"

"Blue cheese."

"Regular or low-fat?"

Needless to say, the black expat population longed for the Wall's return. Yes, the reunification had, as the black security guard and others like him had hoped, doubled the number of, pardon the misogynist redundancy, "fuckable white women"; however, it also had the unforeseen impact of quadrupling the number of white male assholes. Not that the asshole-per-capita ratio was any greater among East Germans. Reunification and the rise of neo-Nazi activity had given the West German asshole the freedom to show his true colors.

The personification of black American frustration in post-Wall Berlin was an eccentric black man who'd periodically come into the Slumberland pushing a wheelbarrow filled with assorted pieces of brick, stone, coins, and paper money. He never spoke, preferring to let the cardboard sign dangling from his neck do his talking for him. A placard said, HOW CAN WE READ THE WRITING ON THE WALL, IF THERE IS NO WALL. If you didn't pitch some money or a good-sized rock into the wheelbarrow he'd stick a grimy finger in your drink.

Unlike the brickless brick mason, I had the Schwa to keep me sane in race-unconscious Berlin. Klaudia von Robinson's brick-house blackness helped too. She and Fatima would show up unannounced at my door. I guess that's how they did it in the former GDR. No phones. If I wasn't home, they'd leave a message scrawled on a flier for Korean BBQ and jam it into the keyhole. If I had female company, they'd sit outside in the hallway, wait for the woman to leave, and then in a fit of pretend jealousy bust in demanding to know if I had licked her toes.

"If you kissed her smelly white feet I'm leaving," Klaudia would declaim, examining my lips and tongue for who knows what. Nail-polish chips and toe-jam residue, I guess.

Despite delusions of a potential ménage a noir, the chicken-fucking song didn't work on Klaudia and Fatima. The first time I played the tape, the only articles of clothing that came off were their shoes.

"Hey, that's the man who suggested I go to the Torpedo Käfer that night we met," Klaudia said, flinging her espadrilles at the man on the TV screen.

"Stasi," growled Fatima, pointing at him.

"So offensichtlich!" Klaudia said, which is German for "Duh!"

While not devotees to the Schwa in the historical sense that Lars was, the von Robinson sisters, at first familiar with his music, soon became deeply fervent fans.

His music seemed to call out to them, especially Fatima, who more than once showed up at my place with a medical bracelet tied around a bloodstained wrist bandage. Sometimes in the middle of a tune Little Sis would hyperventilate. Gasping for air, her eyes would roll into the back of her pretty head and her chest would heave in time with the song. Once she OD'd on his music, passing out and falling to the floor unconscious with the cultic smile of a Beatlemania-stricken coed plastered on her face. It took a loud, cold, bracing splash of Joy Division to bring her back, and the first thing she said upon regaining consciousness was, "When I die I want to be listening to Charles Stone." I didn't see the von Robinsons for a while after that. Then one Sunday night Klaudia showed up at my door alone.

Most women think they're strong. They like to wrestle men down to the floor and put them in what they think is some inescapable choke hold. Instead of tossing these delusional wannabe grapplers effortlessly out the window, we males humor them. Feign submission. Praise their yoga-toned physiques. "Whoa, look at those muscles! No, really, I couldn't breathe."

When I opened the door that fateful Sunday night Klaudia stormed inside, a kiai blur of martial arts expertise unseen since the likes of Lady Kung Fu. Little Miss Fists of Fury kicked off her shoes and judo flipped me over her shoulder, slamming me hard onto the living room floor. Before I could ask what I had done wrong, I was knee dropped in the groin, elbow struck in the larynx, and nearly strangled to death with my own shirt collar, all in rapid succession.

With a belch redolent of fine tequila, she clambered off my contorted heap of flesh and bone and announced she'd broken up with her boyfriend and that Fatima was in the hospital. Without asking permission, she stuck the chicken-fucking song into the VCR and poured herself a drink that she obviously didn't need.

I parted the curtain of stringy clumps of dirty blonde hair that covered her flushed red face.

"Was ist los?"

She told me Fatima was in the hospital. She'd swallowed a bunch of pills and chased them down with a bottle of tequila.

I pressed the play button and the chicken-fucking song lifted her out of my arms. She began to dance. Arms cocked at oblique angles, she moved as if the song had been written for her. Her lithe body the spindle, the record playing around her.

Slowly, almost contritely, she corkscrewed herself into and out of the ground. There wasn't much room, but she managed to express herself. The black soles of her bare feet slapped and pawed softly on the hardwood floor. As she danced, she told me the story of the von Robinson sisters.

Growing up black in all-white East Germany—a totalitarian state where there was free education, no unemployment, and no discrimination—the concept of race didn't officially exist. Being proletarian and, as Klaudia put it, "inofficially black" was hard. At least she had her judo and her studies. She was good on both the mat and in the classroom. She had heroes like East German judo champion Astrid Timmermann and Valentina Tereshkova, the first woman in space. She'd contemplated a run at the Olympic games until her late mother made a big show of taking away her vitamin supplements and mentioning that Astrid Timmermann had a clitoris the size of an earthworm. She considered majoring in physics and applying for the Soviet space program until her quantum mechanics teacher told her that the Russians had already sent a monkey into space.

Fatima didn't have hobbies or interests. All she had were pronounced bouts of depression and her sister's broad shoulders to lean on.

It was hard being black in red East Germany. But the von Robinson sisters were determined to find out if they were indeed black. And if so, how black were they, and did it matter? They set upon developing a self-taught black curriculum. Theirs was an extremely independent course of study that consisted of lots of Pushkin and the Voice of America radio show.

"I've come to understand love wasn't made for me . . ." was a favorite quote from the black Russian poet, one that carried them through many a lonely and dateless weekend night. And when their tired eyes could no longer focus on the books, Willis Conover's Voice of America radio program tucked them into bed. Conover's voice was indeed America. "This is the music of freedom," he'd say, enouncing each letter with propaganda perfection. At first, all the then non-English-speaking sisters understood was "Duke Ellington." They could, however, hear the respect Conover had for the music and the musicians. The way he said, "This week the immortal Zoot Sims is in Seoul, South Korea, at the Matchstick Club. Oscar Peterson, Caracas, at the Mephisto." They loved the music, but his interviews with the musicians were best. Unhurried. Measured. They could hear colors in the language, the relaxed whiteness in Conover's shirt, his teeth and skin, the black cautiousness in his subjects' voices and minds. Other than the Muhammad Ali rants on the news, and Pushkin's poetic voice in the poems of which they'd grown so fond, these interviews were the only times they'd ever heard a black man speak. They reminded them of the father neither of them had ever seen. They sounded so close. Maybe Conover was a Soviet-bloc jazz fiend disguising himself as an American disc jockey, thinking it would never occur to the authorities to look for him in a rooftop studio in Prague or Belgrade. One night, Conover introduced a record with such anticipation in his voice that Klaudia looked up from *Eugene Onegin*. "Here's a song you have not heard before," Conover said, his voice cracking. His voice never cracked. "Charles Stone with 'Darn That Dharma.'" When the song came on Fatima literally shook with happiness. She had found her blackness. After that it no longer mattered that her mother never told

them who or what their father was beyond being "asshole-colored."
White, black, Arab, Mexican, asshole, it didn't matter. They'd been
reborn black. Pushkin black. Black belt black. First-woman-in-
space black. German black. That was their story.

It was my mother's feet that drove me to white women. Every
other Sunday she'd drop those crusty appendages in my lap. Her
toes hammered and gnarled at the knuckles with corns harder
and darker than tree knots. Her nails were ridged like party-dip
potato chips, and the ones that weren't black were spectrograph
bands of fungus brown. On Sundays I was forbidden to leave
the house until I'd clipped her nails, filed down every bunion,
barnacle, and callus, scraped the lint and gummy grit from her
cuticles and crevices, chiseled the dead skin from her cracked
and dried-out heels. Afterward my hands would smell like wet
leather and my shirt would be caked with filings, rolls of toe
jam, nickel-sized flakes of dead skin, and baby powder.

Klaudia's dancing feet could pass for white. Her toes plump
and unhammered and corn-free, they smelled like fresh-cut grass.
When she was in the mood she'd hoist her pants above the knee,
place a cool sole on my face, and with my cheekbone framed in
the arch, massage my temples with her big toe.

"I can tell you're in tension," she'd say.

I'd deny being "in tension" and pop that toe into my mouth.
Marshmallow soft and tasty as children's vitamins, I'd suck on it,
tracing every loop and whorl. Dip the tip of my tongue in ink
and I could sketch her feet from memory.

As a result of her judo training, Klaudia experienced the
world with her feet. When they weren't touching the ground she
was an uprooted tree, listless and silent as the romantic poet's
fallen bough.

> *If a woman has an orgasm and there isn't*
> *anyone to hear it, does it make a sound?*

Klaudia believes that all vibrant energy, from the human heartbeat to music, emanates from the earth's core. Though she's never been in an earthquake, she theorizes my deep sense of foreboding comes from always waiting for the big one to hit. There's some sense to that. Anyone who's grown up in the ring of fire never crosses a high suspension bridge or reaches the apex on the Ferris wheel without thinking, "What if an earthquake hits right now?" Supposedly I've got it all wrong. An earthquake isn't a catastrophe, but is simply stress leaving the planet. A 5.5 on the Richter scale that spills the dishes from the cupboards and topples thatch huts in Micronesia is just the earth cracking its knuckles after a long day. The 7.7 tremor that derails Japanese bullet trains and levels the business district of a major city? That's the earth arching its back and popping its vertebrae.

Making love to Klaudia was like having sex with a snooker player: No matter how contorted the position, she had to have at least one foot on the ground. Her orgasms were loud, rumbling moans, quivering pelvic seismic temblors often in the same growling key as Coleman Hawkins's tenor. Sometimes I'd ask where a certain passionate grunt came from and she'd say, "That was an earthquake epicentered in the seas off the coast of Sumatra," then she'd close her eyes and announce, "Now I take a short sleep."

I enjoyed watching her sleep, her face resting on her powerful arms, her feet smooth, almost white, and as sculpted as a Parthenon Athena's hanging off the futon and resting gently on the floor. But I liked listening to her sleep even more. She snored loud and sharp as if some miniature salsero were stuck inside her throat, scraping her larynx like a guiro. If I pressed my ear to her heaving chest I could hear the beat of her arrhythmic heart. A rapid *baboompbaboomp baboompba* that sounded exactly like the conga riff that starts "Manteca." While the snoring and the heartbeat were most-satisfying aural pleasures, listening to her nighttime farts was damn near orchestral. Hers were a cool-jazz modal flatulence that featured all the measured vibrato and impeccable intonation of a Ray Draper tuba solo. Sometimes after a hearty meal of cabbage stew and an especially passionate session of lovemaking, Klaudia's irritable bowels would rumble and the nocturnal flatus welled up inside her intestines would be jettisoned with a force loud enough to wake her up. And when that happened, she'd sit up, inhale deeply like a proud farmer at daybreak, and exclaim, "Ah, a fresh wind is blowing."

CHAPTER 4

ONE OF THE BEST THINGS about Europe is that you can cruise the streets pedaling a turquoise women's three-speed with a purple plastic basket attached to the handlebars and not feel effeminate. Secure in my sexuality and prospects of finding Charles Stone, I biked along the route of the old Wall.

About a month before my little bike trek, I was at the Slumberland doing routine maintenance on the jukebox. To fill the void I pumped some of my own music through the in-house speakers. As I replaced the amplifier capacitors and installed a new stylus, a regular or two would stop by to compliment my taste. They liked the music, but their inability to categorize it made them nervous. They needed music that told them in no uncertain terms how to feel, how to behave. My music never ordered the listener to "Dance! Think! Wash the Dishes!" It simply said, "Be! or Don't Be, I Couldn't Care Less!," and the Slumberland couldn't handle that kind of freedom.

"Hey, Dark."

"Yeah."

"Doris says this is your music."

"It is."

"It's really fucking good, man. I mean that."

"Thanks."

"It's too good, really. Like a plum so sweet you can't eat it because it makes your heart beat too quick and you end up throwing it away."

"Okay."

"So when's the jukebox gonna be fixed?"

"In a few minutes."

"Cool."

"Later."

"Late."

I had my head buried in the machine's belly and was delicately soldering in a few replacement chips when I heard the squishing of someone walking across the sandy floor. That same someone kicked the sole of my foot.

"What? I'm busy."

No response.

I never bothered to look to see who it was. At first I figured it was Doris wanting to play a quick game of backgammon, or an impatient and feverish regular in bad need of a Teena Marie fix. But the grainy sloshing was too deep, too leaden. I reran the squishy footfalls in my head. Matching them up against the hundreds of different Slumberland steps I'd had filed away in my head. It hit me. They belonged to the crazy-looking black guy who asked for donations to rebuild the Wall.

Ten seconds later I heard the voice on my answering machine coming from the bar: "For the nigger, it niggereth every day."

The Schwa.

Finally.

As long as I'd been looking for him, there he was, around a corner, no more than twenty feet away from me, and I couldn't chase him down or shout him out. Not with the jukebox doors open wide, exposing its antiquated circuitry to the piles of sand

I'd kick up scrambling to greet him. Not with the white-hot tip of the soldering iron clenched between my teeth, precariously close to melting an irreplaceable quartz crystal.

I heard him lift his squeaky wheelbarrow and head out the door. After I finished my work I started up the jukebox and asked Doris what happened.

She didn't answer right away. She was holding me hostage. Waiting for me to pay the ransom. If I wanted her to set Charles Stone free I'd have to confess my undying love for her. Tell her that our breaking up was the dumbest separation since Frankie killed Johnny.

The jukebox buzzed and flickered to life. Van Morrison began to serenade the barflies. Two lovers standing beneath the overgrown banana tree kissed. I knew when the Irishman hit the chorus she'd cave. Crazy Love. Doris sang softly to herself and I pounced.

"What happened?"

"I give him some money. He bows and says, 'For the nigger it niggereth every day.' And that's it. He didn't say anything else."

"But it was Berlin Wall Guy?"

"Yes."

"But there was a pause between him talking to you and him leaving."

"He was listening to your music. Smiling."

I got light-headed. Smoking-California-homegrown-and-drinking-Hennessy-at-the-beach-my-God-look-at-that-fucking-sunset-how-come-nobody-ever-talks-about-Zen-anymore light-headed.

Not wanting to alarm me, she ran her thumbnail down the length of my sideburns and softly said, "His wheelbarrow was filled with brand-new bricks. I think Mister Stone readies to build his wall."

I cupped Doris's pretty face in my hands.

"Yes?" she asked expectantly.

"Can I borrow your bike?"

They say the Berlin Wall no longer exists on the street but in the mind. When it was extant, the Wall didn't meander through the city, it bogarted. Its inexorable ghost is just as belligerent. It cuts uninvited through vacant lots and pricey new condominiums, rattling its hammer and sickle, spooking the tourists and locals who travel along this invisible barrier.

With one eye out for the chickenfucker, who I knew was somewhere watching me, I cycled through the Berlin spring looking for the Schwa. I popped wheelies as I ran red lights, fish-tailed into clouds of mosquitoes breeding over pools of stagnant water, bunny hopped over long-haired subway buskers who didn't need the money, laid down senseless skid marks in historic plazas, rode no-hands down wide thoroughfares whose street names read like places on a Communist board game called Class Struggle: Paul-Robeson-strasse, Ho-Chi-Minh-strasse, Paris-Commune-Brücke. *You've been accused of Left Opportunism. Go back three spaces.*

In the middle of Leninplatz I cruised past a bearded black man stacking bits of broken brick and ill-fitting rocks into a makeshift barricade. I joined the other onlookers and watched him extend the wall into the street.

I have a tendency to remember the names but forget the faces, and I wished that I'd been born with a photographic memory and not a phonographic one. Because here was a man who, during the interminable time I'd been looking for him, I had heard but not seen. He'd been in the Slumberland, asked me for money on numerous occasions, and this was the first time I'd bothered to truly look at him.

Charles Stone looked nothing like I'd imagined, yet how could I have missed him? A garish, evergreen three-piece suit set off his complexion nicely. The redbone, wrinkled skin, more photosphere than epidermis, still had a faint, rusty, Creole glow and reminded me of the setting sun I missed so much. His hair burst from his skull like an erupting solar flare. I don't know if he or the wind was responsible for combing it, but the gigantic afro swept from back to front, a graying red-tide tidal wave that crested over his forehead as if it were about to crash onto his freckled brow. Emaciated yet exceedingly energetic for his age, he moved in jangled fits and starts like a string puppet.

Though his face and physique were new to me, I already knew exactly what he sounded like. He breathed through a deviated septum in labored, wheezy, whistles. Sometimes when he closed his large, snarled hands, his knuckles popped loud and clear like oily kernels tossed into the frying pan. He gnashed his teeth. His wristwatch ticked softly, like a hushed cricket unsure of the temperature. He always carried large amounts of change that, with each step he took, jingled as if he had sleigh bells in his pocket. When he scratched the back of his dry, bristly head, it sounded like a little boy gathering kindling in the forest.

Heroes. Idols. They're never who you think they are. Shorter. Nastier. Smellier. And when you finally meet them, there's something that makes you want to choke the shit out of them.

Blaze always said that one of my best qualities was that I'm never impressed by anyone. He was afraid that if I did locate the Schwa I wouldn't be fazed, and my lack of acolyte appeal would make him not want to play with me.

"Man, you have to flatter motherfuckers like Charles Stone."

For a second I thought about tearing across the street and calling the Beard Scratchers one by one. Pretending that I was more excited than I was.

"Dude, you'll never guess who I'm looking at right now . . . the Schwa, man . . . I shit you not."

But that would've been like Christopher Columbus returning to Queen Isabella with nothing to show for his voyage save a drippy case of syphilis. No, the Beard Scratchers would be notified when the mission for the Perfect Beat was complete.

The Schwa was serious about his work. After examining his pile of stones, he'd carefully select the rock he felt would best fit into the open crevice. If a block had to be shaved or cut down, he filed it by scraping it over the blacktop or dashing it against the curb. For mortar he used a boundless optimism that was constantly being tested by the rumbling vibrations of the passing trucks.

A motorcycle cop with thin cold eyes stepped off a brand-new BMW K100, and though he knew full well what the Schwa was up to, he asked the gathering what was going on.

"He's rebuilding the Berlin Wall," someone announced.

"Looks more like the Berlin Partition," the officer said, and though it wasn't very funny, the crowd, me included, laughed.

The cop snapped his fingers and Stone handed over a tattered but important-looking piece of paper, which the officer glanced at and quickly handed back. The cop waved a leather-gloved finger at a huge billboard that hung overhead. We all peered up at the advert for West brand cigarettes. Two crude-oil-black "homeboys," dressed in black from sneaker to wool cap, stood against a white background, gangster posing and brandishing smokeless cigarettes over the caption TEST IT.

"Do you remember the watchtower that once stood there?" Heads nodded. The Schwa added a stone, oblivious to the socialist nostalgia. The officer stuffed his cap under his armpit and said something in Russian, which broke everybody up.

Then a haphazardly built section of the wall avalanched onto the street, blocking traffic. A man on the east side of the wall playfully leapt through the opening to freedom. A woman closed one eye and squeezed off a couple of finger shots at his back. A few others grabbed the fallen bricks and set to repairing the breach.

Slowly walking over to his bike, the cop removed two small orange safety cones from the saddlebags and set them down in front of the wall. A sharp whistle blast and a stern look sent the halted traffic around the wall in an orderly fashion.

"Mr. Stone?"

The Schwa clucked his tongue and pouted like a kid who'd been found in a decadelong game of hide-and-seek. He tapped a brick into place with the butt end of his trowel, a trowel that had never seen an ounce of cement and gleamed in the sun. I didn't waver. Fuck the salutations. The ass kissing. I told him a joke.

"What do you call a jazz musician without a white girl-friend?"

I paused for effect, and he, pissed that I'd managed to pique the curiosity of a man who'd thought he'd heard and seen it all, idled for the briefest of moments, readjusting a brick that didn't need readjusting, and asked, "So what *do* you call a jazz musician without a white woman?"

"Homeless."

CHAPTER 5

I DIDN'T KNOW IT THEN, but the afternoon Charles Stone spoke to Doris, he'd broken a vow of silence that was more than twenty years old. It was a sacred pact he'd taken with his larynx and his instrument the day trumpeter Lee Morgan died, shot to death by his fed-up woman, in some long-forgotten New York jazz café. When he entered the Slumberland and heard something in my music that invoked Lee Morgan's hard-bop verve, it gave him hope. Though after I'd gotten to know him it was a vow that I often wished he'd kept.

I wanted to subtly reintroduce the Schwa to the music industry and felt that a "listening session" for the latest album of the apple-bottomed pop star *La Crème* (italics music company's) would be the perfect time.

Lars and a few other journalists (referred to by the company as "music partners"), the sales staff, and a few marketing executives sat in the record company's grandest conference room. Doris was there to cater the drinks. I was there to DJ. *La Crème's* father entered the room to boisterous applause trying its best to sound spontaneous and genuine. A tall, black American, he looked like the best man at a motorcycle gang leader's wedding.

He wore a black leather suit that had Indian frills running down the sleeves and pant seams. His presentation was war room slick. There were charts and projections, battle plans and objectives. On command I played four songs from the album and during each one he'd say, "Crank it up, this is the jam." Between "jams" he explained the concept of the album. There was the crossover club song, the R&B ballad—but *La Crème* hadn't forgotten "her core audience," he insisted, and to prove it he played one last cut, "Soldier," the album's title track. Supposedly, "Soldier" had what he referred to as a "street vibe." When the song ended he pressed his fists into the shiny mahogany conference table and exhorted his minions. "We need, no, we *demand* a number-one album, and I expect all of us in this room to do our jobs: salespeople, media partners, everybody!" He cut his bloodshot eyes at us and asked, "Are you all soldiers for black music? Warriors for neo-soul?" After the meeting ended he grabbed Lars by the elbow.

"Do you know, my man, how many number-one singles *La Crème* has had to date?"

Lars nodded and said, "Sixteen."

Impressed, Daddy La Crème smiled, ran his tongue over a twenty-four-karat-gold incisor, and squeezed Lars's elbow even harder.

"But do you know what they all have in common?"

Lars shook his head.

"The hook is repeated exactly forty times in every song."

He released my pale friend gently, like a considerate fisherman throwing his catch back into the water. While everybody mingled over drinks and hors d'oeuvres, half listening to the rest of the album, I announced the Schwa's existence to the world by interrupting a tune called "Shaking My Light-Skinneded Ass Like a Dark-Skinneded Bitch" with the chicken-fucking song.

An angry Daddy La Crème rushed the turntables, demanding that I put his daughter's "shit" back on. He reached maddeningly for the record and I flung it past his outstretched hands to Lars, who taunted him monkey-in-the-middle style before smashing it to pieces on the punch bowl. The husky European correspondent for *Rolling Stone* tackled the apoplectic stage father and sat on his chest. The others took seats at the boardroom table or stared out the window, quietly noshing on *flammeküche* and fighting back tears. Doris hugged me from behind, kissed my neck, and in French, a language she thought I didn't understand, asked me to marry her.

The tune did what it do, and when it ended two salespeople immediately handed in their resignations and left to pursue their dreams. One by one the music critics filed past the prostrated Daddy La Crème, and as he reached out to clutch at their ankles they freed themselves with swift kicks to his rib cage and spittle-punctuated admonishments.

"How dare you pimp your own daughter?"

"Neo-soul? Don't you mean sans-soul music?"

"For the past five years you people, and I mean 'you people,' have ruined my life. Turned me into a musically unrequited necrophiliac who's been making love to a dead art form that won't love me back."

When the man from *Rolling Stone* released Daddy La Crème there was an unexpected look of contriteness on the impresario's face. He shook out his crushed-velvet cowboy hat and looked at me with an "Et tu, brotherman?" expression. I opened the door for him. "Frankly, dude, I think even her ass is overrated."

Rolling Stone made me a hefty offer for the rights to an exclusive puff piece on this "new resurgent jazz" and I pointed toward Lars, who lit a cigarette and simply said, "I want Hunter S. Thompson money and the name of his drug connection."

"Done."

The Schwa proved to be a truculent subject. His musings were snotty, vainglorious, and in a new grammatical person called "first-person Jesus." Every answer started with the phrase, "Jesus told me to tell you . . . ," and if Jesus was indeed using the Schwa as a medium, believe me, Jesus has some growing up to do.

The interview's greatest contribution was its revelation of Charles Stone's whereabouts those past twenty-some-odd years. Turns out that in the late fifties, the Schwa was a member of Buddy Rich's big band. Buddy Rich billed himself as "the world's greatest drummer," and whether that appellation was true or not, there can be no doubt that he was the world's greatest insulter. On those long transcontinental bus rides Stone, who at the time bore all the typical attributes of the fifties jazzman—talent, smarts, disillusionment, a lightweight drug habit, and a beard— bore the brunt of the drummer's abuse.

Those tour-bus tantrums were more than manic outbursts. They were poems. Found American vitriol from a man who had nothing against talented, bright, heroin-using black musicians, but hated beards. Maybe you've got connections and you've heard Buddy Rich's tirade. It circulates in major league dressing rooms and rock-band tour buses. If you've heard those tapes and wondered, Who's Buddy Rich yelling at like that?—he's yelling at the Schwa.

"Two fucking weeks to make up your mind, do you want a beard or do you want a job? This is not the goddamn House of David fucking baseball team. This is the Buddy Rich band, young people with faces. No more fucking beards, that's OUT! If you decide to do it, you're through, RIGHT NOW! This is the last time I'm going to make this announcement, no more fucking beards. I don't want to see it. This is the way I want my band to look, if you don't like it, get OUT! You got two weeks to make up your mind. This is no idle request, I'm telling you how my band is gonna look. You're not telling me how you're gonna look, I'm telling YOU. You got two weeks to make up your fucking mind, if you have a mind."

Two weeks later a bearded Schwa, having been kicked off the tour, found himself standing on an Alpine mountainside outside Salzburg. Still dressed in his Buddy Rich Big Band tuxedo, a tailcoated burgundy-and-camel ensemble complete with top hat and white gloves. Against the glacial backdrop he looked like a lost minstrel who'd taken a wrong turn at Albuquerque. The monkey suit was a perfect metaphor for jazz: old-fashioned, worn-out, pressed and starched to within an inch of its life. Six days a week. Same tux. Same arrangements. Same ranting of an ebullient madman. He stripped off his clothes and walked back into town butt naked, playing "Lover Man" with both his dick and his music swinging in the wind.

After that he gigged his way through Europe, playing the new music for whoever'd listen. When he got to Eastern Europe, he was surprised to find an especially receptive audience. What he loved most was that the kids danced to a music even his staunchest admirers deemed eminently listenable but irrevocably undanceable. In Prague, Art Farmer and Ray Brown sat in and the kids shimmied around their white linen-covered dinner tables for three hours straight. And the more out he played, the louder the applause, the harder they got down.

In time his name began to ring out. In Krakow he was a proverbial Ornette Coleman. Antwerp welcomed him as Cecil Taylor incarnate despite the nearsighted pianist being very much alive and well. "The personification of cultural independence" was how he was introduced to Tito before playing at the dictator's fourth presidential inauguration. In East Berlin, however, he was nobody's free-jazz allegory or the embodiment of a musician too famous to play for socialist factory workers and peat farmers. He was just Charles Stone. Black genius. Billed around town as "*Der sensationelle amerikanische Original-Mulatte.*" Yet that adoration wasn't what kept him in Berlin; it was the conversation. How he enjoyed running into Klaus, the fungi-obsessed horticulturalist who, despite the lack of any demand, had devoted his life to cultivating the first shiitake mushrooms grown outside the Far East. The complicated growing process involved a series of sonorous and captivating gerunds. There was the plunging, the spawning, the pinning, the shading, the incubating, and, of course, what should've been the fruiting, but Klaus had trouble growing the prized mushrooms, too many spoiling nouns: the contamination, the moisture, the decay, the strain, the mycelium, the money, the time, the missus, the kids, and the fucking Japanese.

On Tuesdays he'd meet his small circle of friends at the Prater biergarten. Gabi the voice actor, Ernst the math teacher, and Felix the architect were eager to have an American musician join their *English Stammtisch*, or English-language discussion group. Theirs was an algorithmic roundtable that, with the addition of the Schwa's urbane skepticism and superbad speech pattern, took the Kaffeeklatsch to such conversational heights they eventually found general discussion too easy and had to make a pact to limit their discussion to only subjects that started with the letter *p*. And still there was no shortage of insights and snide witticisms about panthers, plutonium, Palestine, phrenology, the piccolo, and the pimento. Folks, even those who couldn't understand English, often stopped by the Prater just to listen to them talk, sometimes shouting out topics as if shouting out sketch ideas to an improvisational comedy troupe: "Paleontology! Plankton! Puppies! Pupae! Paraguay! Placentas!"

On a bright August day in 1962, Klaus shyly offered his musician friend an oily wedge of steamed shiitake sautéed in garlic butter. Other than the gizzards his grandmother used to make on Easter Sunday, the mushrooms were the only delicacy the Schwa had ever tasted. The Schwa looked into his friend's eyes, expecting to see satisfaction, and found rheumy, hazel-colored apprehension blinking uncontrollably back at him.

"The end is near, my friend."

"What?"

"The end is nigh."

He could see that Klaus was serious, so he grabbed one more piece of the tasty mushroom cap before asking, "How near is nigh?"

"Tomorrow," he said.

A confused Schwa chalked up his friend's apocalyptic mind-set to the rigors of an overwrought empirical methodology, and watched him walk west, disappearing into the afternoon glare. The next morning when he decided to go to the city's American zone to pick up some of the bananas that, along with nylon stockings and political satire, were becoming increasingly harder and harder to find in the east, he found that he couldn't leave. The Berlin Wall had been erected. The border guards who once begged him to tell stories about Bud Powell and Chick Webb now pointed guns at his chest.

Tuesday. In a panic he ran to the Prater thinking about the *p*'s he'd never see again: Pittsburgh, Patti Page, Satchel Paige's palm ball, Bob Petit's pump fake, PayDay candy bars, pizza, the Pacific, Pontiac cars. Gabi sat alone at the table. She had garlic-buttered shiitake on her breath.

Perpetuity, she said, sliding a pen and exclusive lifetime recording contract with the German Democratic Republic toward him. The Schwa quickly signed and left it on the table. Gabi thanked him and went to her grave never mentioning that other p-word, *pregnancy*. Stone liked to think that he had sacrificed his freedom for hers, but in truth he signed because the Wall inspired him like the Skinner box inspires the rat. He spent the next thirty years as an operant-conditioned jazz musician circumnavigating the boundaries of his box, pressing psychic levers and retrieving his retrieving rewards.

Sometimes he explored the sections of the walled border that divided East and West Germany, a barrier fifteen feet high and nearly nine hundred miles long that ran from the northwest tip of Czechoslovakia to the Baltic Sea. The Wessies euphemistically referred to it as the *Innerdeutsche Grenze*, or Inner German border. The paranoid Ossies didn't have time for such Cold War genteelism. *The Antifaschistischer Schutzwall* was what it was, the Anti-Fascist Protective Wall, a rampart against bullshit. It felt good to be trapped.

Legend has it that Sonny Rollins honed his chops on the Brooklyn Bridge; well, Charles Stone found his voice while seated at the base of a moss-covered tree stump, moved by the absurdity of a metal wall bisecting scenic Lake Schaal.

It never dawned on me that Charles Stone was the only artist on Kill the Czar Records, a small self-distributing label supposedly based out of that bastion of ultraleftism, Ann Arbor, Michigan. Maybe the East Germans saw the Schwa as a jazz earwig who'd crawl down the American ear canal and lay eggs of indoctrination in our brains, turning us into mindless Manchurian Candidates. I'm told Charles Manson, Squeaky Fromme, Big Bird, Huey Newton, and Henry Kissinger were all big fans.

Maybe the East Germans viewed him as a sort of socialist van Gogh, an undiscovered iconoclast whose transformative genius, though destined to be unappreciated in his lifetime, would one day come to define their great society. As Rome had been to the Renaissance, Paris to the Age of Enlightenment, Greenwich Village to postmodernism, so would East Berlin be to the glorious Age of Unpopular Antipop Populism.

To everyone's (except the Schwa's) disappointment, Lars's interview didn't result in the expected tsunami of adulation. There

PAUL BEATTY

was some talk of selling the movie rights to his life to Oprah Winfrey.* But in the end, the only places where the article caused a serious stir were among the jazz cognoscenti and in the avant-garde and arrière-garde† communities.

In order to meet the needs of his faithful, we installed the Schwa in a corner booth at the Slumberland. And for two months every free-jazz musician, alternative rapper, filmmaker who'd never made a film, and disgruntled downtown poet whose epigraphs were better than his poems and whose poems were better than nothing made the hajj to the Slumberland to pay tribute. The list of pilgrims was like a who's who of unknowns who among the counterculture homeless are household names: Steve Lacy, Billy Bang, Bern Nix, Milford Graves, Anthony Braxton, William Parker, Cecil Taylor, David S. Ware, Peter Brötzmann, Jameel Moondoc, Butch Morris, Henry Threadgill, and many others.

Those men of my father's generation, especially the black men, were a different breed. Fiercely independent, brilliant, and slightly touched, they were the type who'd represent themselves in court—and win. Children of the civil rights movement, they were the first generation of African-Americans with the freedom to fail without having to suffer serious consequences. They're the Negronauts the black race sent off into the unexplored vastness of manumission.

Race, the final frontier. These are the voyages of the mother ship Free Enterprise. Its five-hundred-year mission: to explore strange,

---

*Oprah Winfrey was then in the process of buying the rights to the life story of every black American born between 1642 and 1968 as a way of staking claim to being the legal and sole embodiment of the black experience from slavery to civil rights. Thus carrying the historical burden that only she has the strength to bear.

† arrière-garde *noun* (usu. the arrière-garde) unacted-upon ideas, esp. in the arts or among the people who have such ideas: Roland is a writer who's never written and thus a longstanding member of the Venice Beach arrière-garde. Coined by Ferguson Sowell, inclusion in the *Kensington-Merriwether* Fourth Edition pending.

162

new, previously segregated worlds, to seek out new life and new civilizations, to boldly go where no niggers had gone before.

And like the first men to walk on the moon, to have gone where no man has gone before, these men, if they come back at all, come back changed. They come back humbled. Discouraged that they'd seen all there was to see and that it didn't amount to much. Yet finding out the Schwa was still alive had restored their optimism, and many of them, after they'd left the bar, would go on to do some of their best work. The Schwa had touched all these men just as he'd touched me and Philip Glass.

Lars tells a story. In 1971, Philip Glass goes to see the Schwa in Antwerp, and during the hour-and-forty-five-minute set the band plays a total of four notes, one chord change, an accidental cough, and a chorus of room-tone nothingness interrupted only by the drummer accidentally dropping his sticks and the bassist tapping his toe twice out of habit. Afterward Glass, then in his mid-thirties, still in search of his minimalist musical voice, and thinking of giving up the keyboards for sheep farming, approaches the Schwa backstage to offer his heartfelt congratulations. To his surprise, Stone is sulking in the corner, quietly cursing himself and his instrument. Glass asks the Schwa why he's so disappointed after such a wonderful, groundbreaking performance. *A little too rock 'n' roll*, the Schwa says, *a little too rock 'n' roll.* Glass nods and complains how his synthetic nothingness felt forced, scripted. That his music was neither improvised nor natural but was what was on his mind and not what was in his mind. Glass and Stone go out to the piano, the bouncer is trying to empty the club of stragglers, but Belgians are as stout as their beers and they aren't leaving. Glass sits down to play, and thirty-two bars of that pounding serialism crap does the bouncer's job for him. The place empties. Glass looks sickly. Van-Gogh-self-portrait-with-the-bandaged-ear sickly. Billie Holiday sickly.

Kurt Cobain "It's better to burn out than fade away" sickly. The Schwa takes out pen and paper and writes out a prescription. "Beckett." That's all the paper says. "Beckett." First thing the next morning, Glass runs out to Standaard Boekhandel on Huidevettersstraat off the Meir. When he enters, the ring of the bell above the door is nothing; he barely hears it. When he exits, *Godot, The Collected Poems in English, Rough for Theater, Krapp's Last Tape* in hand, the ring of the bell above the door is nothing happening twice, and Philip Glass understands minimalism.

Without fail at the end of the night the visiting musicians would take out their instruments and tell the Schwa they'd be honored if he would play with them. I always hoped he'd say yes. If he said yes to Charles Gayle or Peter Kowald, then maybe, if I begged him long enough and promised him the world, he'd say yes to me and agree to bless my beat. But he'd always turn them down.

He turned everyone down except Fatima. Fatima and Charles had some special connection. They seemed to lighten one another's moods, and the Schwa doted on her as much as a broke nonplaying musician could.

Klaudia and Fatima were the Rosa Parkses of Slumberland integration. To my knowledge, before them no black female had ever set foot in the place. Whenever they came through, the regulars treated them like black-hatted gunfighters blown into town by an ill wind. Petrified, the locals would duly deputize a couple of brave white women to find out what the dark strangers wanted. At the first sign of trouble I always backed off, imagining the conversations from the safety of the far side of the room.

"In this here saloon we don't cotton to strangers looking for trouble."

"We ain't looking for trouble, but we ain't runnin' from it neither."

Then the stare down until the Schwa brokered an uneasy truce by buying a round of drinks with my money. After one narrowly averted bar brawl, Fatima said to the Schwa, "How about a song?"

Unable to refuse her, he achingly kicked his way across the sandy floor to the center of the bar and scanned the room with those baggy auburn eyes. It took me a second to realize that he was looking for an instrument to play. Gauging the chair backs, swizzle sticks, and beer bottles for their kinetic musicality. Seeing nothing that met his needs, he removed a paperback book from his jacket pocket and cleared his throat.

"What's he doing?" I whispered to Lars.

"He's going to accompany himself with a book."

I hurriedly took out my minirecorder and pressed the record button. Visions of bootleg riches danced through my head.

Lars giggled.

"What?"

"They say you can't record him without his permission. It's like taking a photograph of Dracula, you're not going to get anything."

The Schwa ruffled the pages of the book over his pant seam, and the resulting sound rivaled that of the best Max Roach brushwork. I nearly fainted. He lifted the book to his mouth and played chapter seven like a diatonic harmonica; blowing and drawing on the pages like leaves of grass in the hands of Pan. Who knew a Signet paperback was in the key of D? For the more percussive sounds he rapped the spine on his elbow, thumb drummed page corners, pizzicatoed the preface, flutter tongued the denouement, and bariolaged the blurbs.

Brothers, will you meet me.
John Brown's body lies a-mouldering in
     the grave;

John Brown's body lies a-mouldering in
the grave;
John Brown's body lies a-mouldering in
the grave;
His soul's marching on!

His voice. His voice was a magical confluence of Louis Armstrong, the thrush nightingale, and Niagara Falls at midnight. After he finished there was no applause. Applause wasn't a deep enough show of appreciation. People called their lawyers and had him written into their wills. A South African diplomat approached him about running against Nelson Mandela in the next election. A widow from Wilmersdorf gave him her mother's secret recipe for *Choucroute Alsacienne*.

I immediately went to play back the concert, but to my dismay couldn't find my minirecorder. Panic stricken, I asked Lars if he'd seen it and he stopped composing the ode he was dedicating to the Schwa long enough to point his pen at the floor. There, coated in sticky wine-soaked sand, was my minirecorder. Too cowardly to hear the results, I held the recorder to Lars's ear and pressed play. He shrugged his shoulders.

"Nichts."

Fuck.

I put the speaker tight to my own ear. Lars was right. Nothing, not even tape hiss, which is impossible—there's always tape hiss. The myth was true: The Schwa could be recorded only when he felt like being recorded. I was having trouble breathing, too much magic realism, idolatry, and *Color Purple* mysticism for one night.

Stone dropped some coins into the jukebox. A breezy Bob Dylan tune filled my lungs with air. After perusing the song list for a moment, he ambled over to me, a devious thin-lipped sneer slicing across his freckled face.

"*Whikrxx-whikrxx-whurr*," he said. He was mocking me, imitating Grandmixer D.ST's legendary scratch from Herbie Hancock's 1983 "Rockit." "*Whikrxx-whikrxx-whurr*. Taurus the Bull. Taurus the Bull." Very funny.

We never talked much. He never said anything, but he was pissed at me for dragging him into the public light, however dim it was. I think he felt belittled that a DJ, the bane of his existence, had been the only person willing to seek him out and dust him off. To him DJing was single-handedly responsible for the complete ruination of music. His frustration with the concepts of the turntable as instrument and the DJ as musician was understandable.

Niels Bohr once said, "Anyone who is not shocked by quantum theory has not understood a single word," and in the summer of '83 any listener who wasn't shocked by the turntable work on "Rockit" was deaf. That grating chatto rhythm is to modern music what quantum mechanics is to physics, except that D.ST wasn't concerned with the subatomic but the subsonic. He wanted to know not what atoms looked like but what they sounded like. His ministrations on that hit single proved what earlier theoreticians—Kool Herc, Albert Ayler, and every headbanging teenager who played their heavy metal records backward looking for satanic messages—had only postulated: that by manipulating rhythm and pitch, one could use melody to bend the space-time-summer-love continuum that is recorded sound. D.ST had transformed the turntable into both instrument and time machine. For me that *whikrxx-whikrxx-whurr* was a call to arms for an old jazz confederate like the Schwa, the "Rockit" video was an air raid siren signaling a firestorm, and the turntable was Grant burning Atlanta. He heard something in the music, saw something in Herbie Hancock's eyes, the splay of his fingers across the keyboard, that I wouldn't feel until years later. He heard jazz sublimating itself to the turntable; and for the first time in his life he heard a jazzman play something he didn't feel. He heard a jazzman running scared.

Something in the Dylan tune distracted him. Could've been the lyric. Might've been the violin. Or the way Dylan sings "reflection" as if it were a monosyllabic sigh. There was a hint of regret in his face. The now-or-never disillusionment of a lonely man who'd woken up in Germany on his fifty-fifth birthday and wondered what the fuck had he done with his life.

Any day now . . .

Any day now . . .

"That's an excellent jukebox, man."

"Thanks."

"Lars tells me you have a beat," he said.

"I do."

He nodded approvingly. "Here," he said, placing the book he'd just finished playing on the table.

I think he expected more of a reaction from me, as if he were Gabriel handing me the horn he just used to blow down the wall of Jericho, but it was just a book. *The Sound and the Fury.*

"Faulkner is the greatest DJ who ever lived," he said, pressing his index finger to the cover, and again mocking me by jiggling it back and forth.

"Whikrxx-whikrxx-whuurr."

I flipped the book over and skimmed the back cover. Each character was described in two words—*beautiful, rebellious* Caddy . . . *the idiot man-child* Benjy . . . *haunted, neurotic* Quentin . . . and Dilsey, their *black servant*. Apparently Dilsey didn't have a personality, unless *black servant* is a psychiatric disorder. At first I misinterpreted his gift as a passive-aggressive gesture. The musical contemporary's equivalent of offering peppermint candy to a friend who has bad breath and doesn't know it. Then I remembered Philip Glass and Beckett.

I thanked him, and we had our first real conversation. Meaningless Tarantino-like banter about how the compact disc was a waste of silicon because no musician has ever been nor ever will be inspired enough to record eighty minutes of worthwhile music. "In the history of recording, name one good double album."

"*The White Album?*"

"Disjointed, and Yoko Ono. Need I say more?"

"*London Calling?*"

"Great album cover. Overrated band."

"*Blonde on Blonde?*"

"Okay, I'll give you *Blonde on Blonde*, like I give God the narwhal whale—beautiful but fucking incomprehensible."

We were bonding. I focused my chi and gathered my nerves. I wanted to broach a sensitive subject with the Schwa, and it was now or never.

"You want to come to my house and watch a video of a man fucking a chicken with me?"

"I've already seen it."

"You have?"

"Short guy, glasses, humping a Rhode Island Red?"

"That's the one."

"I rented it a while back. I have a little fetish for what the German freaks call fowl play. I went to the video store checking for *To Fill a Mockingbird*, starring Gregory Pecker, it was out, and the clerk handed me that one. Surprised the shit out of me when I heard my music on there. Needless to say, that flick is long overdue."

"Did you know the guy in the movie?"

"You know what? He did look familiar. Back in the day there used to be a crew of young, totally square, suit 'n' tie cats that for the longest showed up at my gigs on the regular. Sit in the front row, grooving they no-rhythm asses off. I remember them because when they were in house, all of a sudden my band couldn't play for shit. Asked my drummer how come when these guys show up you motherfuckers start clamming all over the stage. He says, 'They're Stasi agents.' I was like, 'Then be about your business, and play better, so when shit goes down, they'll want to keep you around.' Anyway, I think he may have been one of those cats. Hard to say, you know, because secret agents don't look like James Bond, they look like plain old ordinary motherfuckers who'd get lost in a crowd of two. They have faces you forget."

Before I could ask about playing with him, "Outstanding," the Gap Band's show-stopping tune, took a cautious peek from around the corner and, like a furtive, funkified pimp, dipped garishly into the Slumberland. "*H-e-y-y-y,*" Fatima said, grabbing the Schwa and pulling him away from me and toward the dance floor.

In a way I welcomed the intrusion. I wasn't ready to jam with the Schwa. We both knew it; that's why he gave me the book.

I enjoyed watching them gyrate and twist in the sand. I'd almost forgotten how effortlessly some women ride a beat. That shake. The way their feet glide over a floor, even a sandy one, as if shod in newly sharpened ice skates. A rather large woman, Fatima was no figure skater. Her face etched in bomb-defusing concentration, she danced like a Zamboni machine circling the floor in wide sweeping circles. She was efficient, powerful, and boogied with a smooth grace that belied her size. I couldn't take my eyes off of her. She reminded me of the way L.A. women got they Westside groove on.

In a twinge of homesickness, I wanted to smarmily creep in behind her, press up against her denim derrière, and grind away. Ask her in a not-so-hushed whisper what was happening back home. But I knew the answer. She'd say, "Nothing is happening back home. The word *widget* has lost its ineffability, the computer companies having given it groovy functionality. This generation's young people are the first since the dawn of the jazz age whose music sucks and they know it. And most galling, after all these years, there still has never been an Asian-American male on MTV's *The Real World.*"

Klaudia caught me looking wantonly at her sister. Using a wristlock, she twisted my arm into an ampersand and asked me what I was thinking.

"I was thinking about being back home."

She released my arm and asked me what America was really like.

I told her I once heard a comedian say that if you put an apple on television every day for six months, and then placed that apple in a glass case and put that on display at the mall, people would go up to it and say, *Oooh, look, there's that apple that's on television.* America's a lot like that apple.

CHAPTER 6

IT TOOK ME FOUR TRIES to finish *The Sound and the Fury*. I nearly drowned in Faulkner's stream of consciousness, but once I got past the fact that in Faulkner's world literary existentialism never extends to blacks, the book's technical construction did offer some guidance. Taking a cue from his style, I decided to remove all the punctuation from my life: commas, quotation marks, periods, one-night stands, midday naps, ellipses, and the evening news.

Like Quentin Compson I too stood at an important crossroad. My junction was tri-forked; three life-altering gigs lay ahead of me. Gigs that were to me what *The Ed Sullivan Show* was to the Beatles and the Newport Jazz Festival to Muddy Waters. They lifted my confidence and shaped my style and affirmed my phonographic voice. I traveled down these paths lain with vinyl only to find out that all roads lead to the Schwa.

The Left Fork

Bleary-eyed and fighting a severe case of cotton mouth, I was returning home from an all-night gig in East Berlin wondering if my favorite German boxer, Dariusz Michalczewski, had won his fight for the light-heavyweight championship the night before. My question was answered when a gang of skinheads, still drunk and charged up by the German's victory, forced open the car doors of the fast-moving elevated S-bahn train. A frigid wind and laughter chilled the compartment. Not knowing what to expect, the passengers held tight to the overhead handrail like frightened paratroop trainees. As the treetops of Stralauer Allee whooshed by, the skins flicked their cigarette butts into the expanse, then looked at me. I looked down. Not at my feet but theirs, regretting that there was no Roy G. Biv mnemonic to help me remember the colored-shoelace spectrum of skinhead ideologies. *White laces; white power. Is green gay or vegetarian? Red . . . is red commie skin or neo-Nazi?*

"Did you see Michalczewski beat the shit out of that nigger last night on television?"

Neo-Nazi.

The alpha asshole smashed his fist into his palm and whistled a militaristic tune. He interrupted himself to call me a gorilla, then returned to whistling. I ignored the lame insult, not out of prudence but because the song's title was on the tip of my tongue.

"Torpedo Los!" I shouted, naming the once-popular U-boat tune ("Fire Torpedo!") he was whistling. He blanched and quickly launched into another whistled march. After about three notes I buzzed in with game-show-contestant alacrity, "Hitler's People!" The answer unballed his fist.

"Sit down, kamerad," he ordered.

I should have replied, "I'm not your kamerad," but I simply motioned that there weren't any open seats.

"Do you like fascist music?" he asked.

"Not especially. I like the exclamatory titles: 'Under the Double Eagle!' '70 Million Strike!' 'Farewell to the Gladiators!' 'Germany Awake!' 'I Don't Believe Hitler Can Fly, I Know He Can Fly!'"

"But you don't like the music?"

"No, not really, it's all kind of gay. I love this guy. He loves me. He died in my arms, our blood commingling."

"But why do you know this music?"

"I collect records—those fascist 78s are worth money. A collector in Salzburg offered me two thousand dollars for 'The Book Burning March' and 'If Mother Won't Give You a Nickel, Ask Neville Chamberlain for Czechoslovakia.'"

In a delirious fit of tolerance and gratitude, the neo-Nazi reached out, grabbed me by the shoulders, and pinned me to the wall of the car.

"Kamerad, hast du diese Schallplatten?"

"Klar. Ich bin Schallplattenunterhalter . . ."

A week later I DJed a skinhead rally in Marzhan, a high-rise ghetto twenty-five minutes east of downtown Berlin. The wind-up Victrola phonograph I'd brought lent the festivities an eerie beer-hall putsch authenticity. Scratchy parade marches and brownshirt encomiums bellowed from the machine's mahogany horn. To my ears it was buffoonish kitsch, but the earnestness with which the crowd sang the songs matched the shouting-hallelujah devoutness of the best black American gospel.

I spent the night turning the phonograph crank and watching the bald and milkmaid-braided hellions hoist beers, sieg, and heil, celebrating as if the morning papers had announced the Anschluss, praising the reannexation of Austria, Mississippi, and Redondo Beach in one fell swoop. I felt like a Class D war criminal, but being a DJ is like being an ACLU lawyer arguing for the Klansmen's right to march: If they pay, you play what the crowd wants to hear. Besides, it was going to be the first and last time I'd ever get the chance to play those records. So whenever a pockmarked, punky fraulein spat at me and asked to see my *Schwanz,* I patted the knot of deutschmarks in my pocket and reminded myself that I knew which "tail" she *really* wanted to see.

Thorsten, my employer, leaned on the table. I motioned for him to back off. "Don't do that; you'll scratch the record," I cautioned.

He apologized, then with a wicked look on his face said, "Do you know why the Irish celebrate St. Patrick's Day?"

I shrugged. "Isn't it because St. Patrick got rid of the snakes in Ireland?"

"There never were any snakes in postglacial Ireland. The snakes are a metaphor."

"For what?"

"For . . . hey, that's a catchy tune, what's this record?"

" 'People to the Rifle.' "

"Powerful stuff, makes me want to . . ."

I steered him back on course. "The snakes, the snakes are a metaphor for what?"

"For niggers. St. Patrick kicked the Moors out of Ireland, not the snakes."

I clucked my tongue and pointed out that one or two of his neo-Nazi brethren seemed to be of mixed-race stock. This time it was Thorsten who frowned.

"Look, I hate the blacks, the Jews, and all the other others, but I'm not so stupid as to believe in racial purity. Come on, after two, three thousand years, and not one of my ancestors was a non-Aryan? How do you Americans say? 'No way, dude.' "

"So the half-black guy over there in the SS jacket . . ."

"It's the hate that's important. It doesn't matter who does the hating, but who you hate. Gerhard hates niggers. We hate him. He hates himself. Alles in ordnung."

"Does he think he's inferior?"

"He *is* inferior *and* he *knows* it."

PAUL BEATTY

I ended "People to the Rifle" prematurely with an abrupt record-scrapping lift of the stylus.

Over the complaining murmurs I said to Thorsten, "I want you to hear something," and played the Schwa's version of the Horst Wessel Song, the Nazi national anthem. Even before I'd placed the needle on the record Thorsten had sussed out my intentions.

"This is going to be a black man, isn't it? I've heard your Miles Davis, *Sketches of Spain, Porgy and Bess,* 'My Funny Valentine,' nice music, but its artistry was mostly due to the efforts of his white impresario, Gil Evans. The Negro doesn't have the organizational necessities..." The opening salvo of kick-drum beats shut Thorsten up. As the Schwa's band turned his anthem inside out, he sat there holding his head as if he had a headache. I imagine Adolf Hitler had the same expression on his face when he witnessed Jesse Owens pull away from his vaunted supermen in a blazing mastery of muscle. Subhuman or what have you, there was no denying the apelike man was fast as hell and that Stone's music was no shitty Orange County racist-punk-band cover. The Schwa was doing to National Socialism what Warhol had done to the Campbell's soup can. A few partygoers blubbered nostalgically in their drinks, but most stood at a slouching attention, unsure if the bop rendition of the song was an honorific tribute or an insult. To be honest I didn't know, and neither did Thorsten. When the tune ended it was evident from his downcast gaze that he'd been deeply moved, but he was too embarrassed to praise it and too dumbfounded to trash it. He pressed a fifty into my palm and asked me to play it again. After the fourth playback Thorsten finally spoke. "Did you know that before World War II, the percentage of Jews in Germany was zero point eight-seven-two? To blame such a small percentage of people for the world's problems, it's embarrassing. To be threatened by primitive races like yours that can't think, or heathen races that can only deceive and nothing else, this

176

shows our own inherent inferiority, and I hate the Jews for this, I hate you for this. I've never even met a Jew, and who knows, I might even be Jewish, but I hate them anyway. Who is this?"

"Charles Stone."

"A nigger?"

"If you're an Aryan, he's a nigger."

"There are no 'Aryans,' it's a fake race, a marketing tool. It's ethnic branding."

"Exactly, so are 'niggers.'"

"You know, monkey man, one day there will be no races, no ethnicities, only brands. People will be Nikes or Adidas. Microsoft or Macintosh. Coke or Pepsi."

Thorsten Schick was the scariest person I'd ever met. An intelligent man who sees through the media thought control, the myths of race and class, and free market propaganda only to have become a guileless man who now hates without compunction and speaks perfect English. At evening's end the skinhead egghead bestowed upon me the highest compliment he could give a non-Aryan when he said, "Just remember, DJ Darky, I don't have a beef with you, just your people."

The Right Fork

The *Bundestreffen* is the annual Afro-German get-together. A thousand native-born black *volk* from all over the country weekend at a spa in Ettlingen, a small resort town in the Black Forest. Klaudia and Fatima were reluctant to invite me, knowing that it'd be almost impossible for me to resist the innumerable puns I could make about a gathering of blacks in the Black Forest. But when I offered to DJ for free, even they laughed when I joked, "When we get to the Black Forest, we won't be able to see the niggers for the trees."

In many ways the Afro-German is W. E. B Du Bois's Talented Tenth come to life. They're almost a Stepford race. Unified as only an invisible people without a proximate community to turn one's back on can be. Human muesli, they're multilingual and multikulti, exceedingly well mannered and groomed, and, though most show the telltale sign of biraciality—the prominent shiny forehead—on the whole they're a stunningly handsome and intelligent people.

While Klaudia played volleyball, Fatima played sideline reporter and gave me periodic updates on the game's participants.

Making the side out calls was spunky Friederike Lutz, the nonagenarian referee. During World War II, Friederike avoided the concentration camps by working as a topless ooga-booga extra in German imperialism films such as *Auntie Wanda from Uganda* and *Nine Little Nubian Nubiles.*

On one side of the droopy volleyball net stood Maximilian, Bertolt, Uschi, Axel, Effi, and Detlef, all second- and third-generation descendents of the French colonial soldiers who occupied the Rhineland after World War I. Their ultratraditional names a noble effort to make them, if not more German looking, then German sounding. In the service court, younger and hipper, were the offspring of the black American Cold War occupiers. Their fathers mantelpiece Polaroids, their namesakes jazz legends and blaxploitation antiheroes. Miles, Billie, Dexter, Superfly, Shaft, and Buck and the Preacher stared into the net, knees bent, arms raised. Liberos, middle blockers, or outside hitters, there was something forced in the players' broad smiles and hearty laughter. They seemed as out of place in the Fatherland as black women in shampoo commercials.

Klaudia preferred the outdoor activities and spent her days playing ping-pong and tetherball. Fatima, on the other hand, reveled in the bleakness of the Afro-German experience. She dragged me to countless workshops, lectures, and films where I'd watch and listen to a people construct an identity from historical scratch.

Strangely, the whole affair reminded me of being on a porn set, and I couldn't shake the idea that porn stars and black Germans are a lot alike. Two neglected and attention-starved communities of people who, despite their public nakedness, remain "invisible" to a society that pretends not to see them. In a class on the history of Germany's blacks during World War II, the lecturer flashed a slide of a sandy-haired black boy in pleated shorts and mohair vest complete with swastika button standing next to his mother and saluting Hitler's passing motorcade with a prim nationalist pride. Another Afro-Junge, someone's precocious black child, stood in front of the projection mimicking the salute to crying laughter. I came to the sober realization that the disquietude of forced sterility is the common underlying subtext to porn and Afro-Germanness. In porn menstruation is nonexistent and semen isn't lifeblood, it's slander. A gooey expression of political and interpersonal barrenness, and in comparison the history of the Afro-German is literally one of forced sterilization. A systematic sterilization not only of people but of memory. No wonder Fatima was so sad. No wonder they were people in desperate need of a good party.

I'm proud to take credit for introducing the concept of the after party to Afro-Germany. *After party*—I love that expression. The party after the party. It's one of those ignoble black-American idioms that, along with frontin' and *turned out,** I wouldn't sell to Cutter Pinchbeck and the boys at *Kensington-Merriwether* for a million dollars. The words wouldn't do standard English any good anyways. They're nonstandard words for

---

* Properly pronounced *turnt out* regardless of educational background or geographic locale.

nonstandard people.* And no one's more nonstandard than a tall, abyss-black German named Nordica still workshopping her existence at one o'clock in the morning.

"Can you turn down the music?" she said. "I need to ask you something."

I eased down the volume of Charles Stone's "Berlin Skyline #45" to a level that allowed the party people to continue tapping their feet and ruminate in the flickering fireplace light about German blackness.

"What is happening?" Nordica asked, sounding just like a Hollywood runaway on her first Ecstasy trip.

I didn't answer her. I was too caught up in her afro. A billowy natural so huge it had its own atmosphere, gravitational pull, and a 37.89 percent chance of supporting intelligent life.

"I need to know what is happening to me. Why do I feel so unsecure? Afraid, and yet not frightened."

The room rumbled with agreement. Overcome with German inquisitiveness and black paranoia, these sons and daughters of Hegel and Queen Nefertiti wanted an answer. I wanted to tell them that the Schwa's music leans heavily on semitone, that tiny musical interval that's a half step between harmony and noise, for a reason. He wants to show us that the best parts of life are temporal semitone, those nanoseconds between ecstasy and panic that if we could we'd string together in sensate harmony. If only we could be Wile E. Coyote walking on air for those precious few moments before the bittersweet realization he's walking on air. Before falling to earth with a pitiful wave of the hand and a puff of smoke.

---

* Sure, anyone can say 'hood and *nigger* with a modicum of credibility, but the infinitive *to front* implies a contextual and historical betrayal that goes back to the days when Java Man first fronted on Peking Man at the water hole. *Big-brained motherfucker hoggin' all the arrowheads 'n' shit.* Today when most people say *frontin'*, they don't even know they frontin' on themselves.

I didn't say any of that because I didn't know the German word for *semitone* or if my audience knew who Bugs Bunny was. I simply said, "What is happening is that you've been turnt out, baby."

The Schwa turns us all out sooner or later.

Straight Ahead

My next gig of note took place at the Free University. It was there that I finally answered the cult artist's eternal bugaboo, *Who's your audience?* I can't count how many times a reporter, a fan, or me myself has asked that very question. Who's your audience? Who listens to that wild, screaming, arrhythmic, keening, vinyl-scratching capriccio anyways?

I set up my turntables in a Department of Ancient American Studies classroom. Behind me, on the chalkboard, was Professor Fukusaku's breakdown of what he termed "The Global Battle Royale," a chicken-scratch list of countries and sovereign states that America had invaded in the past two hundred years. Korea, Turkey, Haiti, Honduras, Egypt, the list almost exhaustive but, as recent news reports had shown, was missing one key territory. I grabbed a piece of chalk and in the tiny space between Samoa and El Salvador I squeezed in "Los Angeles." Now with the list complete, can't we all get along?

Clapping the chalk dust off my hands, I turned to face my audience. A pretty, vaguely Mediterranean-looking woman sat patiently in the front row, her hands folded neatly in her lap. It was well past the start time and obvious that no one else but her was going to show up. I scratched my head, wondering whether or not to go on.

"Fuck it," I told myself, "I'll play."

I don't know how long I played for, but I was inspired. I dedicated every note to that woman in the front row.

I can't count how many times a lazy writer for a northwestern music zine, a nosy fan boy, or a stodgy music teacher has asked me, "So DJ Darky, who is your audience?"

Well, I finally had an answer to that ol' bugaboo. Who's my audience? The chick in the blue dress, her hands folded neatly in her lap, that's my audience!

My melodies stomped through the room overturning every unoccupied chair, ripping in half every unsold ticket. Throughout the torrential sheets of sound I rained down upon her, she never moved. Never lifted her head, smiled, or tapped her feet. But she didn't leave either. I couldn't have spun any better. Exhausted, my eyes burning with sweat, my ears ringing, my mind turned inside out, I flung the last Super Ball–dense, illbient-bluegrass-deep-house mash-up of the evening against the back wall. Spiraling in and out of madness, the beat bounced off the walls, it screamed and writhed, a naked patient in the state hospital for the insane fighting against the bed restraints. Eventually it died in a corner with its mouth open, bequeathing nothing to the world save a ghostly silence that, in the absence of improvisational clamor, was hauntingly piercing. The woman in the powder-blue dress never applauded. She stood up, looked at me meekly, and asked, "Are you finished?" I nodded yes, and she exited into the hall only to return moments later bearing a mop and bucket of sudsy water. What if you had a concert and nobody came?

PART 4

THE LISTENING EXPERIENCE

CHAPTER 1

N<small>O ONE BELIEVED</small> she'd do it. Fatima. Her charred skeleton sitting in the lotus position in the middle of Bernauerstrasse, creaking in the wind.

When I got there I could literally see through her, but the bile that rose in my throat forced me to stop looking. Every now and then, from behind my back, I'd hear a sharp crack that sounded like a potato chip being snapped in two and I'd know that a piece of burnt flesh or a tuft of crinkled hair had peeled off her body and was tumbling in the street, being chased down by Klaudia.

I suppose ultimately that was what Fatima wanted, to be skinless and hairless. Featureless really.

Since reunification Fatima had lost a lot of weight, becoming, as Klaudia so accurately described it, "heavily anorexic." Her kilo-shedding despondency grew deeper with each passing day. What had been the healthy fear of white people shared by most of the country's colored inhabitants had recently morphed into full-blown leukophobia, or fear of all things white. It was debilitating at first. She stopped answering any mail that arrived in white envelopes. Refused to drink milk or eat mashed potatoes. Polar bears, snowstorms, and Danes had to be avoided at all costs because they were bad omens. And, in blessed irony, toilet paper scared her shitless.

Her only solace from this all-encompassing pallidity was Charles Stone, and she found it not so much in his music but in the man. Klaudia and I never spoke about how much her sister and the Schwa looked alike. And as far as I know, neither did they. All we knew was that the two became inseparable. Whenever he was in the streets rebuilding his wall, she was right there next to him, blasting his music on a boom box. And conversely, whenever she was hospitalized he was at her bedside singing lullabies and helping her tear down her mental walls. He encouraged her to confront her fears, and for a while she listened. Taking up nursing even though the uniform caused her to break out in hives. For a while she even dated a Kenyan albino she met at the Slumberland. But the grind of being black in Berlin wore on her.

I'd last seen her a few weeks before on Russian disco night at a popular nightspot in Prenzlauer Berg called An Einem Sonntag im August. Fatima, Stone, Klaudia, and I queued up for over an hour waiting to get in. If you've ever heard Russian disco you'd stand in line too. An amalgam of Gypsy hip-hop, Siberian soul, and Moldavian ska, it's an underground music so unabashedly commercial and cheesy that it takes awfulness to heights unexplored since Lawrence Welk covered the Beatles' "A Hard Day's Night." The effect is truly lobotomizing, and Fatima looked forward to her and the Schwa dancing their troubles away to classics like "Vodka Revolution," "Generation @," and "Vassily's Groove."* When we finally reached the entrance, the doorman said he could let the women in, but not me and the Schwa.

---

* *Generation @* is pronounced "Generation At."

"There's a new club policy," he said. "No black men." I followed his finger to an exclusionary sign that, if you'd struck out the *No*, would've been the *entrance* policy at the Slumberland. The sign read:

No Admittance To Black Men
Who Meet Any Of The Following Criteria

- Under 25 years of age
- Wearing expensive and grotesque American sportswear, gold chains, and pricey watches
- Bloodshot eyes
- Bad teeth in conjunction with unusual body hygiene for an African (i.e., strong-smelling deodorant and aftershave)
- Not in the company of white females or locals
- Frequent the drug scene
- Exceptions will be made for tourists and black men with intelligent eyes

While we protested, the doorman shoved us into the street, explaining that the club was having problems with black men selling drugs and sexually harassing the female help.

"We aren't racist," he shouted, addressing the crowd more than us. "We respect our multikulti brethren in the neighborhood far too much for us to suspect *all* black people. Our policy is only directed toward drug dealers."

Peeking over his shoulder I could see Doris and Lars inside, boogying on down totalitarian style to a polka-punk ditty called "Dancing on the Airplane." I felt less insulted by the place's discriminatory illogic than by the fact that he failed to notice the glint of intelligence in my eyes.

While Fatima had a breakdown sitting on the hood of an Opel station wagon, I walked up on the scruffy gatekeeper and batted my brilliant peepers smartly in his face.

"Come on, man. You mean to tell me you don't see at least a hint of intelligence in these eyes?"

Fatima never recovered from the insult. Among the daily affronts—the squirt gun assaults, dirt-clod bombardments, subway gropes, and "compliments" about her excellent German and her good fortune in having grown up in Germany and not Africa—the incident at An einem Sonntag was the snub that stopped the cultural chameleon from changing colors. There is no camouflage for being black.

When the cops asked the crowd about the smoldering corpse, they were really addressing Thorsten, as he was the only white person present. Since my gig the cold-hearted neo-Nazi couldn't get the Schwa's sound out of his head no matter how many Turks he beat, Chinese he stoned, Jewish ghosts he exorcised, and niggers he flicked lit cigarette butts at. On days off from his piano-moving job, he'd call me.

"Where is he?"

I'd call Fatima to find out, relay the info to him. He'd bus in from Marzahn just to sit curbside and listen to the music, hoping to catch the Schwa before he was shooed away by the authorities. The *verdammte Neger* across the street, who since the *Bundestreffen* also followed the Schwa, sometimes gave him dirty looks, but Stone and Fatima never paid him any mind.

As Thorsten explained himself to a sympathetic cop, the paramedics floated a plastic sheet over Fatima's body. It wasn't hard from the evidence (a singed metal gas canister and a melted boom box) to figure out what had happened.

Thorsten told the cop that when he showed up and took his place on the bus stop bench, it was as if she had been waiting for him. She stared him down with those large, distant, camel-brown eyes, then silently toted her gas can to the nearby station.

Splurged on two liters of high octane. Returned to the scene. Sat down. Drenched herself in gasoline. Jabbed her earphones into the radio. Turned up the volume. Adjusted the treble. Held up her lighter rock 'n' roll–concert style and lit it. Hell of an encore.

The Schwa and Fatima had gotten a lot of work done that day, and I admired their handiwork. At nearly five feet high and fifteen feet long, the wall was higher, longer, smoother, and sturdier than I'd ever seen it. Stone remarked that Fatima had studied some architecture books and had taught him that before building he should sort the stones into piles and that the base of a freestanding wall should be about half its height with the bigger stones at the bottom.

By this time the police had barricaded the good-sized group of increasingly agitated blacks behind wooden horses. Seeing the *Schwarzen* had been contained, the coroner whipped the sheet off Fatima's burnt corpse and began pounding the remains into ash with a shovel while two cops prepared to sweep her up into a body bag. The callous treatment of the deceased set the black Germans off, and from behind a phalanx of riot police they hurled rocks and curses. Thorsten, with his ball-peen skull and Nazi chic attire, drew his fair share of both the stony fusillade and abuse. The rocks were your standard fare: hard, metamorphic, and amorphous. But the invective was uniquely German: wonderfully smart, deeply emasculating, and with a dash of U-boat sailor's brio thrown in for good measure. Whether you call it snapping, capping, or bagging, the insult the beach-ball-afroed Nordica unleashed on Thorsten was one for the ages: "It's your fault she died, you cowardly, warm-shower-taking, satin-testicled, spotty-dicked onanist who stinks like a lion's cage, saves every fucking e-mail, answers every fucking e-mail, compares gas prices, drives an automatic car, uses his brakes when driving uphill, and is a fish-faced, poor excuse for an evolutionary mishap who waves back at the Teletubbies and only swims near the edges of the pool."

A lesser man would have joined Fatima in suicide then and there, but Thorsten just stood there, hands on hips, ignoring the barrage of rocks and insults like some cocksure army officer oblivious to the war going on around him.

He took a small, neatly folded piece of paper and tossed it to Klaudia, who tucked it safely behind the wall.

"Your sister gave me this before she killed herself."

"Is it a suicide note?"

"I don't know; I can't read. I didn't give it to the bulls because I thought maybe it blames me for her death. Read it to me, but cover your ears so that you don't hear it, okay?"

The cute, twisted logic of thinking that if she couldn't hear herself reading the note she wouldn't know what it said caused a tight, almost morbid smile to break out on her tearstained face. The Schwa and I scooted in next to her and peeked over her shoulder. Though the note was in German, Thorsten made us cover our ears too. Klaudia started to read: It was a stanza from a poem, "They're People Like Us," by May Ayim.

"We really believe
that all people are the *same*.
No one should be discriminated against,
just because he's *different*."

The stanza's sarcasm hit Thorsten about the same time as a grenade-sized rock pegged him right above his eye. A thick rivulet of blood ran down his cheek and dripped from his chin.

The wind and the rioting kicked up Fatima's ashes, scattering them in black swirls about the street. Klaudia, her fingers feverishly nimble, folded the suicide note into an origami paper cup complete with tuck-in flap and sprinted toward the last pile of ashes. Someone javelined a tree branch into the fracas; meant for the police, it boomeranged into my girl's rib cage, knocking her down. A beer bottle landed at her feet. Unbowed, she scrambled through the broken glass. Thorsten turned to the Schwa and said, "This city really does need a new Berlin Wall, only this time it should be transparent," then whipped his shirt off and stood in front of Stone's wall.

"Heil Hitler!" he shouted, drawing the attention of all those who hadn't already been transfixed by the life-sized tattoo of the führer inked across his muscular chest. It was an exact likeness, but if you looked closely you could see the mustache was a splotchy, fuzz-covered birthmark just above his belly button. Thorsten snapped a fascist salute, clicked his booted heels, and then stiffly goose-stepped to and fro in front of the wall like a storm trooper target in a Coney Island shooting gallery circa 1942.

Some bumptious carnival barker shouted out the rules.

"You have to stay on the curb. Legs and torso—ten points. Head shot—twenty-five points. Groin—fifty points. The swastika on his neck—one hundred points! Five rocks for one mark!"

The crowd loved it, and soon directed all of its energy to hitting the freak, pelting him with bottles, rocks, batteries, and whatever else they could find to throw. Whenever he was hit, Thorsten would shout a metallic "Bing!" and make an abrupt about-face.

The antics created the diversion that Klaudia needed to retrieve the ashes of her sister. And as we watched her scoop the flesh granules and bone chips into the paper urn, the Schwa turned to me. "You know, the bald-headed guy's right."

"About what?"

"About the wall. I can build a transparent wall—a wall of sound."

The intensity of the stone throwing picked up. One of the

blacks accused Thorsten of killing Fatima, and without a trace
of bitterness in his voice, Thorsten kindly pointed out to them in
so many words that in some moral court of law with broad psy-
chosomatic jurisdiction, that accusation might be true, but the
one thing they were all guilty of, black monkey and white super-
human alike, is that they all watched her die.

The stones stopped pinging against the wall.

Exhausted, Thorsten slumped to the ground, his Hitler tattoo
covered in blood.

CHAPTER 2

F OR HIM IT isn't about the way a musician sounds. He could care less whether or not he or she has the "goods." How they dress. For him the assemblage of a band is about some bizarre teleological holism whose main precept seems to be "the whole is a grater on some of its parts."

He conducted his rehearsals like a basketball coach who, in order to emphasize conditioning and defense, puts his players through two weeks of grueling practice before they ever touch a basketball. He auditioned and rehearsed his band without once hearing a musician play.

"How do you know if someone can play without even checking out his embouchure?" I asked him.

"When you see someone holding the steering wheel at ten and two, exactly how they teach you in driving school, what's the first thing you think about that driver?"

"That motherfucker can't drive."

"Okay then, I don't need to see nobody hold, bow, blow, pound, sound no instrument."

Instead he plotted their horoscopes, gave them psychometric tests for group compatibility, and made them sit through team-building exercises. My favorite part of the auditions was when he presented the musicians with his universal sheet music.

"But isn't sheet music already universal?" they'd invariably ask.

"It is for musicians who can read music. What about the cats who *can't* read music?"

Even the most forward-thinking musician would turn to the first page of "universal music" and freeze.

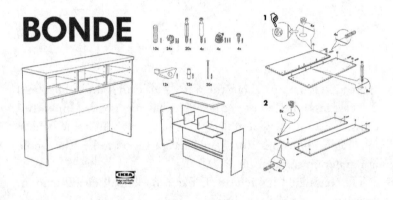

"Hey, man, Ikea instructions? I'm sorry, but I don't get this."

"Ikea's instructions for furniture assembly are the closest thing we earthlings have developed that approaches a universal language. Okay, people, on page two, when we attach the left panel to the top shelf, I want the horns to come in on a D-flat major chord, and trombone, as you're putting in the dowels, tonic the chord at the top. From there we'll count sixteen bars, segue back to the intro, and nail the back panels down. Saxes, I want you to give out with that old Phillips-head-screwdriver, good-timey feeling. Now let's play this fucking hutch, hit it on four."

Most guys ran out the door screaming, but the ones who stayed were special.

There were like-minded guys like Willy Wow, a violinist whose music I'd greatly admired. His talents were retrograde in a very modern sort of way—he could make a violin sound like a synthesizer. During his job interview, the Schwa didn't ask him what was the last book he'd read or what he felt was his worst quality. He looked at Wow's mangled hand and said, "Tell me about Nam."

"Vietnam wasn't so bad. It's what freed up my mind. I used to sit on top of the PX and listen to the sounds of battle. It was like going to the Laos philharmonic. Like sitting at Minton's bar during a late night cutting session. It was the freest of free jazz. The Viet Cong would open up with this light-arms staccato. And the U.S. would return fire with artillery legato, mortar fire. Pound the hillside with 150mm and 175mm rondo and drop the napalm coda and blow away the whole stage, you dig? You'd think after that display of firepower there'd be no more shit for Charlie to play, right? Hills burned to a crisp. Not even a bird in the sky, much less a tree for one to fly out of. Any other normal motherfucker would have walked off the bandstand never to play again, but Charlie Cong let off three little mortar bursts, *pop pop pop!* And the cutting contest was over. They'd won the day and I knew they'd win the war. Right then and there I decided to sound like Vietnam."

Needless to say Willy Wow was the band's violinist, insomuch as there was a band. You never knew exactly who was in the band. The Schwa never summarily dismissed anybody or castigated his (and sometimes her) manhood and musicianship. Cats would simply know if they were wanted or not and would decide for themselves if they could hang. Permit me to introduce some of the regulars: Soulemané Eshun, a black-American bass player with an excellent bow technique and an annoying between-song habit of uttering cryptic African proverbs that only he and the Schwa seemed to understand.

"*Gbawlope nane a gipo ni ton ne a gipo ta-ton.* Alligator says: We know a friendly from an enemy canoe."

"Yeah, baby."

"*Lã asike legbe meflo dzo o.* A long-tailed animal should not attempt to jump over a fire."

"Right on."

On piano and percussion, Uli Effenberg. An expert aerophone player, his eclectic collections of wind instruments included a cage of bees, a propeller hat, and a human skull, which when he waved it in the air produced the eeriest glissando through the eye sockets and missing teeth. Uli didn't play the piano so much as he fucked with the piano. Sometimes he'd just move the stool back and forth, augmenting whatever the band was doing with the squeaks of the roller wheels and the slamming of the lid. He'd strike the pedals with a hammer; play the keyboard with a beach ball. Once, to the Schwa's great amusement, he threw a mouse onto the piano strings, then went to sleep while the little white rodent comped the band.

On drums, Sandra Irrawaddy. Despite holding the sticks as if she had the palsy, she could do things on a drum set Philly Joe Jones could only dream about. The Schwa, stealing a Duke Ellington line, called her an "exponent of drum-stickery," but her footwork was no joke either. Once during a cigarette break Sandra played a more-than-reasonable facsimile of John Bonham's infamous "Moby Dick" drum solo with no hands. Instead of using drumsticks she kicked out the jam on the bass drums and spit tangerine seeds at the cymbals.

And then there's Yong Sook Rhee. Ever wonder whatever happened to that stuck-up-looking Korean kid with the slicked-down hair who was known as the world's smartest boy? The one who at age five had an IQ of 210, could speak nine languages, program in five, recite pi to ten thousand places, and composed poetry?* I'll

---

*My own IQ is said to fluctuate between 89 and 174. A quotient categorized as "haphazardly intellectual."

tell you what happened to young Yong Sook, he plays trumpet in the Schwa's band. Not much of a musician, he plays with a shameless naïveté reminiscent of Halle Berry trying to act. Just as the starlet's insufferable overacting is about to drive you insane, she flashes a perfectly parabolic expanse of flesh and all is forgiven; and when you listen to Yong Sook play he'll miss ten thousand notes, but the one he hits is crazy beautiful.

My role in the band was undefined. There were always turntables and a mixer in the studio, but I never touched them and no one ever asked me to sit in. In the days leading up to the concert someone asked if I was in the band.

"Yes," the Schwa said.

"Well, what the hell does he do?"

"He's our secret weapon. The grand finale that'll bring down the house."

Then he strolled over to Fatima's melted radio, which he always kept nearby, turned it "on," and began to dance a tango with an invisible partner.

As the Schwa caminata'd around the room, Soulemané tapped me on the shoulder and said, *"Brow tron lo, eta ne a ne won oh gike.* The world is too large, that's why we do not hear everything."

The concert couldn't come fast enough. The African proverbs were starting to make sense.

CHAPTER 3

I T TOOK THE EAST GERMAN GOVERNMENT more than three years to build the Berlin Wall. Once we got the approval, it took us only three days to rebuild it. The idea was to bisect the heart of the city from Treptow to Pankow with a wall of sound ten meters thick and five meters high, a sound that, if everything went according to plan, would be a continuous loop of the Schwa's upcoming concert. The music would be so real that anyone within earshot would feel as if they could reach out and touch it. They'd have to figure out for themselves if the wall of sound was confinement, exclusion, or protection.

Given Germany's reputation for being a bureaucratic quagmire where one needs a stamp of approval in order to get the stamp of approval, we walked into the Senate for Urban Redevelopment fully expecting to get the infamous civic runaround. To be, as the Germans say, sent from Pontius to Pilatus.

The Schwa handed the clerk his proposal, a tersely worded, one-sentence document written in English on a sheet of notebook paper wrinkled as an elephant's ass. Herr Müller calmly spread it over the counter, ironed it out with his forearm, and read it aloud. "I want to rebuild the Berlin Wall with music instead of concrete, barbed wire, and machine guns 'n' shit."

Without so much as a snicker, Herr Müller put a bearded chin in his hand and said, "In some ways that's not a bad idea." His muted enthusiasm shouldn't have been a complete surprise. Berlin newspapers often poll their readerships as to whether or not they want the Wall back. At least 20 percent of the respondents answer yes. So we had Herr Müller's tacit approval, but surely that wouldn't be nearly enough. True to form, he slapped a small stack of various pastel-colored application forms on the counter, rattling off in very official German which ones had to be sent where and addressed to whom. It didn't take long for Müller to see that his Byzantine bullshit wasn't registering with Herr Stone, so he tried English.

"Excuse me, sir. If you aren't a German citizen and lawful resident of Berlin, this is going to be a problem. I need to see your papers."

At the mention of papers, both Klaudia and I panicked, thinking that at any second a squad of crew-cut *Polizei* would come barreling in and escort the Schwa to the border. The Schwa, sensing he was at some bureaucratic impasse, coolly took out the same frayed piece of paper he showed the motorcycle cop the day I first discovered him. Herr Müller scanned it, skeptically at first, then he lifted the pair of librarian glasses from his chest and placed them over his slowly unwrinkling nose. Suddenly he was handling the paper by the edges like it was the fucking Magna Carta.

"Udo!"

Udo, an eager boy of about eighteen, appeared at his side, straightening his rayon tie and his unruly forelock at the same time.

"Yes, sir?"

"I want you to make a copy of this document and bring it back to me straight away."

Udo reached for the paper, Herr Müller slapped his hand away.

"Gloves!"

When Udo returned with his identification papers they were encased in a plastic cover. A buzzer sounded and Herr Müller beckoned us to join him on the other side of the counter. Briskly, he escorted us into the bowels of the system, marching us down a cavernous hallway until we reached the frosted glass door to Frau Richter's office. We could see a short, insanely busy woman who, judging by his trepidatious knock and newfound stammer, was Herr Müller's superior.

Frau Richter was on the phone yelling something to the effect of, "Tell I. M. Pei that Potsdamer Platz makes the architect, not the other way around!" when Herr Müller passed the proposal and the mysterious paper under her pug nose.

"Das ist eine geniale Idee," she said, hanging up the phone. She fingered her pearl necklace for a moment and made another phone call.

For the next two hours we were shuttled up the chain of command, marched from building to building until we finally found ourselves in a Reichstag sitting room, waiting to be seen along with an elderly and very dapper gentleman. The antechamber of the elected federal official, whom I am legally barred from naming, was ornate. Interspersed between historical tapestries were exquisitely framed portraits of high-ranking politicians whom I'm also not allowed to identify, but as a hint of the echelon of portraiture facing us, think "unsinkable" World War II battleship.

Now that we had time to rest, we asked Stone to see his identification. He removed it from the protective sheath and flung the plastic into the barrel chest of a bespectacled leader whose German surname in English means "cabbage."

The ID paper was written in that interlocking old-German script that looks like a wrought iron fence. I barely managed to decipher the letterhead, "Verfolgte des Naziregimes," a bold declarative that had been embossed with the screaming red insignia of the German Democratic Republic.

"No, it's not possible," Klaudia said, absentmindedly slipping into the Saxony accent she always tried so hard to hide. "There's no way."

The nameless politician stepped through the tall, walnut doors accompanied by a man with a suitcase handcuffed to his wrist. If the Chinese had attacked Germany at that very moment I could tell you the color of the proverbial "panic button" that unleashes unholy hell.

But Germany doesn't have nuclear arms.

Sure they don't.

Anyway, since China didn't attack, I can't tell you what color the "button" is, but suffice it to say the suitcase is brown. Yeah, I would've thought black too.

"Herr Stone?"

The Schwa stood, hat in hand, except that he didn't have a hat.

"Do you mind, Herr Gleibermann, if I see this gentleman first?" Our anonymous statesperson was smooth yet commanding. It was easy to see how he or possibly she carried North Rhine–Westphalia with 86 percent of the vote.

"Kein problem . . ."

After the brass-handled doors clicked behind the Schwa, I asked a still-pale Klaudia what was the deal with his identity papers.

"What does *Verfolgte des Naziregimes* mean?"

Klaudia cupped her hands around my ear and whispered. Whenever she discussed matters referring to "the former East Germany," she whispered. A survival instinct from the days when the walls had ears and best friends had microphones taped to their chests.

"*Verfolgte des Naziregimes* means 'persecuted by the Nazi regime.' It was an identity the DDR gave to Holocaust survivors as recompense. Of course, in the government's eyes the war was West Germany's fault."

"How so?"

"We were good, innocent Communists, and don't forget, the Nazis hated Communists. My history teacher used to say, 'Remember, class, they gassed Communists alongside the Jews, and if you were a Jewish Communist, forget about it, they gassed and burned you twice just to make sure.'

"Anyway," Klaudia continued, "if you have this Verfolgte des Naziregimes, you got party favors . . ."

I grinned, picturing a bunch of survivors in conical paper hats, tossing confetti and blowing paper whistles, celebrating life, but she meant special privileges. "They could start a little private business, sell food or umbrellas, open up a bicycle-repair shop, even though any kind of open capitalism was strictly forbidden. Maybe they got a little stipend. Maybe they only had to wait six years for a car, I don't know. But anyone who carried this paper basically didn't get fucked with."

I never could figure out how the Schwa supported himself. Now I knew. I mean, so what if the guy basically defected to East Germany—what was the current German government going to do, leave an honorary Jewish black jazzman to die?

The Schwa exited the office with the politician's arm around his shoulder, a substantial check, and written carte blanche to build his wall in any shape or form he saw fit so long as it didn't obstruct traffic or violate any noise-pollution statutes.

Old Herr Gleibermann, clutching a paper certificate of victimization exactly like the Schwa's, touched his hand and in a halting English asked, "What camp were you in, brother?"

"Camp?"

"Sachsenhausen? Buchenwald? Bergen-Belsen?"

"No. Never."

"I thought maybe you were a survivor. Your eyes."

"No, sorry."

"No camp?"

"Stephen S. Wise Day Camp when I was a young'un, that's about it."

The old man took his joke in good humor and entered into the chancellor's inner sanctum complaining that his neighbor's dog was still barking at all hours of the night.

The East Side Gallery is a mural-covered remnant of the Berlin Wall that runs along the north bank of the river Spree between the Oberbaum Bridge and the Ostbahnhof train station. It's a kilometer-long memorial that simultaneously tries to erase and preserve the Berlin Wall's legacy. Knowing that in this case the art is the canvas, the best of the faded and peeling panels incorporate the Wall into their themes. Birgit Kinder's three-dimensional Trabant sedan crashes the through the Wall to freedom. The artist Suku simply lists the Wall's achievements on a concrete résumé.

Curriculum Vitae

1961 1962 1963 1964 1965

1966 1967 **1968** 1969 1970 1971

1972 1973 1974 1975 1976 1977 1978 1979

1980 1981 1982 1983 1984 1985 1986 1987

1988 1989 1990

The last two entries are painted in a screaming red and cautionary yellow, respectively.

It was here, nailed into the butt end of the Gallery, that the cornerstone of the new Berlin Wall, Fatima's melted boom box, was laid. In many ways our wall was an extension of the Gallery—but one immune to the neglect and the countless coats of graffiti defacement that in recent years had rendered the original artwork almost invisible.

With the Schwa who knows where, Lars, Doris, and Klaudia gave me the honor of turning on the old radio, which had been hollowed out and stuffed with Fatima's ashes and new electronic gadgetry. It buzzed with an antiphonary static that carried about thirty meters into the middle of the wide sidewalk.

The sound cut right through Klaudia.

"Was ist los?"

"This is freaking me out. I just realized what we're doing."

She removed a small radio from her satchel and fiddled with the power button. The red light flashed off and on.

"The sound makes the Wall more real."

"More real than the gallery?"

"In a way, yeah. For you guys the murals are a kitschy tourist attraction, but for me, sometimes I walk past them and remember things."

"You're saying we're trivializing the repression?"

I looked up and down Mühlenstrasse. It was getting harder to tell the differences between East and West. Back in the day it was easy. Border streets such as Mühlenstrasse were like the river Styx. Concrete tributaries not to be crossed because on the other side was Hades, a backward underworld where the living dead lived in prefab housing. I dashed across the six-lane street and tried to imagine what West Berlin looked like from an Eastern vantage point. People died attempting to cross that street, so I supposed it looked like the Elysian Fields: still part of the underworld, only the markets carried bananas.

"You're forgetting the chicken-fucking song," I said, somewhat out of breath from the return sprint. "The guy takes an improbable bestial coupling, like man and fowl, and makes it seem like you're watching the secret bedroom tapes of Humphrey Bogart and Lauren Bacall. Whatever his reasons, it's impossible for his music to trivialize anything. His music is an honorific to life—the good, bad, and the ambiguous."

"There's no denying the chicken-fucking song," Doris said, her voice inflected with a sexual nostalgia I thought Klaudia might take offense to. She didn't. Instead she erased any apprehensions we had with an ironic memory of totalitarian life.

She held out the radio.

"See this power button? In East Germany we didn't have power buttons. The word 'power' was too aggressive."

"That's hilarious."

"We had the 'Netz' button."

"What does that mean?"

"It's like 'network.' So when you turned on the television or whatever, you were plugged into the people. Everybody was sharing the power."

"That's deep."

Klaudia handed me the radio.

"Here."

There was a little bit of resignation in her voice that I took for the residue of thought control.

"What now?"

"There's no place to put it."

She was right. We were standing on the only thirty-meter stretch of Berlin sidewalk without trees. The closest thing we had to a tree was a street-lamp stanchion. A truck zipped passed us, illuminating our dumbfounded faces in bright xenon light.

The plan was simple. For the most part the old Wall ran along existing streets. Berlin is easily one of the most tree-lined cities in the world, so we'd stick satellite radios in the trees, where they'd dangle from the branches like transistorized fruit. In the treeless places where the Wall's footprint had been erased by progress in the form of condominiums or vacant lots that would soon be turned into condos, there was no shortage of local artists who were willing to fill in the blanks. For instance, Steffi Rödl strung a clothesline made of barbed wire across the trash-strewn vacant lot that sat behind a row of apartment houses on Stallschreiberstrasse. Using wooden clothespins, she hung a twelve-foot-high curtain of shiny charcoal-gray silk that billowed majestically in the wind, a brilliantine representation of the Berlin Wall aired out like so much dirty laundry. In Potsdamer Platz, where the Wall had been eradicated by commercialism and skyscrapers, in lieu of radios—which would never have been heard over the din of downtown traffic—Michael Harnisch projected a musical stave across the white limestone base of the Sony Center. A computer instantly annotated the music and projected the notes onto the wall, the concert's score running through downtown Berlin like a ticker tape opera. Using the Brandenburg Gate as a backdrop, Uwe Okulaja lined up a bank of high-powered green and red lights that, like a giant equalizer, shot a pulsing LED readout 250 meters into the night sky. There were other installations: a dancing fountain, an oscilloscope, and pushcarts where you could rent a set of those chintzy museum headphones and take a sonic tour of the new Berlin Wall; of course, none of these things would mean much if we couldn't find somewhere to place the second speaker. It'd be like the Union Pacific and the Central Pacific coming up a few tracks short at the joining of the first transcontinental railroad. Some top-hatted CEO pocketing the golden spike with a "Fuck it, that's close enough" shrug.

Overhead the telephone lines buzzed. A car cruised past at that odd not-too-fast, not-too-slow L.A. street-corner drive-by speed that made me instinctively duck behind the streetlight for cover. There, crouched behind the stanchion, I remembered the telephone lines buzzing on a warm night back in Westwood, California. We were playing hooky from Emerson Junior High. Lounging in Julie Koenig's spacious backyard celebrating Martin Luther King's birthday before it was a holiday. Bong hits. Two cases of Hamm's beer. Devin Morris listening to the Eagles' "Take It Easy," and declaring that, just like Glenn Frey, he too had seven women on his mind. A spirited Steve Martin's *Let's Get Small* versus Richard Pryor's *That Nigger's Crazy* debate. Sneaking off into the guesthouse to lose my virginity to Lori Weinstein (and Bobby Caldwell's "What You Won't Do for Love"). Blaze and the rest of my boys finding out about it and jumping me into manhood, pinning me to the ground, snatching off my bleach-white Converse All-Stars and tossing them overhead onto the telephone wires that crisscrossed Comstock Avenue. Those shoes were loyal to me. Twelve points in the Robinson Park rec league. Hopped the fence when Loretta White's Doberman pinscher attacked me for no good reason. Sneaked me down glass-strewn Sherbourne alleyway past the Crip-ass Boyd family. So loyal were those shoes, I expected them to untangle themselves from the wire and slither down the pole and back onto my feet. But night fell with my size tens still hanging from those buzzing telephone lines like some surreal Duchamp castoff. Walking home barefoot, chewing on a plastic straw, a black Tom Sawyer whistling Rush's classic "Tom Sawyer." *The world is, the world is . . .*

The patrol cop calling me over to his black-and-white squad car with a crooked finger and a sneer.

Love and life are deep . . .

"What are you doing over here, boy?"

"I was visiting my girlfriend; she lives . . ."

"I don't give a fuck where she lives, I don't ever want to see you in this neighborhood again. Now get the fuck out of here—and where in the hell are your shoes?"

His eyes are open wide.

Klaudia caught me daydreaming. "What are you thinking about?"

"I was just listening to the buzz of the telephone wires and thinking about 'Tom Sawyer,'" I said, kicking off my shoes.

"The book?"

"The song."

They watched as I knotted the shoelaces around the radio handle, and then bola'd the three-piece menagerie over the telephone wire, gaucho-style.

The New Berlin Wall of Sound was nearly complete. All that remained was for the golden spike to be driven: the first note struck by the Schwa during the next day's concert. Until then the Berlin Wall of Sound would remain silent.

We pressed on home. Mühlenstrasse felt warm beneath my tired feet. It felt just like Comstock Avenue or Robertson Boulevard. It felt like home.

CHAPTER 4

LARS COOLED IN front of the Slumberland, checking his watch and taking notes. Above him, strung between two trees, the concert banner sagged in the middle like a rainbow tweaked on angel dust. THE BLACK PASSÉ TOUR—BUILDING WALLS, TEARING DOWN BRIDGES. He looked proud. If everything went according to plan, in two hours he'd have saved blackness.

Doris sidled up to us to say hello. She was proud too. Proud of her man who, since his newfound purpose in life, had seemingly stopped drinking—*seemingly* being the key word. She leaned in for a peck on the lips, more a Breathalyzer test than a show of affection.

It was a good try. Unfortunately for her, Lars had a tampon stuffed up his ass. An ultra-absorbent, soft-scented tampon, designed by a woman gynecologist to provide eight hours of day or night protection *and* that little something extra. His tampon indeed had that little something extra the packaging promised, because it'd been soaking in absinthe for the past two days.

The alcohol suppository is a technique passed down to journalists and music-industry insiders the world over by Finnish rockabilly bands. "Besotted" is an ethnic group in Finland, and those Stratocaster hellions are the country's most notorious drinkers. It's their alcoholic ingenuity and the recent advances in the menstrual sciences that have allowed many music-industry peons to show up for work stone-bachelor-party drunk with no one the wiser, because their breath is odorless.

I've tried consuming alcohol through the rectum. It's the dipsomaniac's equivalent of a hype's mainlining junk. The porousness of the rectal walls and their proximity to the digestive system make the onset of insobriety instantaneous and deeply spiritual. The flash flood of drunkenness must be what it's like to be born with fetal alcohol syndrome.

"You drunk?"

"Yeah, man, I'm high sky." Lars answered. "You want one? I have vodka, gin, and a really nice single malt back in the car."

The offer was tempting, but I remembered that I had to play tonight—and besides, removing a tampon from a dehydrated anus involved rubber gloves, scented lubricants, tweezers, and a high pain threshold.

"That's okay. Unlike you, I don't drink to get drunk; I drink for the taste."

Most of the concert reviews in the next day's paper would describe the crowd milling about the Slumberland as "diverse" without saying what made them so. In polite democratic society it's important to note stratification but impolite to label the layers. For the journalists in attendance, *diverse* meant that they had gone to a concert in a small venue on a narrow West Berlin side street and didn't know everybody there. The astute reader looked at the concert photo of the nappy-headed Schwa and surmised that *diverse* implied the concertgoers were of various ages and class backgrounds, with a significant percentage of them being of black extraction. But not even an expert cryptologist would be able to infer from the word that the streets surrounding the Slumberland were jammed with a cross section of Berliners who'd come together to celebrate the city's resegregation. A black African peddler vainly tried to sell roses and sandwiches to a platoon of Iron Cross skinheads who were without money, appetites, or lovers. Three Japanese hep cats, bearing gifts and unsigned memorabilia, traipsed over the grounds in open-toed sandals, dutifully upholding the legacy of the Eastern magi being on hand for the birth (in this case resurrection) of every musical messiah from Scott Joplin to DJ Scott La Rock. Yippies, yuppies, hip-hoppers, and pill poppers gathered on the stairs of Saint Matthias church and shared joints and stories. In the center of the plaza, next to the marble likeness of the patron saint of alcoholism, an unkempt beat junkie of about sixteen pressed a set of headphones tightly against his skull. Red eyed and wired, I knew the look—he was a DJ. A fledging turntablist subsumed by melody. Strung out on overdub. Trying with all his might to prevent even a single hertz of sound from escaping his purview.

Although he didn't have a deadline to meet, Lars took notes out of habit. His notations were bare-boned, mostly one- or two-word phrases in German and misspelled English. A young Arab woman wearing a head scarf and a black Stooges T-shirt moonwalked past us. She glided over to her friends, locked eyes with a white dude in a Yankees cap, and started pop locking. After a medley of double-jointed moves, she laid hands on the boy's head and, like a healing evangelist, passed the energy to him. The boy broke out into a spasmodic shock of electric boogie. Pressing down hard with his pen, Lars wrote "Dali-esk."

"Is this a crowd, a mob, or a throng?" he asked.

I'm used to his questions about the subtleties of the English language substituting for real conversation. "Which is more, *some* or *a few*? When someone tells you they are happy to find you safe and sound, what does *sound* mean? To express the indirect object of an action do you use an objective pronoun directly after the verb, or a prepositional phrase?"

"I'd say it's a throng."

"Why not a mob?"

"In English you label groups of people by their moral intentions and collective needs. A mob tries to convince itself it's right and needs to prove it. A crowd knows it's right because if it weren't right, they would all need to be someplace else. A throng doesn't give a fuck about moral imperatives, it just wants and needs something to happen."

Most of those folks were there thanks to Lars's efforts. I imagine the scene wasn't much different along the old Wall's borders. In light of all the hoopla around the Berlin Wall of Sound, his interview with the Schwa had been reprinted in *Der Spiegel,* and suddenly the rediscovery of Charles Stone was akin to the unearthing of the Delta blues musicians in the mid-sixties or Dr. Leakey finding a heretofore theorized hominid species. To many, the Schwa, like Muddy Waters, Mance Lipscomb, and Ötzi the five-thousand-year-old iceman found in an Alpine glacier, was a well-preserved mummy, a music primitive seemingly unspoiled by commercialism and modernity. Lars was the musical paleontologist and I his pickax-wielding native assistant. I didn't mind that he garnered the fame and the credit; all I wanted from the Schwa was a song. He wanted answers. He wanted to test his DNA and carbon-date his instrument so he could theorize about when and how exactly blackness became passé.

Lars removed a pack of Drum tobacco from his pocket. The crinkling pouch reminded me of the radio static in the days when radio KROQ was good. Me and DJ Blaze parked on the Malibu bluffs at dusk ruining our minds with Thai stick and Jane's Addiction.

Exhaling a measured plume of cigarette smoke, Lars jotted down the word *Throng* in his notebook. The gathering was indeed a throng, and depending on how the night went, the shit could've ended in melee or orgy. In either case I figured I'd need some energy, so I decided to buy a sandwich from the peddler. He pushed me to buy a rose in addition to the sandwich, and he almost had me, but I couldn't figure out, Who do you give a rose to at an orgy? Your first fuck or your last?

As we shouldered our way inside, Lars pointed out the cables worming through window transoms and under doorjambs. "That one's for the international radio simulcast . . . DAT recording . . . check this out . . ." He flicked some lever and a matchbox-sized switch box attached to an electrical cord quietly descended from the ceiling.

"When Stone presses that red button, the Berlin Wall of Sound will come to life."

I wasn't worried about the audiovisual technology. I'd long gotten used to the fact that in this country everything works. The vending machines never shortchange you, the pay phones unfailingly deliver that tinnitus-inducing European dial tone, and the suction of the vacuum cleaners is so powerful that vacuuming the living room throw rug gives one the same don't-fuck-with-me rush as filling a human silhouette with bullet holes at the gun range. Charles Stone, on the other hand, was about as reliable as an American bank pen.

I scanned the crowd. Though the Schwa wasn't among them, most of the faces were all too familiar, and I became overwhelmed with heart-searing guilt. Local musicians, tavern owners, regulars, bartenders, and groupies, I owed nearly every single person in the room something, various combinations of money, return phone calls, apologies, and my life. In today's Germany the interpersonal bridges don't burn as easily as those that spanned the Rhine in 1944; the more selfish my actions, the more irascible my behavior, the more those people were drawn to me.

Many of my past one-night stands were there, and Ute, Astrid, and Silke, women whom I'd forgotten even existed, all stared at me as if I'd just gotten out of prison. Bernadette, Karin, Petra, Ulrike—those women were heiresses, herbalists, radio engineers, bookbinders, milliners, but I'd treated them like gun molls. Day after day I swore at them and swore myself off them. Only to return to their arms, a pussy recidivist doomed to repeat my crimes.

I didn't have time for the guilt.

I only had time to blow air kisses and whispered witticisms.

"Where's Stone?"

Lars lifted his chin toward the back. There, perched above us, on the thickest branch of the banana tree, was the God of Improvisation. The sight and twisted symbolism of a black genius in a banana tree unnerved me, but I understood why he was up there—the mental *Lebensraum*. Sometimes you have to elevate yourself above the fray; bananas, monkey inferences, and misappropriated Nazi terminology be damned.

He was talking to a reporter, shyly fiddling with his cuff links and addressing his shoes. I couldn't hear the conversation over the murmur and the Rahsaan Roland Kirk blaring from the jukebox.

"What do you think they're talking about?"

Lars dubbed the dialogue in the affected pitchy drawl particular to the black thinking man. "Rothko . . . harmonic translucency . . . Gerhard Richter, right, right, chromatic color fields . . . exactly . . ."

Stone looked ashen, shell-shocked. There was even more of a paranoid bulge to his eyes than usual. Between questions he blinked at me with the deliberateness of a POW trying to convey some coded message to the boys back at the command center. Not sure if he was looking at me or past me, I wavered between soul-brother salutations—a light thump of my fist to my heart or the chin-up nod—finally settling on a discreet peace sign.

". . . Leibniz . . . an alphabet of thought . . ."

I imagined that Stone, like any guest of honor, wanted to arrive fashionably late, avoid the hoopla, but the pro forma punctuality of the German transportation system wouldn't let him. That's one of the drawbacks of German reliability: There are no excuses, and that's half the fun of being black, the excuses. The negative attention.

"Pollock . . . linear harmony . . . visceral pointillism . . ." Lars was on a roll. "I've interviewed a hundred jazz musicians, and every time I ask them, 'What are your influences, Mr. Blackman?' they come back with the same impress-the-white-boy-with-white-boys shit—Rothko, Bartók, Pollock, John Cage."

Lars looked at me expecting an answer, but I couldn't tell him the other half of the fun in being black is name-dropping Rothko and Liebniz in an interview. Crediting abstract impressionism and the stoics as the biggest influences on your avant-garde art, and not your two tours as a machine gunner in the army, Muhammad Ali, or the white ingenue (aren't they all) who broke your heart by choosing economic stability over eight and three-quarter inches of dick.

"What's he talking about now?"

"Heidegger."

"Heidegger?"

"Heidegger, nigger!" Lars shouted, jokingly snapping out a fascist salute that guilt lowered almost immediately.

"Wow, that's the first time I ever did that."

"Yeah, the first time out of uniform."

"We start after the song's over, okay?" With that Lars withdrew to the bar, leaving me to my thoughts and the Roland Kirk.

At the moment, I needed Rahsaan Roland Kirk more than Ronald Reagan and Eazy-E had needed their ghostwriters. Kirk, as is his recalcitrant wont, was blindly misbehaving like a country cousin at the Thanksgiving dinner table, chewing with his mouth full. I shut my eyes and concentrated on his blowing. Stritch, tenor, and manzello, he played three saxophones at once, somehow braiding each instrument's distinct timbre into one tensile melody. Rather than playing his notes, he played *with* his notes; chewing and gnawing on them until they were sweetened bubblegum chaws that he pulled pink and sticky from his horns, then reeled back in just to chomp on it and start the process all over again. Rahsaan Roland Kirk was telling me to relax. Letting me know that it's okay to misbehave. Perfectly fine to once in a while play with your food, your blackness, and your craft. It was a message I needed to hear, especially since when the song ended I was going to have to introduce the Schwa, in all his musical rudeness, to the world.

Introductions are a serious matter, the import of which I think only the Mafia truly understands. In the criminal underworld there are consequences to expanding the sewing circle. You introduce somebody to the family and your goombah from the neighborhood turns out to be a fuck-up or an undercover cop, you're held responsible, and the person who vouched for you is held responsible for your transgression, and so on down the line. I feel the same way about music: Problem is, there are no repercussions. Some irresponsible uncle drags you to a GBH concert at the Roxy before you're ready and it's like going on a bad acid trip. You're never quite the same. Yet given all my misgivings about making an introduction, I insisted on being the one to introduce the Schwa to the world and I was willing to assume full responsibility for what ensued.

I had prepared by studying all the great emcees. Brave toastmasters like Symphony Sid, whose houndstooth-sport-jacketed "Oh, man, daddy-o" afternoon-radio equipoise ushered in the swing era. I sat up nights staring at album covers and lip-syncing Pee-Wee Marquette's slurring, whiskey-breathed "Welcome to the Birdland" castrato. I thought that these masters of ceremonies would inspire me, but when I sat down to write my intro, nothing past the mundane came to mind; lots of words that start with *in-* and ended in *-able*: *in-domit-able, in-defatig-able, in-dubit-able*, and I swear I took my hand off the pen and, like a player piano mechanically reproducing a hokey Bourbon Street rag, it scribbled out, "Ladies and gentlemen, a man who needs no introduction . . ." If anybody ever needed an introduction, it was the Schwa.

I had half a notion to reverse protocol and introduce the audience to the band. Clear my throat and say, "Over-rehearsed and underpaid musicians, allow me to present your fawning fan base. Charles Stone and members of the band, I give you the last group of people on earth with an attention span—the free-jazz audience."

I finally phoned the Schwa and asked him how he wanted to be introduced.

He simply said, "In German."

His answer surprised me because I'd never heard him speak a lick of German. He was the stereotypical lazy expatriate for whom German is a dour, unnecessarily serious language. He feels life is morose enough without the mooing umlauts and throat-irritating diphthongs. Even though I knew better, I asked him politely if he spoke German.

"Thirty-some-odd years," he said proudly, "thirty-some-odd years I've lived in this country, and all I can say in German is, '*Kann ich reinspritzen?*' Can I come inside you? What can I say, man? The language just don't taste right in my mouth."

He had managed to offend what few sensibilities I have, and I was about to hang up the phone when his voice sputtered through the receiver. "Wait, I can say something else," he said in an excited pant, " *'Kann ich in Ihnen kommen?'* May I come inside you, woman whom I don't know well enough to address in the informal variant of *you?"*

"If you don't speak German, why do you want me to introduce you in German?"

"So I don't understand the fucking lies."

"Lies?"

"Are you going to say, 'Ladies and gentlemen, I'd like to introduce Charles Stone, an old, persnickety, impotent everyday-except-Thursday, muscatel-in-a-plastic-cup-at-four-in-the-afternoon-drinking motherfucker. Let's give him a warm welcome and hope this jazz dinosaur completes the set before he dies'? No, you're not. So whatever you say, say it in German. Bullshit sounds good in German."

He was right, bullshit does sound good in German. In any of the dialects high, low, middlebrow, or guest worker, I can never tell if a person is lying. Come to think of it, I never even suspect them of lying. I think it started with the cigarettes and Günter Grass, but more so the cigarettes. I never had much of a habit, a pack a week, pack and a half if I was waiting on the results of an HIV test, but as my German improved I began reading *The Tin Drum, The Rat,* and the cigarette warnings on my Marlboro boxes. The print was the size of a newspaper headline and just as starkly worded: SMOKERS DIE EARLIER, SMOKING DAMAGES THE SPERM AND DECREASES FERTILITY, SMOKING IS A SIGN OF LOW SELF-ESTEEM, FEELINGS OF INFERIORITY, AND IS SCIENTIFICALLY LINKED WITH GROUP THINK AND MOB VIOLENCE. There was none of the microscopic wishy-washy wording of the American warning labels. No "may causes" or "might lead tos." Gradually I stopped smoking and began to believe everything I read and heard as long as it was in German or the *New York*

Times (a paper printed in a font that looks suspiciously like German). However, agreeing to introduce him in German didn't solve all my problems. I still didn't know what to say. It's no accident that I'm a DJ: I'm a copycat at heart, and as a plagiarist of rhythm I need a source. Someone else's idea that I can cut and paste into an "original" creation, but I couldn't translate Alan Freed, Funkmaster Flex, or Symphony Sid—there's no words for *daddy-o* or *fresh new joint* in German. I tried to think of a German impresario and could come up with only one name. Ruldolf Hess, the master of ceremonies for the master race. His signature line echoed in my head. "Hitler ist Deutschland! Deutschland ist Hitler!"

I winced, yet with a little alteration and less flying spittle it'd make a fine closing statement. I'd be paraphrasing the Third Reich's publicity agent, who himself was only paraphrasing Keats.* I'm rationalizing, I know, but I take some comfort in the fact that humanity is united by its latent fascism, and that is as true now as it ever was and will ever be.

I stepped in close to the microphone, enjoying the sensuous tease of the cold crosshatched steel on my lips. Nothing sounds as believable as little white lies told in amplified German.

"Ich bin sehr stolz, jetzt den Star unserer Show zu präsentieren. Sein Klang ist der Klang des Jazz, der Klang der Freiheit—ein Klang, der nicht zu imitieren ist, die durch hundert berühmte Platten in aller Welt bekannt geworden ist. Er wird von Uli Effenberg am Piano, Yong Sook Rhee an der trompete, Sandra Irrawaddy, Soulemané Eshun, und Willy Wow begleitet. Meine Damen und Herren—Charles Stone ist jazz. Jazz ist Charles Stone."

The applause was gracious, warm, and buoyant, and though it wasn't mine to bask in, I stepped off the stage and waded into it,

---

* "Ode on a Grecian Urn": "Beauty is truth, truth beauty."

letting the clapping and huzzahs lap at my body in small, exuberant waves. The lies were nothing serious, exaggerations of opinion more than falsehoods. What I said was, "He's the sound of jazz, the sound of freedom, a sound that cannot be imitated, that has become known worldwide through a hundred celebrated records. With Uli Effenberg on piano, Yong Sook Rhee on saxophone, Sandra Irrawaddy, Soulemané Eshun, and Willy Wow accompanying. Ladies and gentlemen—Charles Stone is jazz. Jazz is Charles Stone." Okay, the "hundred celebrated records" was an outright lie. And, I confess, I cribbed the intro from Leonard Feather's 1954 introduction of Billie Holiday to Cologne.

The Schwa took the stage before an audience as still as a herd of antelope who'd caught a predator's scent. It was that rare absolute stillness that occurs only after accidentally breaking a neighbor's window, shooting your best friend in the belly, or before the creation of the universe. And having busted many a window, witnessed a shooting or two, and created more than a few mix-tape universes in my day, I knew that that preternatural silence is usually momentary and often followed by earsplitting frenzy. So as a man haunted by a lifetime of sound, the silence was a condition to be cherished, held onto, and appreciated the way an overwrought mother appreciates a sleeping baby.

The band had been onstage for more than ten minutes and hadn't played a solitary note. Thus far the concert consisted of the star attraction Marcel Marceau-ing across the stage in his socks. I didn't care if the quiet was stupefied awe for his tipsy traffic-cop Butoh minuets or impatient politeness for his double-jointed Thai stripper contortions. This was as close to the tranquility of deafness as I would ever get. For the first time in my life I'd forgotten my sonic past. My head hushed as the eighteen minutes of erased Watergate tape played in deep space. It was the blissful quietude of being buried alive in cotton. An indelible nothingness I would remember for the rest of my life.

The Schwa's body began its physical decrescendo. He weaved across the stage like a concussed Movietone stooge slowly regaining his slapstick equilibrium after a blow to the head. He stepped back into his oxfords as if they were bedroom slippers and shuffled to center stage. From the back of the room a cry went up. The skinheads, led by Thorsten, whooped and stomped their feet in appreciation because the silence had finally broken. I turned on my digital recorder. In the gradually dimming room the red recording light glimmered like a distant star in a pitch-black universe.

The Schwa pressed the red button and it was, World, meet Charles Stone. Charles Stone, World. How do you do? Nice to meet you. It's a pleasure.

The Listening Experience

Defying all the laws of acoustics and containing only the barest characteristics of tonality and melody, the Schwa's sound was music in the sense that prison gruel is food. The opening composition, a dirge deluge entitled "Fatima," was a profane flash flood of auditory tyranny that hurtled downhill with such force it literally knocked me off my feet. I felt like I was listening to a family of hillbillies reading Philip Roth aloud in a backwoods mountain hollow; each movement an endless filibuster so dense and pedantic that any one speaker, one paragraph, one instrument became indistinguishable from another.

As I struggled to stay afloat, I wondered how the lay listeners on the outside were coping with the free-jazz tsunami. I imagined a scene quite similar to the one that opened *2001: A Space Odyssey*—the Berlin primordials, in the ill-fitting monkey suits of the day, growling and bounding around the unwelcome-sound monolith. It'd be chaos until one brave soul reached out to touch the wall; then there'd be change. Fundamental no-turning-back change.

There's an old Buddhist saying, "Before enlightenment, chop wood, carry water. After enlightenment, chop wood, carry water." So I picked myself up off the floor—fought back against this torrential downpour of pig calls and tuba bellows by going back to basics. Desperately I tried to wrap my mind around the drumming, but Irrawaddy went into this flimflam paradiddle sextuple ratatap, and the tenuous grip I had on sanity and the tune were broken. Thirty more seconds of her impeccable drum work caused my ego to slide off an inverted ratamacue in the obstinato voice as if it were a wet, slippery, moss-covered river rock in an Appalachian class-five rapid. Barely able to keep my head above water, I gave myself up to the current. Surrendered to the sound, waiting, praying, for the next eddy of cacophony to pick me up, smash my head against the rocks, and put an end to my misery. However, floating among the flotsam of brassy detritus, rushing past my ears—a simple elongated note. A distant overhead trumpet screed that had more in common with the ominous drone of a B-52 flying at twenty-five thousand feet than it did with jazz.

I latched onto this heaven-sent piece of Acadian driftwood, but it wasn't heavy enough to support me. Another wave of diatonic chords, and I was resubmerged in the horn section's slipstream. Too tired to surrender, I decided to just sit there on the floor until the storm subsided. Knowing that in the morning the authorities would find my bloated, improvisation-logged body on the Slumberland floor buried under alluvial layers of sedimentary jazzbo. From behind, just as I had given up all hope, a suntanned-lifeguard-brown arm wrapped itself across my chest and dragged me to the river's edge. Backs against the wall, we slumped to the floor. The hand tapped a beat on my heart. *Doomp-doomp tshk da-doomp-doomp tshk doomp-doomp tshk . . .* And there it was, a sardonic sonic pun buried beneath the pounding piano, the keening horns and the epileptic bass line: The violinist quietly quoting Eric B. and Rakim's "My Melody" was the melody. *Doomp-doomp tshk da-doomp-doomp tshk doomp-doomp tshk . . .* Her hand still tapping my chest, Klaudia von Robinson and I headed back out into the rushing waters, determined to ford the unfordable.

CHAPTER 5

You know how when a soprano hits that note and the wineglass breaks? The Schwa's music does that, except instead of breaking glass, it shatters time. Stops time, really.

Whenever I hear about a method of time travel that involves wormholes, flux capacitors, or cosmic strings and no music I'm not impressed. If there is such a thing as a vehicle for time travel it's music: Ask any brokenhearted Luther Vandross fan.

I used to be obsessed with stoppages in time. Whenever I saw the dog acting funny, I'd think he was forecasting an earthquake. So I'd run inside and set the kitchen clock precariously on the nail nubbin, so that when the big one hit, our fractured family clock would join the famous timepieces stopped by cataclysms, like the frozen wall clock from the Great Alaska Earthquake and the smashed Waiakea town square clock lying in the rubbled aftermath of the 1960 tsunami. In high school I was an above-average athlete who rarely saw the field of play because I'd call time-out for no reason other than to see the scoreboard clock come to a halt. Every spring and fall at the onset of daylight savings time I'd call the time, hoping to hear time stop and repeat itself. In L.A. the number was 264-1234; three hollow rings, and the time would answer. The time was a woman. A husky-voiced female who got straight to the point: "At the sound of the tone, the time will be eleven thirty-three P.M. and ten seconds." *Beep.* No hello or nothing. "At the sound of the tone . . ." Man, I miss her. With the Schwa's band tearing a hole in the space-time-music continuum, I felt like calling the time right then and there. Press the receiver to my ear so I could hear her say, "At the sound of the tone the American Negro will be passé, and I for one couldn't be happier." *Beep.*

When the Schwa called me onstage for the encore, I somnam-bulantly approached the bandstand. The carnage was every-where. It was as if some suicide sound bomber had detonated his explosive belt in the middle of the room. People, seats, and sensibilities were scattered about the room. Though the band had stopped playing, the music still rang in everyone's ears. The audience still tumbled and swayed in the eerie disharmony of a North Korean gymnastics troupe celebrating May Day on acid and half rations. In the darkness I found myself stepping over prostrate bodies and bumping aside zombified audience members. The Schwa's set had blown minds, and all that re-mained was the smithereens of a pre-Schwa, post-commercial consciousness.

I took my place behind the turntables, my hands shaking so uncontrollably I could barely put the record on the spindle.

"PTSD!" someone shouted.

A peal of laughter rippled the room. They were right, of course; we were all indeed suffering from post-traumatic stress disorder. My case being especially acute because I had to follow in the Schwa's brilliant wake. To ease my nerves I did what we all do in times of crisis: I turned to the cliché. Peering through the dark-ness into the packed house, I imagined the audience naked, but in this case the old adage was of no help because half the audience really was naked. In back of the room couples clung to each other in the infamous Yoko-and-John-Lennon *Rolling Stone* pose. A conga line of streakers, including Thorsten and Nordica, molted from their clothes and deliriously snaked their way through the audience. A man stood at the front of the bandstand wincing as he pulled the hair from his nipples. The sympathetic African sandwich peddler gave him a rose and a hug.

Cuff links sparkling in the spotlight, Stone raised his arms and hushed the crowd.

"On those days when I wake up realizing my life has been lived in vain, I come here to the Slumberland. Let me rephrase that: I never knew my life had been lived in vain until I came to the Slumberland and heard that jukebox."

"Die größte Jukebox in der Welt!" someone, who sounded suspiciously like Klaudia, shouted.

From its corner the jukebox flashed and flickered its lights in appreciation.

"This is a man who's turned the jukebox into a modern-day oracle. You put your money in the slot and Bill Withers answers a question you didn't think you had, Aretha Franklin distills advice you didn't think you needed, Tom Petty and the Heartbreakers predict your future. He's a man who's synthesized every sound ever heard and every feeling ever felt. Ladies and gentlemen, I give you . . ."

He never finished his sentence. He'd forgotten my name, hoping "the look" would suffice as an apology for his mental lapse and my anonymity.

"The look" sufficed. I'd waited all my life for someone to give me that look. The look Duke gave Johnny Hodges. Bob Marley gave Peter Tosh. George Clinton gave Bootsy. Benny Goodman gave Charlie Christian. Billie Holiday gave Lester Young. Chuck D gave Flavor Flav. Alvin gave the Chipmunks. The look that said, "Do your thing, motherfucker."

I didn't mince music. I slapped the crossfader and hit them straight with the beat. No grease. The room went reverential. Folks sat down and listened with the rapt attentiveness of campers hearing their first fireside ghost story. Those on the outside pressed their regretful faces against the windows and the skylight. I knew, somewhere, my boy Blaze was listening in on the international feed, clapping his hands and nodding his head. "Oh, hell yes. It's about time, fool."

I was scared. Scared that I would die before we finished. I wanted time to stop but not forever.

The Schwa was frightened too. Even though he'd been expecting a miracle, he wasn't quite ready for the thoroughness of the boom. His hands shook. He was faltering, unsure of himself. It was then I shot *him* the look. *Do your thing, motherfucker.*

The Schwa leapt onto the track. Tackling and attempting to subdue his instrument as if it were a wild swamp gator roused from a deep, satisfying sleep. The first note he hit was pure paterfamilias. Its sound wave so concussive it flapped my clothes, shook the walls, and caused one audience member to exclaim, "Yes, Father?"

If you ever attend a poetry or jazz workshop to learn the mystical art of improvisation, invariably the instructor will say to you, "First thought, best thought." It's a faux-Buddhist axiom that has led to nothing more than some wildly uneven Beat literature and some shaky second-half play calling by the Los Angeles Rams in Super Bowl XIV, but it sounds good. Personally, I never believed in improvisation. Listen to any cat freestyle or solo—Dizzy, Biggie, Bessie, or Ashbery—they're not playing the way they want to play, they're *trying* to play the way they want to play. No one ever sounded exactly the way they wanted to sound. But that night the Schwa convinced me otherwise. Without trying, he played exactly the way he wanted to play, and when I say he wasn't trying, I don't mean he wasn't putting forth any effort, I mean there was no pretense. He simply played his ass off, blessing my beat with brilliant new neo-bop and retro-cool interstices that filled voids both musical and spiritual.

In the advanced poetry and jazz-improvisation workshop the instructor will invariably say, "Don't think. If you think, you're dead." Of course, it's the obverse that's really true. If you're not thinking, you're dead, and I didn't need to look at the Schwa's knitted brow and gritted countenance to know that Charles Stone was deep in thought. I just had to listen.

He was switching up the tempo. Segueing from a frenzied fortissimo to a languid legato by quoting from "Lift Every Voice and Sing," the Negro national anthem. It's a beautiful yet trepidatious song, and especially so in his hands. Musical mason that he was, the Schwa erected a series of African-American landmarks upon the foundation I had laid down. The contrapuntal effect of our discordant architectural styles meshed together wonderfully. One moment the beat was a towering black obelisk, the next it was an ebony-walled Taj Mahal. The music was so uniquely majestic I felt like stepping outside of the song. A disembodied DJ floating out into the audience, putting a proud arm around his unborn child, and saying, "See that song? Hear that music? Daddy helped build that."

Despite the tune's genius, in my mental landscape where blackness is passé, his quoting the Negro national anthem was a blatant violation of the zoning laws. By constructing a new black Berlin Wall in both my head and the city, he was asking me to improvise. Prodding me to tap out an unpremeditated beat on the drum pads, compress the bass line, and add some *shama lama ding-dong* to the groove. He was daring me to be "black."

But blackness is and forever will be passé and I held my compositional ground, hit my presets, and leaned on my turntables, furiously scratching the coda. The audience roared and shouted for more. Hands so sweaty that my slippery fingers had trouble staying on the vinyl, I continued to scratch, lacing the beat with a dense, undulating buzz that I cribbed from a nest of agitated hornets I found during a late-night stroll along the Spree.

> *I shall not be moved*
> *Like a tree that's planted by the water*
> *I shall not be moved*

Forced to relent to my racial and turntable obstinacy, the Schwa deconstructed "Lift Every Voice and Sing" by laying out like a suicidal Acapulco cliff diver who could give a fuck about timing the tide. He paused, then took a deep breath and cannonballed into his own tune, unleashing a voluminous splashing salvo of triplets that shattered and scattered the song into a wave of quarter, half, whole notes that fluttered to the floor in wet, black, globular droplets.

My beat parfait complete, I leaned into the microphone, "Ladies and gentlemen, Charles Stone. Thanks for coming out, drive home safely, and remember, 'All art is propaganda.'"

Each of us exhausted and covered in sweat, the Schwa and I met at center stage. Over those past two and a half minutes we'd spilled more inner secrets than Anna Freud and Deep Throat combined, but having been in Germany too long and deeply influenced by a country where one has two or three friends and everyone else in your life is an acquaintance, we didn't know whether to hug, shake hands, or kiss.

From outside I could hear police sirens blare and kids, amped up on caffeine drinks and our extraordinarily powerful encore, jumping on cars and setting fires. It wasn't a case of the devil's music spurring the youth to act a fool. It's not rock 'n' roll or hip-hop that's to blame: After all, Daniel Auber's opera *La Muette de Portici* set off the Belgian Revolution, and long before the Paris rap riots, a wolf pack of rich old ladies went absolutely buck wild on the Champ-Élysées following the debut of Stravinsky's *Rite of Spring*. It's the touch of sound. Sound is touch and nothing touches you like good, really good, music. It's like being masturbated by the hand of God. Having the siroccos cooing softly into your ear. It's Mama's lullaby gently stroking the neurons in your auditory cortex.

The cops were getting closer and Doris tried to hurry us outside before we would get arrested. The Schwa gripped me by the shoulders like a man trying to be fatherly and keep his distance at the same time. Our conversation was short and sweet.

"Thanks, man," we mumbled to each other.

"No, really," he said, "the wall, the concert, Fatima, I want you to know . . . you know."

"Yeah, man, likewise."

"Beautiful."

"Say, can I ask you something?"

"Sure, go 'head."

"During that last solo, what were you thinking about?"

"I was thinking about the phrase on the banner, 'Black Passé.' How being passé is freedom. You can do what you want. No demands. No expectations. The only person I have to please is myself."

"You'll never be passé."

"Shit, you keep spinning like that and neither will you."

"I don't know about that. To be passé you have to have been happening at some point in time, and I never was nor never will be happening."

The Schwa laughed. Doris finally got us outside. Burning cars filled the streets. People crowded around the Schwa and begged for his autograph. Behind him I could see the towheaded boy who years ago had written "Ausländer Raus!" on the dewy Slumberland window standing in a circle of Sudanese skateboarders. A flash of light and the circle parted, leaving the white kid standing there holding a Molotov cocktail. He tossed it into the church plaza, then stood there transfixed by the spreading flames.

"Lauf!" I shouted at him. Run!

Tyrus, the Slumberland librarian, came out of nowhere, shaking me by the elbow. I expected him to give me a book. And I wanted a book. I needed a gratuitous, multigenerational tale of colored-people woe that would assure the white reader and the aspiring-to-be white reader that everything would be okay despite the preponderance of evidence that nothing is ever okay.

"Dude, do you know what you've done?"

"Huh?"

"You've turned this motherfucker out. Permanently fucked shit up. Shit is no longer okay, but that's a good thing."

"Huh?"

Sensing my confusion, Lars handed me a tampon soaked in absinthe. In the middle of Goltzstrasse I dropped trou, and in the greatest act of love since Juliet tried to drink Romeo's hemlock backwash, Klaudia took the cottony dagger and rammed it up my ass, thusly. Thank goodness for the gentle-glide design.

The wormwood buzz kicked in immediately, and for the rest of the night any conversation was subtitled in bright pink-and-green variety-show Japanese.

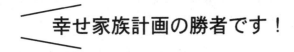

幸せ家族計画の勝者です！

And that was most definitely okay by me.

EPILOGUE TO THE DAY
BEFORE YESTERDAY

T HEY SAY THE Schwa's wall sounds different depending
upon which side you're standing on. Experienced from the
west, the replay of the concert invokes the West Berlin of thirty
years ago. It gives the city a sense of the old intimacy that once
made it so special. Standing on that side of the wall the music
makes you feel safe. It's the sound of inspiration, encourage-
ment, and hope. On the other hand, if you walk ten meters east,
the same music stirs up a different set of emotions. You're overcome by a power-ballad wistfulness that leaves one reflecting
upon how far the city and its citizens have come. In contrast to
those on the west who take from the wall, listeners on the eastern side are moved to give of themselves. They treat this wailing
wall like a musical temple. Prayers hang on nearby trees. The
ground around the wall is wreathed and strewn with offerings
ranging from photos of missing relatives to antiquated East
German appliances like the RG-28 Mixing Device.* That's been
the wall's impact on the city. At least until the speakers get

---

*Formally known as the Schaumschläger-28, but the "beater" in Egg Beater-28 was
too, you know, aggressive.

shorted out by the rain and snow, and Christo or some other installation artist decides to dye the Spree river orange and wrap the Reichstag in flypaper.

Apparently my perfect beat has had a far less reverberatory effect. Not that I expected much, though an instant Grammy airmailed to my bedside would've been a good start. Is a call from the U.N. secretary-general asking if it'd be okay to commission my track as the anthem for planet Earth too much to ask? A show of appreciation from the sick and crippled children who were healed by the curative powers of my creative cut mastery would've been nice. Shit, it was only the day before yesterday that I transformed modern music from this very bar, and no one's even bought me a drink. I bought my first drink tonight. I'm not buying another.

Doris and Tyrus slip into my side of the booth, squeezing me against the wall, crashing my pity party without so much as putting a three-mark beer on the table. Tyrus can't contain his excitement. He's flapping a Guggenheim Fellowship check in my face and insisting that I'm the only one who can do justice to his new musical.

"What's it called?"

"*Real Recognizes Real.* It's a one-man performance piece about an African-American expat from Los Angeles who returns from Germany with the perfect specimen of white womanhood in tow, a blonde Saxon named the Venus Hot-to-Trot. He and Venus tour the chicken 'n' waffle circuit charging sexually frustrated black men to touch her corporeal peculiarity, a completely flat ass. A condition the scientists refer to as no-shapeatallpygia."

"I'll think about it," I lie. I'd never score anything titled with black street vernacular. But it's the only compliment I've gotten, so I'll placate for now. Surely if I string him along long enough there's a beer or two to be had.

"Hey, we went by the wall today. Sat there for two hours and never heard your beat. What's up with that?"

"I erased it from the loop. I didn't want my beat to be just another brick in his wall."

"So where is it?"

"It's on top of my refrigerator."

Doris says nothing. She knows the space atop my icebox is where I keep my most precious valuables. I'd put my dreams up there if I could. Silently she hands me two pieces of paper. One a telegram from DJ Blaze that just says, "NIGGER!"* The other a long list of musicians who'd called the bar asking to get in touch with me. The list smells strangely familiar. I hold it to my nose.

"Your . . ."

She winks.

Now Lars hurtles himself into the booth. "Black is back, baby!"

Groan.

"Don't you want to be relevant?"

"No way. Who needs the fucking pressure?"

"That's the beautiful thing about you people. You stay bitter. I bet when Martin Luther King Junior got on his first integrated bus, he said, 'C'mon, can't you make this motherfucker go any faster?'"

Thanks to my misguided efforts, blackness is back. The Schwa's musical munificence hadn't rendered blackness irrelevant, only darkened it in even further. They say fifty is the new thirty. Iraq is the new Vietnam. Gin is the new vodka. Now that black is the new black, Lars had plans. Big plans.

---

*Funny, you can convey tone in a telegram, but you can't in an e-mail. I think it's because it costs money to send a telegram. If somebody cares enough to pay cash money to tell you something, it's not so hard to infer what they mean. And if you can't properly intonate Blaze's telegram, well . . .

He'd already conspired with a major computer manufacturer to take the Schwa on a concert tour of cities with a history of being bisected by walls. Tentative dates had already been scheduled in Jerusalem, Baghdad, Belfast, and the Calexico-Mexicali border. The Schwa would play a series of cutting contests against the company's latest showpiece, Deep Blues. A jazz-playing computer that rumor has it has already beaten Wynton Marsalis three jams to none.

In comparison, my itinerary is rather limited. Apparently I'm booked to appear on *Wetten, dass . . . ?*, a German game show whose title best translates as *Attention-Starved People with No Discernible Talents Doing Seemingly Amazing Things*. I love that show and it's easy to imagine the prime time course of events.

I'll be pitted against a man who claims he can distinguish between brands of mineral water from how the carbonation bubbles settle on a spoon placed inside the glass. He can't. Next week I'll best a crane operator who brags that while standing in a dark room he can identify any car made after 1978 simply by the brightness and layout of its headlights and the blinking pattern of its left turn signal. He can, but no one will care. Then, in a long-awaited semifinal showdown, I'll embarrass a blind girl from Bremerhaven who insists she has the ability to identify any bird indigenous to continental Europe by touching a single tail feather. The sympathy vote will be hers until her delicate fingertips betray her on the plumage of the Bulgarian blue-breasted swamphen.

Undefeated and unbowed, I'll face Karl-Heinz Schmidt, a telemarketer from Cologne who can identify the color of a colored pencil by taste. Going first, I'll dutifully impress the judges and studio audience to no end with my phonographic recall. "That's a McDonald's straw being inserted into a vanilla shake . . . a video gamer vanquishing a turtle, capturing a star, and eating a large polka-dotted mushroom in world one, level three of Super

Mario Brothers . . . one more time, please . . . Norma Desmond sashaying down the stairs on the way to her close-up . . . that's the sound of the other shoe finally dropping, and yes, that's my final answer."

Blindfolded, Karl-Heinz will then take center stage to a live orchestral accompaniment of *Boléro*. The host will hold up a sharpened brown pencil for all to see, and as *Boléro*'s insidious melody shifts from the flutes to the piccolos, he'll doodle on our savant's lumpy, outstretched tongue. There'll be lots of wet lip smacking as if our star were tasting a delicate fine wine, then a dramatic pause and a ventured guess: "Burnt Sienna?"

"Unglaublich!"

Germany will be flabbergasted. Ravel's oboes shall sing out in celebration. He'll cleanse his palate, and as the melody increases in intensity the host will switch pencils and scribble.

French horns.

"Dark Gray."

Correct.

Bass clarinet.

"Moss Green."

Correct.

Bassoon.

"Turquoise Blue."

Correct.

Violas.

"Light Malachite Green."

Correct.

It'll be an amazing display, no doubt, yet it'll still be anybody's game until the host simply places a pencil under Karl-Heinz's nose. He'll take two deep hound-dog sniffs and in perfect synchronization with *Boléro*'s crescendo, correctly proclaim the color to be Salmon Pink.

* * *

Still no one has offered to buy me a beer. I'd buy one myself, but it'd be like giving myself a surprise birthday party by turning out the bathroom lights, flicking them back on, and yelling, "Surprise!" in the mirror.

Look at Klaudia, her judo bag slung over her shoulder, kicking up sand and smiling that sheepish we-have-to-talk smile. I'm already imagining our post-breakup encounters. When most couples stop fucking they meet for tea and pretend to be happy with one another's successes or content with the lack thereof. Our run-ins will be more spontaneous. They'll be attempted robberies and sexual assaults that'll take place in darkened stairwells and twenty-four-hour Laundromats. Frame-by-frame surprise attacks straight out of the self-defense textbooks. I'll have to brace myself for a lifetime of pellet guns pressed to the small of my back and kitchen knives to the gullet.

True to form, Klaudia grabs my wrist in a gonorrhea-piss-painful hold and climbs atop the table, pulling me up behind her.

I hadn't noticed how crowded the bar had gotten.

Even Thomas, the place's absentee owner, whom I hadn't seen since he handed me the keys to the place, was there. Catching his eye, I tip an invisible glass to my lips, the universal sign for "Can I get a free brew?" He gives me the finger.

Klaudia plants a hard, wet Leonid Brezhnev *Bruderkuss* on me, flattening my nose into my lips and my lips into my incisors.

"May I have your attentions, please?"

Standing there, unable to avoid the stares, I realize the past thirty minutes of my life have unfolded like an episode of *This Is Your Life*. I half expect Ms. Belfour, my third-grade teacher, to make an appearance. *Young Ferguson was a good student, not a great student.*

"Ferguson Sowell, we, the regulars of the Slumberland Bar, in honor of your outstanding service to the arts, culture, and economy of the Slumberland and to the country, are proud to present you with the Order of Karl Marx and this proclamation designating your status as a Verfolgter des Selbstgenuss und Selbstsabotage, or victim of self-indulgence and self-sabotage." With that she pins the shiny gold medal to my chest and shakes my hand and gives me another *Bruderkuss*, but I bet Brezhnev never slipped Nixon the tongue.

I finger the likeness of Karl Marx embossed on a red Soviet star and whisper over the applause.

"This thing is solid gold? Where'd you get this?"

She points to the vestibule. There the Stasi chickenfucker stands under the Ausgang sign, sipping a mojito. I'd never noticed the resemblance between him and Klaudia before.

"Is that your . . ."

She cuts me off and hands me a coin.

"One last thing . . ."

Lars whips a bedsheet off a gleaming, brand-new, state-of-the-art Wurlitzer 2100 and with a gracious bow bestows upon me the honor of playing the first song. Leaping off the table I pop the coin into the machine, eager to peruse what I'm sure will be a massively wonderful song list. There's only one selection. 0001 – THE PERFECT BEAT/DJ DARKY.

The song caravans through the room. A young brother whom I've never seen before, his gray pullover bearing the imprimatur of Yale University, steps to me with an awkward soulshake.

"Hey, man, I just wanted to tell you your beat's thrown the entire School of Music into a tizzy."

"They don't like it?"

"No, everybody's blown away. They just can't agree on what it is."

We talk briefly about Germany. He's getting his doctorate in African-American studies and has come to Berlin to do research for his dissertation. "Did you know that seventy percent of scholarship on African-Americans is in German?" I didn't know that but I'm not surprised. There are many similarities between Germans and blacks. The nouns themselves are loaded with so much historical baggage it's impossible for anyone to be indifferent to the simple mention of either group. We're two insightful peoples constantly looking for reasons to love ourselves; and let's not forget we both love pork and wear sandals with socks.

This novitiate doesn't want to hear this. He wants what all the Negro newbies want, some advice on how to pick up white girls. If he'd only offer to buy me a beer I'd drop pearls of wisdom on him like, "White women with nose rings love black men. A diamond-pierced nostril and you're in, man."

I excuse myself and step outside. There's a line of people waiting to get in so that they can hear the beat. Not a long line, but a line nonetheless.

A stout woman with her auburn hair matted into spiky plaits offers me an unsolicited cigarette, which I accept. If I wanted to I could light it with her stove-flame-blue eyes.

"Have you heard the beat?"

I nod and take a tight-lipped French-resistance drag on the Gauloise.

"Today morning in ethnography class my professor played an African chant, a Negro spiritual, a Robert Johnson ballad, some Louis Armstrong, Charlie Parker, Marvin Gaye, and Kool Moe Dee, and asked the class if we could hear the similarities."

"Did you?"

"No, except for a few *Arschlecker* in the front row, no one heard it. But when I hear that beat the other night, I hear all that music and more. I hear my grandmother raking the leaves. I hear a Volkswagen idling. I hear my father cheering Borussia Dortmund. My sister brushing her hair in the morning. I hear Sade. I hear Motown."

"Naw, no goddamn way. You didn't hear any Motown. Stax maybe, but not no fucking Motown."

"Maybe I don't. But you know what I hear most? I hear America."

"And the rest of the world trying to sound like America."

My curiosity got the best of me.

"What of America did you hear in the beat?"

"I've been to America. I was fifteen. My family went for a month. I hear the La Brea Tar Pits bubbling and chirps of the New York City subway escalator at Lexington Avenue and Sixty-third Street. I hear the nothingness blowing through the Mojave Desert Yucca trees. I hear black men on a Cleveland sidewalk, fighting over ten dollars. I hear Mexican deli workers speaking Korean and teasingly calling each other 'mojados.' I hear the false optimism in the ring and buzz of an Indian-reservation slot machine. I hear the runoff from Mount Shasta streaming through a bed of pine needles. I hear boiling shabu-shabu at Fisherman's Wharf. I hear waves crashing into the Santa Monica pier at midnight under a red crescent moon. I hear my father talking over the tour guide at Universal Studios. 'Welcome to [America]! Before we begin, I'd like to remind you of a few rules we'd like you to follow while [in America] today: First, there is no smoking. Please extinguish all smoking materials [and unpatriotic thoughts] immediately. Second, keep children under forty pounds on the inside seats of the tram; some animated attractions [like ethnics and homeless people] can be intense. Keep your arms and legs [and private parts] inside the tram [and your pants] at all times, and do not stand up [or take your wallet out] while the cars [or any black people] are in motion. If you should require assistance at any time during the tour, pull the cord located above the window on either side of the car. [Most likely nothing will happen, but you never know.]'"

"You heard all that?" I ask this kindred spirit of phonographic memory.

She doesn't answer. Too busy gazing at me with that skin-deep stare I don't get much anymore. In an old gangster movie it'd be the blank, expressionless look Edward G. Robinson shoots a nosy flatfoot while deciding whether to ice him or not. Here on the streets of Berlin, it's deciding whether to insult the black guy or not.

I'm expecting an impromptu ethnographic lecture on Orientalism and black infantilism or the standard "Hitler must've forgotten about you" rebuke. Instead she stands next to me shoulder to shoulder and measures off the difference in our heights.

"Height . . . slightly above average."

Now she takes my chin and yanks it toward the streetlight to get a better view of my complexion.

"Skin color . . . luminescent obsidian with a touch of purple."

Roughly, like a horny sightless woman on a blind date, she begins to knead her heavy friendship-ring-laden fingers into my face. "Leptorrhine nose . . . kumquat-headed dolichocephaly . . . thin, almost Scandinavian lips, the small conchoidal ears, the pronounced prognathism common to most of the Negroid race . . . tufted, no, fleecelike hair . . . I bet you're either from Lagos or Los Angeles. Now, if you show me your penis, I can tell by the size, girth, and curvature what African tribe your male ancestors hail from. It'll be purely for ethnographic purposes, I assure you."

Man, these Germans, they either want to fuck you or kill you.

Sometimes both.

Just like everybody else.

ACKNOWLEDGMENTS

Thanks to Barbara Richter, Thomas Wohlfahrt, Lou Asekoff, Britt-Beyer, Susanne Burg, Nicola Lauré al-Samarai, and Markus Schneider.

Sarah Chalfant and Colin Dickerman, a special thank you for your patience and unwavering faith.